# Purple Alpenglow

## A NOVEL

Craig Boroughs

*For my parents*

# Contents

# Purple Alpenglow

## *Chapter 1 - Visionary at the North Fork Tavern*

Adam turned his head, peered out the small windows of the tavern, and watched the snow, falling more intensely and with large, heavy flakes, pattering on the wet parking lot. If there is one thing everyone lives and breathes by in the Colorado high county, it's deeper snow on the ski mountain, but still being October, it was as tranquil and peaceful as ever in the Spruce Creek valley. With essentially every tavern customer involved in some sort of seasonal employment, revolving around operations of the Spruce Creek Ski Resort and being the heart of the off-season, the collective, subdued, systolic blood pressure of all the tavern patrons was palpable. Resort operations drive the entire economy in the valley, and while the resort was now open with two ski runs covered with man-made snow, the valley was still very quiet and all in the tavern were cherishing a peaceful Sunday before the first big wave of tourists that would arrive in a few weeks.

Adam's legs were extended with his feet crossed and his right arm resting on a table. It was about as comfortable a position as he could achieve with his six-feet frame in the cheap, wooden tavern chair. He took another sip of his beer as he redirected his focus back to the football game that was tuned in on every television throughout the tavern.

A large, old, wooden bar, aligned with the back wall, was the cornerstone of the North Fork tavern – a smoke free restaurant like all establishments in Colorado. Every seat at the bar was taken, and the bar owner, Jake, was seated at the edge of the bar, monitoring the football game but clearly aware of the service being provided to all the customers. The left side wall of the tavern was covered with different relics collected from the ski resort, primarily old ski run signs that were long ago replaced on the mountain. Several signed pictures of former U.S. Ski Team athletes were hung on the other side wall with several large banners and flags, for various sports teams from around the country, draped down from the ceiling and partially covering some of the pictures. A large banner with the Denver Broncos schedule for the current season was hanging just to the side of the bar and behind a foosball table. An old wood stove and single pool table contributed to the somewhat crowded floor plan.

Hannah, sitting just to the side and slightly behind Adam, was also viewing the football game but with limited focus on the latest action. Despite the jumbled audio of football commentators, whistles, and crowd noise from the multiple televisions, a cacophony of potty talk, originating from the patrons at the bar, was resounding throughout the entire tavern. Hannah was comforted by her proximity to Adam, and while Adam would normally feel cramped by someone infringing on his personal space, he had his torso slightly tilted toward Hannah.

Hannah Nelson, a twenty-nine year old demure receptionist for a local real estate agents office, was somewhat disheveled with her blond hair slightly messed up from the cold wind blowing in her face during the walk to the tavern. She was still wearing her winter coat, which was hanging low over her five-feet, eight-inch figure and covering her loose sweatshirt and jeans. Hannah looked over at Adam as he watched the football game. She slowly reached up with her left hand to move a ringlet of Adam's brown hair that was curled up into his left ear, but she quickly pulled back before he noticed and turned her head back toward the football game.

"Skiing tomorrow?" Hannah quickly asked.

"Sure," Adam said, turning toward Hannah. "Why not?"

"You know it will be Halloween. Are you going to wear a costume?"

Adam chuckled. "No, I'm going with Drew. I know he wouldn't care for that." Adam shifted his legs up under the table and turned toward Hannah. He looked right into Hannah's green eyes and continued to chuckle. "There was a time when he would have been all energetic to make a full crazy day of it."

"Well, it's going to be festive. You'll definitely see many in costume. It will be a fun day." Adam smiled and turned his head back toward the football game.

Adam Turner had lived in the Spruce Creek valley for seven years and experienced enough ski seasons to take it all in stride. Now thirty-one years old, Adam worked as a staff architect for a local architectural firm that specializes in designing trophy homes, built throughout the valley for wealthy second homeowners.

With the heat radiating from the nearby wood stove, the joint was plenty warm, and Adam took off his fleece vest, revealing that he was the only person in the entire joint with his shirt tucked in – a button-down shirt at that. While epic days on the mountain were assuredly to come soon enough, the ski season was still far removed from Adam's mind on that October day. While it used to be that thoughts of a powder day on the hill were all Adam needed to have that basic feeling of emotional balance and personal peace that everyone seems to fight for, internally, each day, but such thoughts hadn't been helping him of late.

Adam let out a deep sigh over the status of the football game, slowly leaned his head back, and looked up at some old light fixtures on the ceiling. Hannah turned and furrowed her brow as she watched him, but she did not inquire about his thoughts. Adam then quickly dropped his head back to the game following a sudden roar over the television audio that was followed by some disgruntled mumbling from the tavern patrons. "Why do I watch this nonsense?" he asked.

Hannah, not too genuinely stressed about the game, said, "I don't know. Why do you watch this nonsense? It's only football." Hannah leaned forward and started picking at some remnants from their chicken quesadillas they had just previously devoured within a few minutes. The Broncos were now down by seventeen points with eleven minutes remaining in the game. The game was not really a significant concern for Adam either, especially this year, and Adam's perspective has never been so distorted that he would lose sleep over the latest ballgame, though he was always a devout follower of the latest source for sports excitement – football, basketball, baseball, golf.

Adam turned his head back toward Hannah. He blurted out, "Tell me something," in a tone that sounded like a direct challenge.

"What?" Hannah replied, somewhat confused.

"I don't know, anything."

Hannah rolled her eyes and then looked up, almost as if she wanted to seize an opportunity to see what Adam was evaluating on the ceiling. She dropped her head, started to look out at the snow, but then froze as her eyes got real big. She quickly looked over at Adam. "Voting next month?" she asked, sprightly.

Adam nodded very deliberately. "Yep."

"For who?" she asked. Hannah then turned in her chair so she was directly facing Adam. She leaned in and looked right into his eyes.

"I don't know," he answered.

"Really?" Hannah asked loudly as she leaned back and relaxed in her chair again.

"Nope. Do you have it all figured out?"

"I guess, as much as I can expect."

It wasn't an election unlike any other. It was a presidential election year with an evenly divided nation, and all indications pointed to the net result being continued sheer, utter gridlock. News reporting was deeply focused on every race, with only nine days remaining until election day. Of course all the rhetoric had been on how *this* election was the most significant and most pivotal election of all time.

Adam suddenly stood up and yelled, "Pick-six?!" His cheers were matched by an uproar in the pub as everyone watched a Broncos defensive back easily walk into the end zone. "Ah, yes," Adam said as he clinched his fist in the air. "Ah, the proverbial pick-six," Adam said, turning right toward Hannah. "Hannah, an interception return for a touchdown has broken the hearts of so many speculators in Vegas. It is the single event than can turn a game, instantaneously. Now, we got a ballgame!" Adam high fived Hannah and then plopped back down in his chair. Hannah was cackling though her laughter was directed more at Adam than over the latest development in the game. Grimaces and legitimate stress emanated from a table of Bengals fans, sitting isolated, next to the wood stove. The hubbub continued for a couple minutes as everyone watched the replays, though the Broncos were still losing.

Hannah got up. "I'm going to go check on Cody," she said. Adam loved Hannah's dog, a sixty pound mutt. It would be very difficult to isolate the breed without some laboratory analysis – all white fur, definitely some malamute, maybe some husky and shepherd. Hannah adopted Cody from the local animal rescue after she first moved to the valley, five years ago. Cody had turned out to be about the most docile pet anyone could ever hope for. If it wasn't the fourth quarter in the game, Adam would have joined Hannah.

"Cody will be so happy about the falling snow," Adam said. He then looked toward Hannah but she was already walking out the side door of the tavern and didn't hear him.

Adam completely focused on the football game for several minutes before the server walked by and startled him. "Two more?" she asked.

Hannah was just returning. Even though the server was looking at Adam, Hannah quickly replied, "Yeah," as she sat down.

"How's my boy?" Adam asked.

"Good," Hannah mumbled. "He was awake." Hannah started chuckling. "I think he may have heard the commotion following that pick-six."

Hannah and Adam quietly watched the game for a couple minutes. Adam then turned and was looking right at Hannah. She certainly felt his gaze but kept watching the game. He looked right at her for several seconds and then let out a sigh and started shaking his head. Hannah finally turned toward Adam. She didn't say anything but responded with an inquisitive gesture. Adam shrugged. " What?" she asked. Adam shrugged and turned back toward the television.

They watched the game quietly for a couple minutes, and then Adam suddenly cleared his throat and shifted in his seat. "So, about that question you asked," he said. "I felt this slight sense of euphoria a while ago. It wasn't from the pick-six, or my favorite schwag beer here, but from the realization, that yes, I indeed will get to vote in nine days. Amid all the frustration, rage, and disappointment in society, that basic voting right might be the absolute best result of yet another election."

Hannah nodded slightly as she continued to look at Adam. Adam then looked right at Hannah. "You know," he went on, "it shouldn't be that difficult. It shouldn't be that hard to develop a governmental structure that would work for everyone, or at least the vast, overwhelming majority of people. If that was going to happen, you would sure think it could be done, here in the United States of America." Hannah rolled her eyes, smiled real big, and turned toward the television. "There's a golden opportunity," he continued, "for the absolute perfect system to now be developed, or refined from the current system, that would be the model for the rest of the world for decades. With all the lessons learned from this great democracy and the democracies of other developed nations, it should be possible to now refine the system to provide the essential needed moderate social safety net while also affording everyone the opportunity to get a top-notch education, move on to rewarding, important work, and then have the wherewithal to raise a healthy, happy family. Everyone would be rewarded for their hard work and their extraordinary contributions and every American would have an opportunity, with assured sustenance and basic shelter. The system would, on its own, function smoothly and allow everyone to enjoy time for laughs with their friends and family."

Hannah smiled and mockingly said, "Your vote, Adam, in nine days, will be the difference as to whether this all comes to fruition or not."

Nobody else was tuned in to Adam's comments as Hannah could barely hear Adam herself over the background noise from all the television audio and the numerous other discussions in the tavern. "The system would foster innovation and that entrepreneurial spirit that has made America so great with a moderate, progressive tax system, minimal regulations on business, and a simplified environment for companies to operate that would drive the economy through the end of the twenty-first century." Hannah was looking at Adam as he leaned forward. "The system must include a fantastic education system to assure an abundant supply of workers required to implement new technologies and the innovative solutions to society's challenges. The net result would be a thriving economy and a strong healthy, educated, working society that consumes and utilizes all the great products provided as a result of the entrepreneurship and the innovation of businesses and individuals and with everyone rewarded for their hard work and genius."

"Have you been listening to talk radio?" Hannah asked.

Adam continued as if he hadn't heard Hannah's question. "The problem is that the system that provides that framework for entrepreneurial pursuits and prosperous business ventures, where innovation and hard work are rewarded, requires a full thriving economy built with an educational system for all of society, fully developed infrastructure that is maintained, reliable energy resources that are economical, an advanced communications framework, security from international threats, and numerous basic services to all communities. If you don't have all that, there's no society, no consumer, and no economy for businesses to operate. There are expenses to providing that entire framework, and those, with the resources, have to help pay to maintain the system."

"And there's where it all comes tumbling down," Hannah slowly interjected.

"It's not just that any society must have clean drinking water and a clean food distribution system, infrastructure that provides the means for commerce, and assured safety from local and international threats that allows everyone to focus on their work and their families, but a system with such key elements then creates the entrepreneurs and researchers that develop solutions for all society's challenges, for improving the quality of life for all, and to enhance business efficiency. You end up with a fantastic society where young people can get educated, start careers, and build a fantastic life for their family and do sound, hard work. They then pay it forward to keep the great system in place for their kids and their kids' kids."

"I'm afraid that last part is just not that easy to sell," Hannah said. "There will always be successful people that want to close the door behind them."

"Well, there must be a moderate social safety net. Without that lifeline, you end up with masses of the population, disadvantaged members of society, that do not have the opportunity to participate and be a part of the development and benefit from the use of the nation's resources. With so many members of the economy left out of the system, the result is then a depressed economy that completely holds up business development."

"Well," Hannah said, "if you can figure it out, if you can figure out that perfect system, that perfect balance, and sell it–"

"I believe there is a happy medium that the overwhelming majority of the population can accept, with pride, from the right and left, and the rest of the world would observe with envy. And there would be uprisings from the civilians, business leaders, and labor in other countries, where their people are oppressed under their authoritarian regimes. They would want to see the same fantastic system implemented in their countries."

Hannah laughed. "Are we drinking the same thing here?"

Adam finally started laughing. He looked right at Hannah with a big smile. "What?" he asked. "Okay, okay, but it's fun to think about, isn't it?"

"Are you going to figure all this out before you vote?" Hannah asked. She then blurted out, "Wait," as she scooted forward in her chair. "Okay, here's the challenge for you. Over the next week, figure it out – realistically. How can the current system be adjusted to achieve this perfect system, for our generation, for every American?

And then tell me who will get us there." Adam was still chuckling as he took a sip of his beverage. Hannah shifted her seat back again. "You're not really going to vote for that guy, are you?" she asked, as she looked back at the football game.

"I don't know," Adam said. He looked into Hannah's eyes. "I can tell you that it's outright malfeasance if any policy maker denies that society is now reeling in a malaise over the inaction and sheer refusal of politicians to see much needed, significant updates implemented to important programs and policies."

Hannah and Adam sat quietly for a few minutes but Hannah kept shaking her head, chuckling over Adam's little speech. Adam kept smiling and shrugged a couple times when Hannah looked at him. The server dropped off two more drinks. The Broncos were now down by seven points.

"Going home for Thanksgiving?" Adam asked. A look of sheer dread immediately fell over Hannah's face. "Oh come on, have your parents not forgiven you yet?" Adam asked.

Hannah froze and then slowly shook her head as she stared at some broken chips on the floor. "My mother talks to me. I haven't talked to my father much. Adam, I was all happy about the snow! What do you have to bring that up for?"

"It will be fine. Come on, they're your parents."

"Yeah, but it will always be there," she said. "It will always be a topic that my father will throw back at me, at any moment." Hannah looked up at the television, the football game in commercial break, as Adam looked right at her. Adam let out a light sigh, and with genuine concern, he looked right into Hannah's eyes. Her cheeks had become red and her eyes glossed over as she started to tear up.

"You'll be able to repay him some day."

Hannah wiped her eyes and took a breath. She breathed in, shifted in her seat, and tried to shake off her most recent emotion. "It's not the money so much as his sheer disappointment in me. They had always expected so much from the little girl."

"So, have you talked to Lane recently?"

"Ugh!" Hannah blurted out. "No. I don't know. I think he's back in Wisconsin."

It had still only been a few months since it happened. Hannah thought Lane was the man who would give her everything she ever wanted. It was all set up so perfectly. Hannah dated Lane for eight months before they decided to get married.

"Hannah, what happened?" Adam quietly asked, looking down at the floor.

"Ah, shoot," Hannah shouted loudly. Some others in the tavern heard her scream and turned around. "Do you see the Broncos are about to score again?" Hannah's asked as her cheeks had now turned beet red.

"Okay, okay, sorry," Adam said as he shifted in his seat to focus again on the game.

Hannah hadn't talked about it much with anyone, and she had somehow managed to turn off her emotions over the subject, for the most part. While Adam hadn't expressed too much interest in talking to her about it, he surely enjoyed slipping in a little banter and witticism every now and then. How could he not joke with her – a no-show for her own wedding! Hannah looked up at the television but then dropped her head and gave Adam a sullen look of deep melancholy. Adam shrugged lightly and took a sip of his beverage. Adam was probably her best friend, and oddly, the one person she would really like to open up to about it, but that wasn't an option given their history. Suddenly, another roar resounded throughout the tavern as Hannah looked up to see the Broncos quarterback in the end zone with the ball and being mobbed by his teammates.

"A naked bootleg?!" Adam yelled, looking over at Hannah. He slapped Hannah lightly on the shoulder and stood up. "Are you kidding me?! How tremendous was that?"

Hannah stood up and somewhat half-heartedly gave Adam a high five. "I'll be right back," she said, and then she strolled over to another table to visit with a couple other local residents.

After the excitement over the latest Broncos touchdown subsided, with the broadcast in commercial break, Adam leaned back in his chair. He turned and looked out the window. The snow had eased up and there was a serene sense of calm outside. The storm was inconsequential for building up the base on the ski runs, but it was a nice harbinger of the fantastic, heavy snows to come. Very few people had walked in or out of the tavern during the game, except for a couple guys that had briefly stepped out to smoke.

Hannah returned and before she could sit down, Adam began talking while staring at the television. "Why do people feel they need to brag about where they are at any moment?" he asked. "It's as if they don't actually care at all about where they are or the people around them but are more interested in gloating about their current situation to others, who are not there, to hopefully improve their status in the greater society. Somebody could be cruising a fjord in Norway and be more focused on broadcasting their position to their social community as opposed to enjoying one of the greatest, natural wonders of the world."

"External validation," Hannah quickly replied, scooting her chair up to the table. "It really is rare to find someone who is at peace with themselves and their place in the world and not always obsessed with seeking out some external validation from their peers."

Hannah leaned forward with her elbows on the table and immediately changed the subject back to the upcoming election. "Adam, you're such a tree hugger. I can't believe you don't know who you're voting for. I even have a picture of you hugging a tree! Right there, by definition, you are a consummate tree hugger. You completed the deed."

"Hey, now," Adam said, "that's not fair. I was hugging a specific tree. Don't you knock ol' Felix. Felix is my buddy." Felix is a name Adam had given, years ago, to an old-growth Engelmann spruce tree on one of his favorite ski runs on the backside of the resort, and he developed a habit of religiously visiting that tree, every ski day – well, whenever the terrain was open.

"If this storm keeps up," Hannah said, "you may be able to ski by ol' Felix and give him another hug soon enough." It would actually be a few weeks, but it was indeed a comforting thought for both of them.

"It makes me sad to think that some people don't ski, or have never skied, Gus's Glade."

"I'll give you credit," Hannah said, "it's indeed Heaven on Earth."

Adam and Hannah both focused quietly on the game for several minutes. The Broncos had gotten the ball back with a minute remaining in the game, and they were able to move down the field to set up an attempt at a game-tying field goal. The kicker was lined up for a forty-eight yard field goal to force overtime. The kick narrowly passed inside the right upright, which was followed by another roar from the tavern patrons. Several people got up to head to the restroom as Adam also went over to stand in the short line.

As soon as Adam returned and sat down, Hannah said, "The fact that the current government system is so ridiculously involved and complicated is just a product of democracy." Adam started pulling on a loose thread on his vest, hanging off the back of his chair. Hannah went on, "There's really no reason for anyone to be that perturbed because any system developed, through democracy, for everyone will undoubtedly have an endless list of footnotes as a result of policy makers trying to assure all the various voices are represented. Is it really that much of a surprise?" Adam shrugged as Hannah continued. "Also, there's no way that a complete body of governing legislation can be so simple while continuously funding a first-rate educational system, well developed infrastructure, reliable energy resources, a communications framework, sound national defense, and a moderate social safety net, all necessary as you said. The convoluted system in place is simply what should be expected and shouldn't necessarily be regarded as a disaster. Actually, any other simpler system would be what you would get if we were living under an autocracy of a single king."

Adam grimaced at the television after seeing the Broncos lose the coin toss allowing Cincinnati to get the ball first in overtime. He then looked over at Hannah and said, "I think it can be done. I think old age entitlement programs can be reformed and a much simplified corporate and personal tax code can be developed that would encourage economic growth and provide the needed revenues for the same basic social safety net, currently in place, and the same level of funding for defense, education, agriculture, energy, water, land management, transportation, and veterans' programs and emergency services, all of it."

"Ah, yes," Hannah said, smugly. "The grand plan. You really think he can get it done?"

"Well," Adam said, "I don't know who would be best. I do know that to get it done, all programs have to be maintained with no new taxes. While that can be done, I'm not sure all his fat-cat donors and his ultra conservative base would let him get it done under that umbrella."

Hannah and Adam redirected their focus back to the football game for several minutes. Everyone in the tavern quietly watched as the Bengals marched down the field, scored a touchdown, and won the game under the sudden death overtime rules.

Hannah scoffed. "The overtime rules are so messed up," she said. "Well, I should get Cody home. I'll talk to you later in the week. So, you're skiing with Drew in the morning?"

"Yeah," Adam groaned, still glum over the Broncos loss.

The server dropped off their bill while also handing checks off to numerous other tables. "You getting this one?" Hannah asked with a flirty smile.

"Yeah, I got it."

"And you'll tell me later about your silver bullet plan for leading our country to thriving prosperity that will last for the rest of the century?"

Adam gave a firm nod and smiled.

# Chapter 1 - Visionary at the North Fork Tavern

## *Chapter 2 - Compassion at Spruce Creek Resort*

There's something intrinsically therapeutic about gliding down the snowy slopes on a cool, fall day with the clean Colorado mountain air blowing in your face and the aroma of sweet pine all around. The fresh snow from the day before definitely helped the ski conditions, and one can never complain when you're skiing in October. Drew was an absolutely fantastic skier and while it would be expected that he couldn't actually stomach waiting in a lift line for thirty minutes to ski on a couple narrow, crowded, white strips of chaos, he was in heaven. Drew absolutely loved being outside and always reveled in every opportunity to make turns.

Drew Erickson, six-feet two-inches tall and a solid two hundred and ten pounds, carried himself with confidence and a certain panache and was the kind of guy any other would like to follow if they ever had to head into battle. Now thirty-three years old, Drew kept his hair cut very short and had tan, slightly sun-damaged skin from working outside and playing outside for much of his life. Drew ran a landscaping business that required sixty-hour work weeks during recent summers, and while he wasn't one to take it easy, he cherished being flat-out bored for a few weeks in the off-season and reveled in any available time to play outside. Drew really liked to catch up with Adam during the winters as he hardly saw Adam during summers anymore. They had just sat down on the quad chairlift next to another couple.

"So I assume you watched that nonsense yesterday," Drew asked, referring to the Broncos game.

"Yeah, I'm a glutton for punishment. They'll be alright." Adam responded.

"Where did you watch it?"

"North Fork, of course." Adam didn't really have to say this as Drew would have immediately guessed it.

"Who was there?"

"Oh, all the usual suspects. I watched it with Hannah."

"Dude, I can't believe you still hang out with her after what she did to you. Is she expecting you to absolve her someday or something?"

Adam shifted a bit in the chair. He let out a light yawn, not too interested in discussing Hannah, and he turned around and looked back at the mass of people waiting in the lift line maze below. "I don't know," Adam said. "It's easy to hang out with her. It's fine. Actually, we ended up talking politics, so I suspect that's why nobody else was too interested in joining us."

Drew turned, looked right at Adam, and asked, "You still don't know who you're voting for?"

"Nope."

Drew shifted in his seat and looked right at Adam, "You're not going to vote for her, are you?"

"I don't know." The other couple on the chair adjusted in their seats in discomfort over the sudden focus on politics.

Drew sat back in the chair slowly, looked up the hill, and then began chuckling as he asked, "Hey, so what happened with that guy, Lane?"

"It sounds like he's back in Wisconsin."

"Did Hannah say anything more about it?"

"Nope, I pried a bit more yesterday," Adam said, smiling, "but I got nothing."

Drew continued chuckling. The chair clanked as it passed over another lift tower, and Adam looked over at a collage of stickers that had been slapped on the tower pole.

"Who do the Broncos play this Sunday?" Drew asked.

Adam replied very slowly, "The …Oak …land …Raid …ers."

Drew nodded, acknowledging that it would be another big test for the Broncos. Drew leaned back in the chair, closed his eyes, and turned his face toward the sun. It was about forty-five degrees Fahrenheit, a warmer day for skiing but pleasant weather is a key part to enjoying a day on the hill in October, as it's definitely not about the ski conditions.

Drew suddenly leaned forward, "Adam, some of us are trying to run businesses. You can't vote for her." Adam then leaned back, closed his eyes, and sat quietly. He had no interest in talking about it with the other couple on the chair. Drew sighed and then curtly asked, "How's your work?"

"It's fine," Adam said. "The bosses are worried about us getting slow for the winter, but we always get slammed with way more work than we can handle. I've decided that I'm just going to crank away, get what I can done, and not worry about the backlog anymore. They're definitely fine with me as far as I know." Adam then chuckled. "They're probably not too happy I'm skiing this morning."

Adam worked for a small partnership. The vast majority of the homes Adam designed would be occupied about eight weeks out of the year and sit vacant for the rest of the year. Adam already had a reputation in the valley as an excellent, conscientious architect, but his bosses appreciated his stolid efficiency even more. Adam was endowed with an innate ability to finish superb designs very fast, and while Adam rarely discussed work outside of the office, Drew knew Adam's reputation as well as anybody from working on landscaping projects for many of the same homesites.

"When are you going to break out on your own, start your own gig?" Drew asked.

"Oh, I don't know about that," Adam replied. "I'm fine with my current situation. I like being an architect. I wouldn't like running a business and dealing with all the other hassles: setting up a retirement savings plan, maintaining liability insurance, selecting a health insurance plan, invoicing, making payroll, filing tax forms, hiring employees, firing employees."

Drew grimaced in disgust. "Okay bud," he said, "you just keep letting Henderson and Armstrong take care of all that for you and keep that fat cut from your billing." Drew leaned back again and faced the sun, "Dude, it's easy," he added with his eyes closed. "Heck, you can pay an accountant a reasonable amount to do half of it for you. Do your bosses do designs themselves anymore?"

"Not much, but that's just it. They're too busy with all those other hassles. I don't want to run a business. I want to do architecture."

"I wish I had some suckers like you working for me," Drew said. The chair clanked loudly as it passed over another tower.

"I guess I should consider it," Adam said.

"Adam Turner and Associates," Drew exclaimed.

"Actually, I can't think of anyone that I would want as an associate. I really don't mean that as disrespect to anyone. It's just that you really need to feel great about a work relationship to head down that road with somebody." Adam looked up at the peaks that had become more visible as they climbed in elevation.

"Sounds like that fear of commitment you had with Hannah," Drew said. He looked at Adam with a big smartass grin on his face, clearly trying to get Adam's goat.

Adam figured he would retort. "Well, if we just had government health insurance, maybe I could start my own business. Then I wouldn't have to worry about getting health insurance for me or any employees." Adam looked back at Drew with a matching, big grin.

Drew reached over and grabbed Adam's arm firmly, almost dropping his ski poles. Drew then muttered, "Adam, I'm going to throw you off this lift if you even start with such nonsense." Adam laughed as Drew then released him. Adam had always enjoyed pushing buttons and knew exactly which buttons to push with Drew; nonetheless, Adam was happy they had reached the top of the lift.

The couple beside them had been sitting quietly and clearly had about enough of Adam and Drew they could handle.

Adam and Drew blazed down the primary open trail in about three minutes, slaloming through an obstacle course of skiers and boarders. The open runs at Spruce Creek represented two of just a few runs open in the entire state, so about anyone who wanted to ski that day was now crammed onto those two, narrow, strips of man-made snow. The resort had volunteers that were stationed on the mountain, wearing bright orange coats, blowing whistles at skiers that were skiing too fast and pulling passes for riders that were being unsafe. In past years, Drew carried his own whistle and would whistle back at them with a big smile as he whisked by, but he had outgrown that juvenility after he had his first child.

This day was certainly not going to rank on their list of epic ski days, so Drew and Adam couldn't help but have a little extra fun putting the day into perspective. Adam skied up behind Drew at the bottom of the run and sarcastically screamed, "Work on your turns Drew, not your speed!"

Drew laughed. "Yeah buddy, I'll be sure and do that next run."

"And no straight-lining!" Adam yelled facetiously.

Drew and Adam slid into one of the lanes in the lift line maze to wait for their next lift ride. For a couple minutes, Drew and Adam looked around and laughed at several people in the lift line who were having lots of fun for it still being before noon. Many of the other riders were decked out in some fairly elaborate Halloween costumes, but a big part of the comedy was that costumes and skiing don't go well together. It was such a warm day, many were already shedding layers. Much of the crowd was younger – maybe skipping classes at whichever university they attended down on the Colorado Front Range. The Front Range refers to the urban corridor just at the eastern side of the Rocky Mountains and at the very beginning of the high plains. Within Colorado, the Front Range includes Denver, Colorado Springs, Boulder, Greeley, and Fort Collins.

After quietly watching other people in the lift line for several minutes, Adam leaned down on his ski poles and looked down at the skis worn by riders in front of him. After several seconds, Adam stood back up and sighed as he looked at Drew. "Seriously," Adam said, "if we had government health care, then I could start my own business with the comfort of knowing that I'll have health insurance for me and maybe a family someday."

"Oh man! Adam, don't even talk to me about health care. I've been dealing with such a nightmare trying to provide health insurance for my employees." Drew then froze and looked at Adam as a gap formed in the lift line in front of them. "Wait a second. What do you mean, family?" Drew asked with legitimate concern. "Are you and Hannah getting back together?"

"No," Adam quickly said.

Drew nodded slightly and edged forward in the line, "You aren't still all over that little Icelandic princess that works at the coffee shop, are you?"

"No! They have good coffee there. I like the music they play." Drew dropped his head and started laughing. Adam then quipped, "Also, Iceland doesn't have royalty!" Drew laughed even louder and reached down to his knees to catch himself, about falling down in the lift line.

As Drew finally caught his breath, he said, "Well, I hope she recognizes you some day. You would be much better off with her than Hannah. Now Hannah, that girl can rend the heart of a guy and then she has the audacity to show back up later, looking for a reprieve, some expectation of impunity."

Adam rolled his eyes and shook his head. "How long have you been waiting to throw that at me?" he asked with a light chuckle.

Adam and Hannah had dated for about three years before Hannah skipped off with Lane. Lane came from a wealthy family and was able to take Hannah on nice vacations to New Zealand, Hawaii, and cities in Europe. He had a job with the county District Attorney's office and was able to offer Hannah the future she had always dreamed of. Hannah walked away from Adam with little explanation. After just four months, Lane and Hannah were engaged, yet it was so apparent that there was something unseemly about their union. Adam anguished for a while, but despite it all, he handled it well.

Drew and Adam quietly watched the Halloween revelers for a couple minutes and then Drew leaned down on his ski poles. They were now about two thirds of the way through the maze.

"I'm better off," Adam suddenly muttered.

"It would have probably helped you if you weren't so cynical," Drew replied.

"I'm a realist," Adam said. "Are things good with you and Amy?"

Drew had been married to Amy for eight years. They not only married fairly young, by twenty-first century standards, but they had known each other since they were both in high school together in New Hampshire. They had a six-year-old daughter and a four-year-old son and owned a modest, but nice, three bedroom, two-level place down the valley from the resort – an exceptional property given the cost of living in the community.

Drew snapped, "Hey, things are fine with Amy." Drew knew Adam was looking to revel in any discomfort Drew had in his marriage. "Look, she nags. It's not always easy. I could talk about specific situations. I've made fairly good money with my business, and I don't have too much to show for it yet. I've spent late nights cleaning the garage and working on other honey-do tasks after working eleven hour days at job sites. I don't get to watch much football anymore, but it's all worth it! I love her, and I am happy to make sacrifices for her. She works hard. Dude, she bore me two kids! Adam, she's so good with the kids. And she does my laundry!"

"Okay, okay," Adam said. He dropped his head and mumbled, "Ugh, I hate doing laundry."

"What's it all for if you don't have somebody to share it with," Drew went on. "I know you think it's nothing but a yoke around your neck, but you're wrong."

"No, no, hey, I'm a fan! I'm a fan of all of it. You have such great kids. I know Amy's great. I know! You're going to have so much fun with your kids. Hey, enjoy every moment because they grow up fast." Adam paused and then looked up at the chairs full of skiers cruising up the lift. "I guess for me, it's like that comparison to football. I'm a huge fan, …but I wouldn't dare try to play."

"Agh!" Drew quickly yelled. Drew looked up the mountain at some revelers that were hollering from one of the lift chairs. He then slowly looked back down at his skis. "Adam, everybody's been jilted. Just forget about Hannah. You can't let that nonsense sour your perspective. You'll see, it will come around again for you soon." Drew smiled and added, "Although, I'm not sure it will be your little Icelandic princess down at the Java Alley."

"Ah, come on, I love her, man."

Drew and Adam laughed and chuckled on-and-off for the next couple minutes. As they moved closer to the chairlift loading zone, Drew focused on others in line, including all the lift operators doing a fantastic job to assure every chair was full and keeping the line moving as quickly and efficiently as possible. Drew eavesdropped on a couple conversations as Adam was leaning down on his poles, remaining pensive as he looked down at the snow.

"That deal with Lane was so stupid," Adam suddenly muttered. "Sure I was bereft, but I'm certainly not going to say I was ever envious of what they had. It was just a conquest for him. Hannah obviously figured it out just in time. Lane probably doesn't even really care that she bolted on their wedding day." Drew leaned down closer to Adam. "You know what else?" Adam continued. "There's no scrutiny in the valley on Hannah or Lane. Everybody just looks at me as if I'm some pathetic dweeb and thinks, 'There goes the cuckold.'" Drew couldn't help but laugh a little. "And everyone thinks Lane is just some kind of stud."

"Hey, he was left at the altar and then moved out of state."

"And Hannah's still our little sweetheart," Adam mumbled.

"I don't think her family thought any of it was too sweet."

Drew didn't have much more to add, and after a few seconds, he seemed happy that they had reached the front of the line. They sat down on a chair for another lift ride. A couple younger snowboarders, each wearing headphones, had joined them on the chair. The snowboarders were immediately fumbling in their pockets for granola bars and queuing up different tunes. The gurgle of jake brakes suddenly resonated against the peaks from two oversized trucks coming down the highway pass by the resort.

Drew looked at Adam and asked, "Man, are you really going to vote for her?"

"I don't know," Adam said.

Drew was shifting around on the chair. "You would just be supporting that endless stream of benefits and handouts for all those slackers."

Adam laughed and asked, "Is that really the best you got?"

"Ah," Drew grunted, waving his hand, "wait till you start your own business and start shelling out so much in taxes to fund all that nonsense. If this system continues, they'll never buck up and take any responsibility for their own life."

"I don't think it's that simple. When someone has children and the kids don't have access to good nutrition, comfortable shelter, or even a rudimentary education, they are at such a disadvantage."

"Oh, they need to quit whining," Drew interjected. "I didn't have anything handed to me. I started my business from scratch. I went to the bank, took out a loan, took on all the risk, and worked hard, day after day, to keep it going. It could all come tumbling down, but I keep cranking. That's what you do. You can't wait for anyone to hand it to you."

Drew was a hard worker. He wasn't an Ivy league scholar, but Adam had always felt Drew was an incredible, positive influence on him. It wasn't just the tremendous effort and energy Drew put into his landscaping business, but Adam had known Drew earlier, when they worked together for the resort. Adam also knew Drew had worked at fast food restaurants all through high school and did his time working as a clerk at a grocery store when he was growing up in New Hampshire.

"Trust me, I know you've worked hard," Adam said with a hushed tone, to not annoy the snowboarders on the chair. "You know I know that, but you had a family. You had a community and an excellent, safe public school. You had food and shelter every single day. All those clients that hire you, they wouldn't be there if we didn't have a vibrant economy, that wouldn't be so strong if there weren't services for that segment of society that wasn't born into the same circumstances. Your crews drive on roads to job sites, tap your irrigation systems to an unlimited supply of safe, clean water, take your garbage to a landfill that assures proper clean disposal and storage while assuring clean drinking water years later for your kids and your kid's kids. You go out to lunch with your crew knowing that you can always rely on a safe, clean meal."

Adam, sensing the rage in Drew, looked toward the couple of snowboarders on their chair and asked, "Do you guys mind if we lower the safety bar?" As they lowered the bar, the pungent, skunky aroma of marijuana suddenly wafted in their face from the chair in front of them. Adam, Drew, and the two snowboarders all immediately looked up to assess the source of the smell.

Drew raised his voice and sputtered, "You should go sit with your hippie friends up there! Sure, services cost money, but how does it end up that nearly half the nation gets by without contributing anything for these services?"

Adam paused and quietly muttered, "They don't have anything to pay." Adam shifted back in the chair a bit. "Also, they don't consume. They aren't using near as much of the nation's resources. For those at the bottom of the pay scale, their demands for food, water, infrastructure, and energy are so much less."

"You're stoned!" Drew yelled as the two snowboarders promptly busted out laughing. Neither Adam or Drew seemed too concerned about talking politics in front of these two kids. "The opportunity is there," Drew continued. "They can get up, take on the day, start their own business, or get a job and work hard and eventually move up and be out there utilizing the same services, but that social safety net, those handouts that provide a crutch for them to not even work, it has to stop! The system is designed such that they're better off taking the benefits versus getting their start."

"The formulas can change. Everyone knows that, but notwithstanding that, you have to look at it macroscopically." Drew was seething as he dropped his head. The chair then climbed out of a stand of lodgepole pines and passed directly over one of the opened ski runs, and Adam and Drew immediately looked down to watch the throng of skiers and boarders below. Skiers were whizzing down the slopes in Halloween costumes and all having a great time. "Without that lifeline," Adam went on, "you simply have a society that is not taking care of itself. You have a society with rampant homelessness, malnutrition, and illness, a society with a significant portion of the population that can't read or write. The resulting effect is higher crime and, ultimately, a slackening economy. All the higher income investors and business owners end up losing out in the end if that system isn't there. Their investments and businesses go belly up. It's not even about avoiding some sort of uprising. Everything would just go to crap for everyone if you don't have an insurance policy in place for society. I understand that a working economic system will inevitably have income inequality, but there needs to be a system that provides opportunity equality." Drew started laughing uncontrollably as Adam continued, "Providing opportunity is not as simple as letting disadvantaged members wallow in poverty while assuming that they actually have the same opportunities, when they don't. Without some programs, the chance for many is zero."

Drew was now looking down at the run below and shaking his head slowly. He looked over at the snowboarders, "You boys didn't know you were going to get to ride the lift with the pope today, did you?" They smiled and gave a nervous chuckle but didn't dare speak.

"The biggest problem of all is there's a cycle," Adam continued as Drew scoffed. "The children of this segment of society are at an even greater disadvantage. This is your kids' future society." Adam paused and leaned back some in the chair. "It's easy to get focused on those particular lazy individuals you encounter in life, working for minimum wage, that take ten minutes to bring you a chocolate shake at a fast food restaurant or those that take advantage of the rules for social programs to receive benefits while somehow driving a luxury car. I know it's tough to look at the bums in the city that can't even get their act together enough to find an appropriate place to take a crap. I get all that."

"As long as the crutch is there," Drew interjected, "people will always rely on it. You want to pat yourself on the back for being so righteous, but you have to understand: as long as the crutch is there, they won't ever get their act together, ever. You have to take it away. Then they won't have an option. They'll buck up and get their act together. They'll adapt–"

"Or die?" Adam quickly said. Adam paused and lowered his tone. "Some people would have nowhere to go."

"Oh, there are charities that pay for missions and there are other services available."

"It's not just about coming from unfortunate circumstances," Adam said. "Societies have small segments of people that have slight learning disabilities, mental illnesses, or even permanent physical maladies. Or some people just have lower social skills and lower people skills."

"You sentimental sap! Your people skills are a little sub-par. Actually, I think you left a Y chromosome out in your car."

"I don't think it's even about being compassionate. There simply has to be a system in place, or the entire society is affected. There needs to be an insurance program for everyone. Sure, you likely won't need it, but it's there. It's there for your extended family, or whoever in your community, that might need it down the road. I'm not so sure it's even about caring for the disadvantaged as much as caring for your country."

"So reform the formulas, fix the rules!"

"I agree."

"Look," Drew droned, "since the Great Depression all these programs have been created to pander to the rabble and have insidiously accumulated to where it's absolutely out of control. I know it will be tough to undo things, but something has to be done. This dereliction of people's basic duty to get up, go to work, and contribute to society has gone rampant. All these programs do is beget laziness and foster more and more people to become complete slackers. Who do you think is going to continue to pay for all these handouts for free housing, free food, health care subsidies, disability hoaxes, low income tax credits–"

"Right there, you're talking about shelter, food, health care, and help for disabled people." Drew clenched his teeth as he slowly turned his head away from Adam. "Okay," Adam went on, "Okay, okay, I'll agree that there are isolated cases of abuse and that overall reform is needed, but the only way it can realistically be done is if the system is redesigned to preserve the same initial level of benefits but works better to help people. Such a reformed system would work, on its own, to over time reduce the total expense by further improving conditions for everyone to get a good education and move on to productive work in safe, clean, healthy work places. Sure, there will always be some people with significant disabilities and nowhere else to go that will need a little assistance, but I don't believe anyone, that does not need assistance for the long term, wants to live on the slim pickings from the current social safety net. If the system works, it will become a smaller component of the government. That really is the solution. The number of people on assistance and the cost will decrease as a result of a functioning system as opposed to completely abandoning people that still need help."

Drew groaned in disdain and threw his arms in the air. He was slowly shaking his head, incredulous. "You're deluded," Drew said. "You actually think that will get done?"

"I think it can be done. It could be done. I think it can all be done as part of a grand plan that addresses so much more too: reform to all entitlement programs, changes to the approach for setting discretionary spending, corporate tax reform, and personal income tax reform."

Drew was now laughing loudly, looking up at the peaks, and shaking his head. "You got this grand plan all figured out?"

Adam stammered, "Uh, no, not just yet," as he looked over at Drew with a sarcastic smile and slight shrug.

"I think you just need to toughen up. See, this is why Hannah left you for Lane!"

"Stop it," Adam said, brusquely.

"Here's what you really need for that grand plan. All these welfare programs, have been around for a long time, and there's evidence that they aren't working."

"Just because big problems still exist doesn't mean that the programs haven't been very helpful to so many and to the entire society."

"Go look up the statistics. The cost-benefit ratio is horrendous. Look, I understand that some individuals really do get some valuable help, but what all these communities really need is some restored values: community, family, and hard work. People need to get back to understanding that extraordinary opportunities are right there in front of them. They can work hard and go on to live prosperous, happy lives. There is nothing that is out of reach if they focus on educating themselves, developing skills, and working hard every day. These values are not getting through in some communities. Is your grand plan going to restore these values?"

"If a system is in place that works – that works better – it can go a long way at helping so many realize the opportunities that would also then become more attainable."

"Argh," Drew yelled.

Adam then softly said, "Drew, you know I'm trying to get your goat more than anything else." Adam and Drew were reaching the top of the chairlift ride. "Which way do you want to go?" Adam asked with a chuckle as there was still only one direction to go off the lift. Adam and Drew got off the lift for another blast down the hill. Adam looked to Drew and said, "Actually, I got to get to work after this run. I can't wait in that lift line again."

"Alright, hey, we'll talk again soon," Drew said as he slowly started to scoot forward, and then he yelled, "Hey, do you want to hit the Java Alley on Thursday? We really need to talk man. I have to figure out some way to disabuse you of this warped, noblesse oblige perspective."

"Yeah, right, I know what you want. You just want to check out my girl."

"Hey, just because I've already ordered, doesn't mean I can't look at the menu," Drew replied with a chuckle. "Actually," he added, "I'm seriously looking forward to hearing about your progress on this grandiose vision of yours."

Adam shrugged and then raised his eyebrows in self-doubt. "Okay. Well, I'll see you there." Adam and Drew pushed forward to bolt down the run, and within seconds, their last run quickly became a race to the bottom."

# Chapter 2 - Compassion at Spruce Creek Resort

## *Chapter 3 - The Photographer Weighs In*

Adam and Josh walked into the strength training room at the community recreation center on Tuesday night around 7:45 p.m. The after-work exercise crowd had pretty much cleared out, and it was quieter than normal, still being the off-season in the valley. Classic rock, piped in throughout the entire building by the front desk attendant, could be heard plainly.

"Man, it's getting dark early," Josh said as it was already completely dark outside and the windows offered nothing but a reflection of the inside activity.

"Are we doing our frat boy workout tonight?" Adam asked.

"Heck yeah!" Josh said, playfully. "Chest and shoulders. Actually, my legs are still sore from those dang lunges you had me do on Saturday."

"Are you sure you don't want to just shoot some hoops?"

"No excuses, buddy. It's happening."

Josh Carpenter grew up in the same town as Adam in Ohio and graduated in the same class at their hometown high school. They had been friends for twenty-one years and still played basketball, lifted weights, and watched ballgames together. Josh, five-feet eight-inches tall and stocky with fair skin and shaggy black hair, managed to get by only shaving twice a week.

Josh moved to Colorado a couple years after Adam and worked as a lift operator for the resort for three years, then waited tables at a local restaurant for a ski season, and subsequently got a job with the local newspaper, the Spruce Creek News. Josh didn't make much money working for the paper, but he was happy with the job and relished the opportunity to ski Spruce Creek sixty days a year. He wrote stories on many local community events and other hot topics in the valley such as the Forest Service's efforts to crack down on squatters living in the forest for the summer or the Department of Transportation's work to get the highway pass reopened after an induced avalanche buried a three hundred foot stretch of the road with snow and debris. The truth is that Josh's duties for the newspaper focused on less significant events: local charity golf tournaments, the radio station's heli-skiing trip giveaways, or the annual spring contests to see who can most accurately guess when the ice will break on Lake Labash, ten miles down the valley from the resort.

Josh's forte is definitely his photography and his pictures that show up in the newspaper about every day. He became a fantastic professional photographer through his employment, as the newspaper paid him to take several courses to become their lead photographer, and his personal interest in photography also recently cut into his ski time.

Adam was moving around the gym, stretching his arms. Josh had finished stretching and was loading weights on the bar for military presses. It should be emphasized that neither Adam or Josh was the slightest bit buff; although, Josh always lifted a bit more than Adam.

"Any more thoughts on opening a gallery?" Adam asked as he had his right arm extended and pulled over to stretch his shoulder.

"Nope. Alright, get in there, ten reps." Adam sat down, as instructed, to do a set.

Adam finished his warm-up set and stood up, and Josh sat down to complete a matching set. Adam continued stretching as Josh worked through his repetitions. Josh then quickly stood up and grabbed more small plates to add to the bar, without hesitation.

"Seriously," Adam said, "be sure and keep all the pictures you have so far. I'm telling you, you could sell copies of those pictures you got of that bull moose up by Pine Grove Tarn. You must have gotten up early to get those."

"Stop the chitchat. Next set boss."

Adam pushed through another set of military presses. "Ugh," he grumbled as he slammed the bar back on the rack following his last repetition. "We should have done bench first."

"You ski yet?" Josh asked as he sat down for his set.

"Yeah, I went up yesterday with Drew."

"How was it?"

"It was a mob scene by 10:00 a.m. On a Monday! Lots of Halloween revelers. It was fine. Nice to be outside. I need to tune my cruisers."

"Ah, you won't be needing those much longer. You're going to be riding your fatties soon enough." Josh finished his set and then gazed across the room, in thought, as he slowly said, "Ah, we'll be back there on Gus's Glade in a few weeks, immersed in the sanctity of the Spruce Creek forest. Adam, it's going to snow so much this year." Of course Josh didn't know that, but it was always pleasing to be optimistic before each new ski season. While making turns in October is enjoyable, the deep powder is where lasting memories are made.

"I hope you're right," Adam said.

Adam and Josh quietly finished their remaining sets of military presses and moved over to the dumbbell racks to do some lateral raises and front raises. Even though they were using different weights, they took turns doing sets.

"Is Drew enjoying his off-season?" Josh asked. "What did he have to say?"

"Yeah, he's good," Adam said. "He's relaxed. Well, he was until I got him all riled up. We ended up talking about politics."

Josh grunted, partially from his set of lateral raises and partially from the notion of talking politics with Drew. "Oh man," Josh said as he slammed the dumbbells down on the rack, "you're not really going to vote for that guy, are you?"

"I don't know," Adam mumbled. "Actually, you would have been proud of me. I started arguing fairly intensely with Drew. I don't even know why. I was just looking to have fun and push his buttons, but I think I may have gone too far. Oh boy, I really had him in a snit when our day was over. I seriously may be in the doghouse with him now."

"Good. Drew could use it."

"Oh sure, you got it all figured out?" Adam asked, chuckling.

"After everything that's happened the last few years, are you kidding? Adam, the corporations, big oil companies, and investment banks are absolutely out of control. They don't care, Adam." Adam, having heard all this before, started a set of lateral raises, looking to pass the time until Josh was finished. "The big banks can completely wreck the economy," Josh went on. "They've done it. They'll even bet on the economy tanking. They cash out or even get a bailout while the rest of America struggles to get their feet back under them. The big executives float down from their corner offices with their lucrative, golden parachutes and cruise back to their castles with big smiles on their faces. You don't think they should chip in a little more in taxes to pay for these bailouts."

"Are you through?" Adam asked, annoyed.

"And the big oil companies tap into America's resources, but do you think they care if they spill millions of gallons oil all over pristine lands that don't belong to them?"

"The oil has to be moved somehow, Josh," Adam replied between breathes as he worked through his exercises. "The oil isn't located in the same place where it's used. The refineries aren't located in the same place where they mine for oil."

"I understand that, but it has to be moved safely and without harming community water supplies."

"And done efficiently," Adam interjected.

"Look," Josh said, "their number one goal is to make as much money as possible next quarter. There's no concern for anything or anyone after that. The American taxpayers come along later and pay the huge tab to clean up the messes from these big companies. Do you think the big energy companies deserve loopholes to avoid paying taxes? You don't think those executives, with their fat cat salaries, dropping down onto the helipads on their 200-foot yachts, should give a little more back as recompense? You think these guys need fewer regulations?"

"Alright, alright, just do another set there," Adam said. Josh was suddenly blasting through his lateral raises like a super hero. "Thing is Josh, you can't regulate these industries to non-existence. We need these companies, out there, exploring and developing energy resources and researching new means for meeting the country's energy needs. And there has to be a profit motive to drive these efforts. The banks have to be able to create investment vehicles, open channels for businesses and individuals to get credit, and move money around for the entire financial system to operate. People need to be able to borrow money to buy houses and provide safe, comfortable shelter for their families and to maintain the massive housing component of our economy. Home ownership has proven to be so valuable for maintaining healthy communities all around the country. The financial system has to be able to function under a free market system with little intervention."

Josh finished his set, got up, and slowly walked over to the television in the corner of the room to turn the channel to the Avalanche hockey game. There were three other late-evening regular members in the room that had not been paying any attention to their conversation or the television, for all three of them were wearing headphones.

Josh walked back over to Adam and said, "Okay, I'm sorry for the rant. I understand all that. Of course, I understand that, but there has to be some oversight. We've seen the effects before when these big corporations run amok. The economy has been wrecked before. Financial regulations have to be in place to assure transparency and protect consumers that are directly impacted by what the big banks are doing. Environmental considerations are important too. We've seen fragile ecosystems tarnished before. There have to be some regulations. I certainly don't favor de-regulation."

"It has to be reasonable," Adam said.

"Fine," Josh said. Adam dropped some dumbbells down on the dumbbell rack, unintentionally making a loud clang. "Come on," Josh said, "it's bench press time. I feel like maxing out tonight."

"No, no, no, I don't want to do that," Adam said. "I know my max. Just do your regular sets." Adam sauntered over and glared at the hockey game as Josh loaded the bar on the flat bench rack and worked through several repetitions for his first warmup set.

It should be noted that Josh wasn't always such a liberal. Maybe it was the beautiful Colorado high country that did it to him. He would certainly forever push for stewardship for the wilderness, rivers, and National Parks and has always loved the clean air of the forests, the gurgle of a clean, high mountain stream, and being ensconced in the untouched serenity found throughout the Rocky Mountains. He had evinced to Adam many times before that he would never have faith in private industry to preserve the beauty of this great planet.

"So, are the Avs going to be any good this year?" Adam asked.

"I don't know. It's football season. Your set." Josh and Adam quietly rotated through their sets on the flat bench while monitoring the Avalanche game. Adam managed to somehow use a bit less weight than Josh, without judgment. They then moved over to the incline bench.

Adam was pinching his sides as Josh was putting weights on the bar. "Ah, these dang winter love handles," Adam said.

"Are you suggesting that you don't have love handles in the summer?"

"No," Adam murmured. "Uh, I call those my summer love handles."

Josh sat down on the incline bench to begin a set. "Did you watch that Broncos debacle with Hannah?" Josh asked.

"Yeah," Adam said, listlessly.

"How was that?"

Adam smiled and said, "We also talked about the election. It was actually a nice distraction from the game."

"So, are you two getting back together?"

"No," Adam said, quickly turning away. "Stop with that nonsense. Do your set." Adam waved at Josh as he took a few steps toward the television to watch the Avalanche game. As Josh finished his last repetition, Adam whimsically said, "Hey look Josh, I'm multi-tasking. I'm watching hockey and working out at the same time. I'm simultaneously completing two very productive activities."

Josh got up and, undistracted by Adam's effort to change the subject, said, "You really don't see what's going on, do you?" Adam attempted to completely ignore Josh as he sat back and blasted through his incline presses with gusto.

Josh had been well aware of the time Adam and Hannah had been spending together over the past few weeks. Josh was dating Emily Barnes, who had become good friends with Hannah after they first moved to Spruce Creek and worked together as servers at a local steakhouse for nearly two years. Josh met Emily, who grew up in Atlanta, through Adam and Hannah. Emily was to be Hannah's maid of honor for her planned nuptials to Lane.

Adam suddenly blurted out, "Wasn't it Emily's responsibility to make sure the bride made it to the wedding? Where was she?"

"She was with Hannah the whole time."

Adam moved back over to watch the hockey game even though there was no audio and the game was in the second intermission – the broadcast shifted to analysis and commentary. Josh sat back down for another set on the incline bench, and then Adam quietly took his turn.

"Have you seen or talked to Lane?" Josh asked.

"Nope," Adam said as he finished his set.

"He was your roommate! You got no follow-up, ever?"

Adam sighed and was looking up at the ceiling, shaking his head. "He was my roommate, not a friend," he said.

"Obviously. I don't think I've ever heard of anything so crass. Did you ever catch them?"

"No! It wasn't like that. She just ...hopped in his car one day."

"You know, you didn't exactly fight for her."

"I'm going to get a drink of water," Adam said, miffed. "I can only take so much of this infernal drivel."

Adam strolled out of the room to the water fountain, located down a short hallway and near the front desk. Josh had finished a set on the incline bench and went to get a drink too. As he walked down the hall, he passed Adam, who had a surly expression on his face. Josh lurched toward Adam and pretended to punch his stomach real fast, as if it was a punching bag. Adam subsequently pushed Josh firmly against the hallway wall, nearly knocking down two pictures of personal trainers that worked at the center. The loud thump caught the attention of a couple younger front desk attendants, but they chose to ignore the incident as Adam and Josh were both giggling like seven-year-olds. Adam was nodding his head and smiling as he continued back to the weight room.

Adam promptly finished his last set on the incline bench and was re-racking the weights when Josh returned. As Adam slammed the last plate on the weight tree, he said, "You know, if the taxes aren't reduced for these big corporations you love so much, they're going to keep moving their home offices to Europe." Josh laughed at Adam's obvious attempt to change the subject away from Hannah.

"Hey, Democrats want to cut the corporate tax rates too," Josh retorted. "They are totally on board with implementing significant corporate tax reform, if it includes simplification to the overall tax code and removing the subsidies and nefarious loopholes that so many of these corporations are now enjoying. Adam, I wish the entire Internal Revenue Code was simplified and cut down dramatically, for corporations – well, for all business types, for that matter – and for individuals."

Adam and Josh walked over to the multi-cable unit to do some crossover fly exercises. Adam quietly completed the first set, letting the two opposite weight stacks slam when he was finished. "Significant tax reform would have to be a revenue neutral effort," Adam said.

Josh worked through his set of flys and then grunted as he muttered, "You suppose that could ever be done?"

"Any effort to use tax reform as a means to decrease or increase revenue would kill the effort," Adam said. "There would still be plenty of opportunity to change rates up or down after a reformed code is implemented. Of course, even an overall revenue neutral plan would involve some difficult give-and-take, but it could be done."

"It will never happen," Josh said.

"It's sad," Adam said with genuine sorrow. "It really is."

Josh smacked Adam on the shoulder. "Come on, your set." Adam slowly moved over and gave a lackluster effort for another set of flys as Josh noted, "Somebody would insist on trying to eliminate the progressive tax system and implement a flat tax for everyone while somebody else would inevitably try to bump up marginal rates without any offset anywhere else and that would be it: any chance for a deal is then dead. The whole effort would ebb into sound bites."

Adam and Josh quietly completed several sets of crossover flys, and while Josh finished his last set, Adam sat down on a bench next to the multi-cable unit. He looked at the reflection of the room in the window. "You know Josh," Adam said, "the progressive tax system needs to be maintained with extreme care. I understand that it can't be expected for dishwashers, eating noodles for dinner and riding public transportation to their minimum wage jobs, to fund the world's greatest national defense system, and I understand the basic expectation that those who have benefitted the most from the government's subsidized system of schools and universities, robust infrastructure, and expansive energy network need to return more of their pay, but the system can't be structured such that it discourages entrepreneurship or innovation or discourages employees from working harder or from performing at a higher level to simply achieve a greater return or achieve the standard American dream for their families. The system can't punish people whose entire young lives are devoured in school, training to be doctors, lawyers, engineers, and business people. We would be terribly remiss to not understand that. Many who have done fairly well for themselves are still simply looking to provide a good life for their family."

"I agree," Josh exclaimed. "But the multi-millionaires that reap the massive gains, from others' hard work and innovation or from this country's resources, that do not belong to them, or from a system of laws, regulations, and loopholes that yield big windfalls for their corporations, need to give more back to support the system and all those that contribute so much to this great nation." Josh was waving for Adam to do his last set of crossover flys. "Come on," he said.

Adam stood frozen, ready to complete his exercises. He then lowered his tone and said, "I really don't have any problem with all the CEOs, with their golden parachutes, and the hedge fund titans and our favorite entertainers, actors, and actresses and our favorite professional athletes, while albeit incredibly talented, paying a good bit more for this great society that they have enjoyed so much more, in ways that most Americans couldn't even begin to fathom. And I certainly don't mind if your favorite rap stars give a little bit of their mass of millions back." Josh certainly laughed as he never actually listened to rap.

Adam then quietly completed his set and was suddenly distracted by light tapping sounds against the windows. "Is it raining?" he asked. As soon as he finished his exercises, he immediately walked over, put his face up to a window, and cupped his hands around his eyes so he could see outside. "It's raining!"

"It's snowing up on the mountain," Josh said.

Josh and Adam slowly moved over to mats on the floor in the corner of the exercise room and sat down to begin doing sets of crunches.

Josh was slightly panting as he completed his crunches and asked, "So what did Drew have to say about the election?"

"Josh, I seriously think he may be done with me. I don't know what got into me. I had so much fun prodding him over the social safety net. Josh, it really has such an enormous impact on how so many people think about politics and how they'll vote for the rest of their lives. There are so many people that vote Republican because they just can't stand food stamps and other welfare programs. That's it."

"Good grief," Josh replied, "as a percentage of the federal budget, it's so small."

"Yeah but it's as if that's not even a consideration for many voters. I'm telling you, there are so many voters, most of whom are actually at the lower end of the income ladder, that vote conservative for that one single reason. They just ...can't ...take it. They really don't have a problem with the progressive income tax system, with seeing more focus on developing alternative energy resources, with more emphasis on diplomatic solutions to foreign policy issues, or whether stiffer regulations are placed on big banks, ...but when it comes to food stamps, subsidies, and other welfare, ...they ...just ...can't ...take it. They grind their teeth every night and stew over it all day. They sit around at diners with their conservative buddies, and talk about it, over and over, day after day after day." Adam sat up as he had completed a set of crunches. Josh didn't respond and started a set. "They tell these same stories over and over for years," Adam went on, "about people that received benefits, when it really didn't look like they needed the assistance at all."

"Sure," Josh chimed in, "but in most cases, it's because of the assistance that they are in so much better shape than they otherwise would be. The assistance has helped them so much, and they are subsequently in a better position to further their education or to fulfill the basic requirements needed to get a job or just participate in their communities." Josh sat up. "I don't know. It's as if it's all a big, unfortunate misunderstanding. Good grief, most of the programs are temporary. People only get food stamps for a limited time, and they don't even fully cover the cost for groceries. I think these same voters are getting too focused on some particular stories, isolated cases, of the programs being abused, where the stories may not even be completely accurate."

Adam looked right at Josh and repeated the mantra, "I'm just saying, ...they ...just ...can't ...take it."

Josh and Adam quietly finished their sets of crunches, stood up, and walked over to a unit to do some hanging leg raises. Josh began a long set of leg raises as Adam then took a few steps toward the television to check on the status of the Avalanche game.

As Adam walked back over toward Josh to wait his turn, he said, "I think the country and the majority of the electorate is perfectly comfortable with unions."

Josh dropped his head and busted out laughing. He had to stop his exercises. "You're killing me here," he said. Josh dropped his legs down and was now standing, shaking his head, and looking right at Adam. Adam was chuckling lightly with a huge grin on his face. Josh propped back up to continue his leg raises and grunted a bit as he said, "I don't know that everyone else would agree with you on that."

"Okay, no, but I really believe that many in the electorate are now comfortable with unions and believe they are simply fighting for basic clean, safe working conditions. There's no place in America for sweatshops, workplace disasters, or situations where workers are getting injured doing their basic assignments. There's no place for masses of workers coming down with sweeping illnesses like we see occurring in other countries. I think there's also a collective agreement among most voters that union workers have a good work ethic, for the most part, and work very hard at their jobs, which are very important to the overall society. They don't always get paid well for what they do and they have trouble fighting for good pay on their own, so employees simply need to be able to work together to achieve some basic workers' rights. At the same time, union members have also become very comfortable with the notion of compromise and understand that negotiated terms must allow for a company to remain profitable and competitive and that unions, themselves, also have a key role in reducing the amount of jobs that are offshored. With this attitude among the population, I think you're now going to see a surge in manufacturing jobs in this country and see that surge continue for decades."

Josh dropped down after finishing his set. "Think so?" he asked with a dismissive tone.

"Ah," Adam said with a shrug, "what do I know? We'll see."

"You're saying manufacturing's back?"

"Okay, I definitely wouldn't go that far."

"Well, union rights still need to be maintained," Josh said. "Workers must have that ability to organize such that labor can have a voice in so much that affects them directly: trade deals, labor rules, and other policy decisions. And it may be that very sentiment you expressed that could hurt workers' rights if there is a follow-up tendency to let some basic rights fade. Actually, as the economy has changed and with manufacturing's declining share of the economy, it is now even more important to assure that basic union rights don't get lost in the transition. We know from history how bad conditions can get for workers without those rights. We still see today, in other countries, how bad conditions can get without such rights in place. Also, it's certainly not just about manufacturing. How about the service unions for teachers, nurses–"

"I seriously don't even want to talk about some of the stuff nurses do," Adam interjected. Adam quietly finished his leg raises as Josh sat down on a nearby bench. "Actually," Adam added, "a large part of the struggle is about protecting pensions, right?" Josh shrugged as Adam continued, "But most companies are done with pensions, at least for our generation. The best way to address that for the future is to fix social security, reform the rules for retirement savings to create a more level playing field for all workers, refine the rules to encourage more people to participate in savings plans, and create a program to advance personal finance education for every American. Unions don't need to be involved with that effort, do they?"

"You got a solution for all that?" Josh asked, exhausted over the conversation.

"It can be done," Adam said.

Josh waved and said, "Come on. Tell me later." He started walking out of the room. "Let's go shoot some hoops."

## *Chapter 4 - Headstrong at Eagles Nest Lookout*

Hannah, Adam, and Cody started their hike up the North Ridge at 3:00 p.m. on Wednesday afternoon. The trail climbs diagonally up the ridge, on the north side of the valley, opposite the ski resort, passing through a dense aspen grove about a quarter mile up and then crossing a stream before the ascent becomes fairly intense. The top of the trail is at the summit of Higgins Peak, at nearly twelve thousand feet above mean sea level, after passing the few remaining remnants of an old mining town, Higgins. They wouldn't make it near that high on this hike with the recent snowfall, as even the very beginning of the path was a bit muddy from the cold front that passed the previous night. Cody was in front, leading the way, as Adam and Hannah motored along behind him, carefully watching their steps on the slick trail.

"So, how high do you think we'll get?" Hannah asked.

"Not too high," Adam replied. "Also, it's a new moon, so we won't have any moonlight after dark." Adam picked up the hiking pace a bit.

"So, we set our clocks back on Sunday," Hannah noted. While they were both breathing heavily as they moved swiftly up the trail, Cody was disappointed with the slow pace and stopped to look back at them.

"Ugh, I dread it getting dark so early," Adam said.

"Are you going to do any full moon snowshoeing this year?" Hannah asked.

"Heck yeah," Adam quickly said with a high pitched inflection in his voice.

Hannah was wearing thinner, synthetic hiking pants and a light shell over her frayed pullover sweatshirt bearing the name of the university she attended in North Carolina. After focusing on catching up with her breathing for a few seconds, she smiled to herself and said, "Just think, the election will be long over by the next full moon – no more mail flyers, no more television ads, no more campaign calls, no more phone polls."

"Ugh," Adam groaned. "It's really about so much more than what we've been bombarded with around the clock for the past few weeks."

"Adam!" Hannah quickly blurted out. "You're not really going to vote for that guy, are you?"

"I really wish it was as simple as you and Drew and Josh make it out to be."

"It is simple."

"Well, you're focused on one particular aspect of the bigger picture."

"Well," Hannah quietly uttered between breathes, "it's important." She and Adam were both still breathing fairly heavily.

Hannah and Adam continued on, quietly enjoying their hike. They passed through the aspen grove where all the leaves were already off the trees, affording a nice view of the valley that is not visible from that section of the North Ridge trail in the middle of the summer. The air was cool and the fresh snow higher up and on the trees muffled most of the din of traffic and barking dogs in the valley below. They easily crossed the stream, that was nothing but a trickle, but the babble of the water flowing around the rocks and woody debris was peaceful nonetheless. That same crossing can be downright hairy when encountered in the spring, in the middle of a heavy snowmelt runoff. Hannah and Adam settled into a comfortable hiking pace following the transition to the steeper section of the trail – a grade of around twenty percent. The smell in the air was telling of the short autumn season, that was already on the lam, and the long winter to settle in soon. Hannah and Adam continued on silently for several minutes. Adam was purposefully kicking through the layer of aspen leaves that had recently covered the trail. Cody had previously been exploring all around both sides of the trail but was now settled into a steady walking pace in front of Hannah and Adam.

"Adam, I understand how so many people reach that place with their faith and through their love of people that they feel that they need to intervene, but there are other ways to deal with it. There is so much room to provide a better education to women and young people about the significance of their decisions and their options, but for the options to be ultimately restricted through government rule has so many dire consequences to society. There are so many educational resources and programs that could be administered." Hannah paused to catch up on her breathing before continuing. "Programs that could significantly reduce the number of abortions and properly educate young people about their options." Hannah looked up at a few ravens that were circling high overhead. "I'll just never understand how the Republicans can be so adamant about reducing the size of government and getting government out of the way of businesses and all individuals in every way, except when it comes to this particular, very personal issue."

Adam stopped hiking and was breathing heavily as he looked, through an opening in a stand of lodgepole pines, over the valley below. Hannah stopped a couple steps behind him, put her hands on her hips, and looked down at the ground.

Adam slowly asked, "Hannah, did you ever–"

"No!" Hannah quickly yelled. Hannah angrily lunged at Adam and slapped him hard on the arm. "Why would you ask that?" She punched him hard three more times as he turned away from her strikes. "You know–"

"I know. I know. I'm sorry. I don't know why I asked. I'm sorry." Adam dropped his head. "You know I would never question your virtue." Adam gritted his teeth as he looked away from Hannah. "Hannah, I've sensed and known that you've always been at a such a strong place with your faith and figured you would be outright devout if you weren't out having so much fun on the hill on Sundays, so I just continue to be fascinated by this, that's all."

"Adam, all women are for improving and expanding education so everyone will understand their options for family planning and so they will thoroughly consider the ramifications of their decisions. We just don't need a bunch of old guys in Washington to institute laws to ultimately get it done." Hannah gave Adam another evil stare as she kneeled down to pet Cody, who had finally turned around and walked back to join them. "Adam, this issue affects the health of the entire society."

Adam looked back out over the valley and surmised, "I guess that really is it. There is such a disconnect in understanding. There really is no way that a sixty-three year old man, shoving papers around in a swanky office in D.C., long, long removed from his days of being a teenager and courting ladies." Adam paused for a second and went on, "there really is no way such a man can understand how personal this issue is for so many people, specifically women and young people."

"Courting ladies?" Hannah blurted out, laughing. "You're such a dork." Cody quickly took off up the trail, barking at a chipmunk that successfully scurried up a tree. The chipmunk, still horrified, looked down at Cody from the safety of a high branch. Cody stopped barking but sat down and continued to stare right at the chipmunk. Hannah went on, "We just need to let the health care providers and non-profit groups continue to work to refine programs, with the involvement of conservatives to assure their concerns are reflected, but all the needs, concerns, and health of society cannot be properly addressed with hard rules forced on everyone without consideration for the specifics of each circumstance."

Cody had returned and found a dry spot to sit down to wait for Adam and Hannah. Adam looked at Cody and ordered, "Alright, alright, giddy up!" Cody quickly darted up the trail in excitement as Adam and Hannah moved swiftly behind him. The grade had eased up a bit. A couple inches of snow covered the trail, which actually provided better footing than the slippery mud they had trudged through before.

"You want to stop at the Eagles Nest Lookout," Adam asked.

"Sure."

They hiked quietly for about twenty minutes before reaching the lookout – a large bedrock outcrop surrounded by several sparsely-spaced, old growth spruce trees. Adam and Hannah sat down on a couple spots on the bedrock that were so perfectly configured as seats that they looked like they were molded from a couple lawn chairs. Cody stayed nearby but was moving around, picking up enough scents to keep him plenty occupied. The sun was low in the sky off to the west and the air, twelve hundred feet above the valley floor, was noticeably thinner and cooler. From this location, they could see a long stretch of Spruce Creek meandering through the valley. The stream had been nicely rehabilitated twenty years ago to address the devastating impacts from placer mining, that completely destroyed the river bed, in the nineteenth century.

Hannah pulled out a couple granola bars from her jacket pockets, handed one to Adam, and then looked out over the valley. "Hey, is that an eagle?" she quickly asked.

"Uh," Adam droned, focusing on a bird flying high over the valley in the distance. "I believe that's just another raven." Adam quickly devoured his breakfast bar.

"Younger eagles are all black like that, aren't they?"

"Yeah. Josh would know for sure."

"How's Josh?"

"He's fine. I saw him at the gym last night. I was telling him he should open a gallery."

"He should," Hannah quickly replied. "I was actually thinking about that some the other day. He could set up a coffee stand in there and sell pastries and muffins during the busy season. He could also sell hiking guides and all sorts of other regional travel books."

Adam nodded in agreement. He then drank a big swig of water from his water bottle and handed it to Hannah. "How's your job?" Adam asked.

"Eh," Hannah groaned, "it's alright. I'm basically a secretary." She shifted to find a more comfortable position on the rock. "I don't consider it demeaning or anything like that. I like the agents in the office, but I need to use my degree, Adam. I have to start paying down my student loans." Hannah majored in Business with emphasis in Accounting. She dropped her head and pet Cody on the top of his head as he leaned against the rock where Hannah was sitting, "So, I have an opportunity to go work at my uncle's accounting firm back in North Carolina."

Adam quickly turned toward Hannah. He stared right at Hannah for a couple seconds. "You're not considering that, are you?"

"I don't know. Maybe it is time for me to hang up my powder skis and take my place in the carpool."

"Carpool? What carpool?!" Adam was laughing and shaking his head as Hannah shrugged.

"The lease on my place is up at the end November, so now's the time to make the decision if I'm going to do it."

"Hannah, you can't just hastily make a decision like that because your lease is up." Adam sighed as a raven quickly flew down and alighted on an adjacent rock. The raven looked right at Adam as he froze and stared at it. Adam then loudly blurted out, "Kraaugh!" The raven looked at Adam but didn't budge. Cody took a couple steps toward the raven and barked once but the bird remained on the rock, unaffected, looking around for crumbs. Adam said, "I know they're smart, but dang they sure are ugly."

"Other issues are important to me too," Hannah suddenly said. "But I'll be very comfortable with my vote." Adam, immediately registering the returned focus on the election, gave a firm, positive nod of support.

Hannah handed Adam a soft water bowl for Cody, Adam poured some water in the bowl, and he gently set it down on the ground for Cody. Cody began slurping at the water before Adam could get his hand away.

"So much of it is demographics," Adam said. "If you told me someone's age, gender, race, occupation, annual income, and marital and family status, I bet I could tell you, within ninety-five percent accuracy, how they'll vote." Hannah leaned down and poured some more water in Cody's water bowl. "It sure seems like it should be about so much more than that. People should vote for the good of society, for their children, and for their children's children."

Hannah suddenly looked down and froze. Cody stopped drinking and looked up at Hannah. Adam's eyes got real big. He looked at Hannah. "Hannah," he said, "I never said I didn't want to have kids."

"Oh, no, yeah, no, I know," Hannah quickly said. Hannah quickly diverted the conversation back to the topic at hand. "They still think they're voting in the best interest of future generations, even though they're clearly affected personally and directly in some way or just flat out voting their pocketbook. Older generations think the government should be about Social Security and Medicare and that the government should cut back on other involvements in society. Middle aged people think the government should focus more on spending for energy development, infrastructure development, research, and taking care of all the government facilities – that is, jobs. Younger voters think there should be heavy focus on education and protecting the environment and this great planet, that they plan to enjoy for many more decades, but they don't think about old age entitlements." Hannah started laughing and was stuttering as she went on, "If somebody changes careers during their life, their political convictions will dramatically and completely shift right in tune." Hannah leaned back against the rock and looked out over the valley as she continued, "You add that the political process revolves entirely around a two party system. Each party will try to pander to an expanding demographic while catering to their base. If one party drifts too far toward their base and loses the majority vote, they lose power in policy making. Then, they adjust their platform to pander to a broader demographic to get back to a majority. It's inevitable that you have such an evenly divided electorate where winning with fifty-four percent of the vote is considered a landslide victory. The system does not allow for either party to win by a larger majority, at least throughout the entire nation."

"Oh," Adam interjected, "an entire national election can come down to a few counties or even a few people."

Hannah smiled, leaned back against the rock, and closed her eyes. "Well," she said, "you're one of those people Adam. It's all going to come down to your vote." A cloud drifted east allowing the sun to shine on their faces, but there would be only a few more minutes of direct sunlight left. It was much warmer in the sun, and the breeze had let up. The raven had hopped down on the ground and was moving around, still looking for any crumbs. Cody wasn't currently affected by its presence. Hannah shifted a bit to find a more a comfortable seat on the rock.

"So Adam," Hannah said, "how do you get all voters to think selflessly and consider the greater good of everyone, the greater good of society? That's what you need to see your grand plan realized."

"North Carolina?" Adam asked, perturbed.

Hannah raised her eyebrows and shrugged. "I have to do something, Adam. I'm broke. I need to pay down my student loans. My aunt and uncle have offered to let me stay, rent-free, in their basement for a while." Adam dropped his head and looked at the different colors of lichen on the rock around his seat. "North Carolina's a nice place," Hannah said.

"That's not the point," Adam said. "Hannah, what the–"

"There's no place for me here anymore," Hannah exclaimed.

Adam sighed and mumbled, almost inaudibly, "Yes there is." Cody then immediately thereafter lurched toward the raven and it flew away.

Hannah and Adam sat quietly for a couple minutes, looking out over the valley and enjoying the quiet and sweet aroma of the Spruce Creek forest. "Did you talk about immigration policy with Drew?" Hannah asked.

Adam quickly perked up, opened his eyes real big, and vigorously shook his head. "No, no, no, no," he said. It was a common belief between Adam and Hannah that Drew hired illegal immigrants to work for his landscaping business, but there was no way either would discuss the topic with him. Adam leaned back against the rock. "Actually," he said, "I get the impression that Drew is really good to all his employees. They seem to really love working for him and come back every season. I think he really cares for those guys and also genuinely appreciates how they have relied on him for a job and for money to pay their bills."

"Yeah I've picked up on that too," Hannah said, nodding.

"Now immigration, …now, …that's a complicated issue."

"Yep," Hannah said. "I don't know exactly how to deal with the overall situation. I can tell you this: I'm not going to be a racist."

"Uh, of course not," Adam said, somewhat on the defensive.

Hannah leaned forward, looked down, and began sifting through a pile of pine needles on the rock beside her seat. "Every day," she said, "people get up and make that decision to either be racist or not be a racist. It's not a condition that anyone is born with. It's entirely learned behavior, and every person is perfectly capable of making a change. As soon as somebody catches themselves saying or even thinking in regards to 'those people', they've gotten to a really bad place, but they can still change. They can get up the next morning and simply decide they're not going to be a racist anymore and act and think accordingly." Hannah leaned back. Adam was quiet, seeming almost too nervous to comment. "People that have gotten to that bad place have to recognize that their attitude toward an entire race has been dreadfully distorted. Maybe it was a few experiences with some particular individuals or it was due to some whacked out statistics they heard about, inaccurately or inappropriately presented without proper consideration for history or the broader situation, but they have to acknowledge that their entire perspective is anathema and has become horribly warped. They need to stop and think about where they have ended up and make a solitary decision to deplore racism and make a concerted effort to get to a better place, entirely on their own, without any consideration or influence from anyone else around them."

"Yeah, yeah, of course," Adam said nervously. "Why did you get on that all of a sudden?"

"Oh, I mostly just can't stand some of the rhetoric that you hear when immigration policy is debated, but it's a broader belief that extends way beyond immigration policy or politics."

Adam nodded firmly. "Sure, sure."

"Anyone who carries themselves through life with such an awful attitude, deep in their gut, will in the end, rue that they didn't make a change earlier in life before it would have such a negative effect on so many others around them. I think it's something that anyone, looking back on their life, will regret more than just about any other decision they make, in regards to how they carried themselves. Also, if someone really has a strong belief about some situation in society or their community, that's fine, but as soon as they adopt a racist attitude about the situation, any opportunity for reaching a solution or getting to a better place is dead."

Adam looked at Hannah and gave another firm nod of confirmation. Adam and Hannah looked over at Cody who had closed his eyes. Hannah zipped up her shell and pulled a thin wool hat out of her jacket pocket and put it on. The sun had just disappeared off to the west, and it immediately got much cooler. They quietly looked at the sunset for a minute.

"Woh!" Adam then suddenly blurted out with his head turned to the east. "Check out the alpenglow!"

Hannah turned and looked at the peaks off to the east. "Wow, it's purple," she said.

Alpenglow refers to the light on the mountains to the east after the sun has disappeared to the west. The alpenglow is from the rays of sunlight still reaching the higher peaks to the east and usually looks red or orange but certainly looked purple at that moment. Adam and Hannah sat quietly for a couple minutes monitoring the sunset and the alpenglow.

"Well, we should get moving," Adam finally said.

"Yeah."

They stood up, Adam stretched his back, and they began a quick walk back down the trail. Cody hopped up, bolted down the trail, and was out of sight within seconds. The walk down is always faster, but they had to carefully watch their step in the slush and mud.

After a couple minutes of walking quietly, not breathing hard at all on the descent, Adam said, "You know, it's difficult to accuse any political candidate of being a racist."

"Oh, I agree," Hannah said. "Yeah, I don't think there's any way a person could be in that position, to begin with, if they hadn't already made the decision long ago to resist any racist feelings. Now, some may have a tougher time living up to their decision than others." Adam and Hannah were moving rapidly down the trail, Hannah leading the way, sloshing through the mud and mucking up her hiking pants. "The problem may be more that some candidates will still tacitly pander to prejudiced people to get votes. I know they're just trying to get elected so they can accomplish their objectives, but they will ultimately have a propensity to still pander to that sector of the electorate that got them elected long after they've been in office."

Adam nodded but did not add anything. Adam then called out to Cody a couple times, for they had not seen him for a few minutes. After a few seconds, Cody suddenly popped his head up above a grade shift further down the trail. Cody took a few steps toward them and then sat down, in the middle of the trail. Hannah would never admit it to Adam, but she knew Cody maybe liked Adam better than her. Adam had taken care of Cody many times when Hannah was on long vacations with Lane – awkward for Adam, but it was all about Cody. Cody sat on the trail until they reached him. They didn't slow down as they passed, Adam quickly pet Cody and muttered, "Good boy." They continued on for a few minutes, gingerly making their way down the muddy, steeper segment of the trail.

"Hannah," Adam said. "There was a time when I thought you would always be good to me."

"What?" Hannah said, immediately stopping on the trail as she turned around to look at him. "Of course, I'll always be good to you." She paused for a moment and looked right at Adam. She tilted her head slightly and slowly said, "Adam–"

"I know. I know. I just mean, I felt that in a unique way. I felt that – well, consider a stupid example – if I was out to eat with all your coworkers and friends and spilled my soda all over the table." Hannah started laughing and Adam continued as he was laughing too. "You would sympathize with me one hundred percent. You wouldn't laugh in front of everyone else. That's unique." Adam paused as Hannah furrowed her brow and looked right at Adam. "If I got sick and lost a bunch of weight, if I was in a car accident and wound up in a wheelchair, if I ended up getting early onset Alzheimer's, whatever, you would be there for me."

"Adam," Hannah said slowly as she moved over and gave him a hug. Adam and Hannah hugged each other for a bit, long enough that Cody decided to sit down.

Hannah finally pulled back and said, "Come on, let's go. It's getting dark."

They continued on for several minutes without talking. They hopped across the stream and really picked up their pace on the flatter descent through the aspen grove.

As they walked out of a stand of lodgepole pine trees at the trailhead, Hannah asked, "So are you going to that screening of the new extreme skiing movie tonight?"

"No, I actually have to go back to work for a couple hours and finish up some stuff for a meeting tomorrow."

"Oh, okay," Hannah said as they were splitting up. "So Adam, is this grand plan of yours going to put an end to racism?"

Adam sighed. "I'm afraid that's just going to take some time," he said.

"Yeah but, can your grand plan be designed such that people won't be so bitter and won't be so apt to carry so much hate around with them every day while at the same time still appropriately look out for the long-term good of society and the good of all citizens?"

Adam stopped and looked down toward the ground. "Hmm, interesting," he mumbled.

"Okay, you think about that," Hannah said. "See you later." Hannah gently pulled on Cody's collar so he would know to follow her.

# Chapter 4 - Headstrong at Eagles Nest Lookout

## *Chapter 5 - Ingenuous at the Java Alley*

The scent of freshly roasted coffee beans was powerful and had completely drowned out any other smells at the Java Alley. The floor plan at the coffee shop was fairly small with the counter to the left of the entrance and a large bookshelf on the opposite wall, recently restocked with a wide variety of titles for sale. A fairly large coffee roaster was located on the floor just past the counter and was surrounded by a metal railing. A small sunken seating area was located in the back, three steps down. The joint was more of a coffee and pastry takeout place, but seating was provided for about fifteen people. The chairs seemed to be rearranged differently every day around two square coffee tables and two smaller eating tables. The walls throughout the shop were completely covered with nature posters, eclectic artwork, and numerous old promotional posters for past events hosted by the resort – food and music festivals and such.

Five resort employees, gathered at the front of the shop and each holding takeout coffee cups, were bantering with each other. Light music was being piped in – a typical coffeehouse music mix – which could actually be heard that Thursday morning due to the light, weekday, off-season customer traffic. Adam was sitting in the very back of the seating area, separated from the discussions between the patrons and baristas, reading his latest book. At this time of year, essentially all the costumers are locals and friends of the employees. It's a very relaxing time at the Java Alley compared to the scene in the middle of the holidays. One other local, Justin Hayes, was sitting quietly at the other small table, reading a professional journal, and a family was sitting adjacent to Adam, the parents sharing a large, homemade, blueberry muffin and watching their two young children play with game pieces on one of the well-worn coffee tables. It would be difficult to guess why the family would be there on that quiet Thursday morning.

It was chilly out, but the front door was still propped open to let the shop cool from the heat recently generated by the coffee roaster. Drew entered carrying a copy of the daily Spruce Creek News. He quickly said hello to a couple of the resort employees and walked down the steps toward Adam. Adam was leaning back in an uncomfortable wooden chair with his feet up on another chair, his head down, completely focused on his book.

"Mr. Turner," Drew said in signature fashion as he threw the newspaper at Adam. "Did you see Josh's picture of that white tailed ptarmigan?" he asked as he gestured toward the paper while sitting down.

"Yeah," Adam said as he lightly grasped the paper and quickly glanced at the front page.

"Where did he take that?"

Adam set the paper down on the coffee table. "Ah, I bet he was up on Willow Pass. He drives his old Jeep Wrangler up there fairly often to take pictures."

A server walked back and asked Drew, "Can I get you anything?"

Drew smiled and said, "Just coffee, thanks. Your coffee of the day, whatever."

The server then turned to Adam and asked with a big smile, "Adam, are you ready for your coffee cake yet?"

Adam peered up at Drew and before Adam could answer, Drew started laughing. Drew leaned forward in his chair and looked right at Adam. "Yeah Adam," he said, "are you ready for your coffee cake yet?"

Adam gave a genuine smile to the server. "Sure, thanks," he muttered.

The server walked back up the steps. Drew continued laughing, bent over in his chair, about to fall on the floor. He looked back at the server as she walked up the steps. "She is cute," he said. "I'll give you that. What's her name?"

"Britt."

"Britt? I was expecting her to have some funny Icelandic name with those strange vowels – the As and Os with dashes and dots over them."

Adam laughed and said, "She actually has a degree in Psychology from a university in Virginia. It's a good degree." Adam sat up in his chair, lowering his feet to the floor. He adjusted the bookmark in his book and set the book on the table to his left. "She's smart. Actually, with that degree, she has a lot of options, after she takes a year and enjoys life a bit or whatever."

Drew looked back at Britt as she was pouring coffee behind the counter and joking with one of the resort employees. Britt was twenty-three years old and around five-feet six-inches tall with straight, shoulder length black hair. It was easy to see why anyone would become enamored of her, beautiful with an alabaster complexion that could draw the ire of teenagers. She had only been in the valley for a little over four months since graduating.

"Is she dating anyone?" Drew asked.

"Yeah." Adam paused as he looked up at her. "I think he's got a lot of ink."

"Ah, you should get yourself some ink!" Drew quipped, still unable to control his chuckling. "You need some tats for those guns of yours."

Adam picked up the newspaper and opened it. "I think he's got a motorcycle too."

"Dude, when are you going to get a dirt bike and go ride the old mining town roads with me?"

"You're always working in the summer."

Drew conceded and leaned back in his chair. He hardly ever got his dirt bikes out anymore, especially with his kids growing up and keeping him as busy as ever during the few periods of free time he gets in the summer.

Adam threw the paper back down as he had already read it. "Do you have your snowmobiles ready for the winter?" he asked.

"Yep, they're all good to go. We'll go out some day …before I get busy in the spring. I promise." Drew suddenly grimaced and was looking around for the speakers. "What are we listening to?"

"Uh," Adam droned as he listened for a couple seconds and then said, "this is Billie Holliday." Drew rolled his eyes and looked over at Britt as she was walking down the steps with his coffee, Adam's coffee cake, and another cup of coffee for Adam. Drew smiled as he looked at the additional cup of coffee that Adam received, unsolicited. Britt handed Drew his coffee, and after she set Adam's coffee and cake on the table to Adam's left, she dragged her hand over his shoulder firmly as she walked away and then looked back at him with a flirtatious smile.

Drew's eyes got real big. He waited until Britt had walked up the steps to the front of the shop, and then he quickly leaned over toward Adam. "What was that?" he asked.

"Oh, stop it," Adam said. He tilted his head toward Drew. "They do work on tips, you know."

"No, no, no, that wasn't just some little touch of your arm. She's fawning all over you."

"Stop it," Adam said firmly.

Drew adjusted in his chair but was still focusing on Adam through the corner of his eye. Drew sighed and leaned back a bit. Adam worked through three bites of his coffee cake and then picked up his book. Drew had become focused on the kids at the next table that were scuffling over the way the game pieces were being positioned while both parents looked on quietly, deeply focused on their own thoughts. Drew then noticed the local resident, Justin, with his head buried in a professional journal. Justin, with shaggy brown hair and thick rimmed glasses, only gave Drew a slight nod. Not only was Justin a bit nervous and shy but he could be classified as a complete loner; nonetheless, he was always perfectly nice to everyone.

Drew asked, "Hey, so, what does our little, hipster weirdo over here do again?" There's no way Justin couldn't have heard him.

"He's fine. I've talked to him a few times. He actually has a Ph.D. from Iowa State. He works on small research projects for that non-profit research institute down the valley, studying the effects of dust on snow and stuff like that."

Increasing amounts of dust, attributed to human activities, have blown into the Colorado high country in recent years. The dust is picked up as storms move across the desert southwest and into the mountains and when the dust settles on the Colorado snowpack in the spring months, the snow looks pink and the dust decreases the albedo of the snow, or its ability to reflect sunlight. As a result, the snowpack melts much faster creating specific problems for farmers and water managers, among other issues.

"What are you reading?" Drew asked.

Adam showed him the book, the Fountainhead by Ayn Rand.

"Good for you," Drew exclaimed.

Adam squinted and looked over inquisitively. "Have you read it?"

"Uh, no, but I know the gist. There's a movie – Gary Cooper."

Adam chuckled lightly, positioning his bookmark and closing the book. "You know, this Howard Roark guy wouldn't last three days in the military or working for a private corporation. He would get so burned as soon as he started bucking protocol and letting his individualistic impulses control."

Drew shrugged, clearly naive to the full story. "Yeah, he's no slacker though," he said.

Adam then suddenly perked up and said, "You know, he was an architect."

Drew had looked back over at the kids still scuffling, not registering Adam's last comment. After a few seconds, the kids reached some sort of compromise and were peacefully playing together again. Adam had looked up toward the front of the shop where the resort employees were having fun watching a chipmunk that kept repeatedly darting in the front door of the store to scrounge a crumb off the floor and then it would dart back outside. The critter was scurrying fifteen feet into the store before bolting back outside with its prize.

Adam gestured toward the front of the shop and asked, "So how do you know those guys up there?"

"Oh, I just know the guy on the left there. He's been bugging me for work for the last couple summers, but he's too much of a stoner, so I've been trying to subtly ignore him if I can." Drew took a sip of his coffee as he and Adam both watched the crowd at the front of the shop. Drew continued, "He's not one of those guys that smokes after work on Fridays or at parties or before concerts. My understanding is that he's one of these wake-and-bake guys. I don't know. He might actually be a better worker than some of my current guys, but I don't want to deal with that."

"It really is a shame," Adam said. "I fully understand how folks want to enjoy life, enjoy being young, and play – delay reality a bit if they can. That's great. But they really hold themselves back. Eventually, they wake up and they're forty years old and many opportunities to make their lives truly extraordinary have passed. I know it's harmless. All the late night talk show hosts, morning radio jockeys, and commentators on the twenty-four hour new channels wouldn't be having so much fun with it if it was a more serious problem …like coke, crack, heroin, meth, or even prescription pain killers."

"Oh gosh," Drew interjected, "yeah, I guess nobody jokes about that stuff."

"But eventually," Adam continued, "it's time to put down the bong and go take on the rest of your life."

Drew smiled and said, "I really think it's funny how some pundits and news commentators act as if nobody is smoking weed anywhere else in the country. It's only happening in Colorado." Drew and Adam were laughing loudly and then noticed the parents beside them were eyeballing Drew. Drew gritted his teeth, a little mortified, and looked back at Adam. Drew sat up in his chair and slapped Adam on the shoulder. "So, are you going hunting with me on Saturday?"

"I don't have a hunting license." Drew shook his head, considering this to be more of an excuse than a reason. Adam looked right at Drew. "I want to go someday. I really do."

"Did you and Hannah see any elk up on North Ridge yesterday?"

"No, but they were bugling up there a few weeks ago."

Drew suddenly popped up, almost spilling his coffee, and looked Adam right in the eyes. "Where? Where?" he whispered.

"I don't know. They were up there somewhere. I could hear them bugling for hours one night when I was out on my patio a few weeks ago. It was loud. But with the echo in the valley, I really couldn't tell you exactly where they were. It was a few weeks ago anyway. Are they still in rut?"

Drew leaned back in his chair and said, "Nah. Well, if I get one this weekend, will you help me eviscerate it and haul out the meat?"

"Of course," Adam said. He then smiled and added, "well, that is, if you set me up with a few steaks."

"Absolutely," Drew said. He started rummaging in his pocket for his phone. "Hey," he said, and then he paused as he start looking through the pictures on his phone. "So, check out this picture my buddy, Jim, took of one of his kills way down in the San Juans a couple weeks ago?" Drew fumbled quietly for several seconds, finally found the picture, and handed his phone to Adam.

Adam looked at the picture for a couple seconds, squinted, and then tilted his head a bit. He furrowed his brow, looked over at Drew, and then looked back at the picture. Drew was smiling real big. "Really?" Adam said. The picture was taken at night with a flash. Drew's buddy was kneeling behind the rack of a large bull elk he had killed, but a mountain lion was crouched about twenty-five feet behind him in the picture. Adam said, "What the–"

"After he shot it, he tracked that elk long after dark. He set up his camera on a rock to take the picture. He didn't know the cat was there until he looked at the picture the next day."

"Maybe I don't want to help you haul out a kill if you get one."

"He camped there overnight. He gutted the elk the next morning and brought home a load of meat. He seriously never saw the cat when he was out there."

"Wow," Adam said. Drew put his phone back in his pocket and leaned back in his chair again. Adam took a few sips of coffee and leaned back too. "Well, heck," Adam said, "I don't mind seeing a reduction in the elk population, that's for sure. I still don't know how I missed that elk on the highway outside of Samston last November. That beast was still standing dead center in my lane after I finally came to a stop. I got sideways in my car yet still somehow stayed on the road."

"I don't know what to tell you: turn on your brights."

Adam finished his last bite of coffee cake. "How about bow hunting?" he asked. "Have you ever done that?"

"No, actually, archery season's over for the year, but if you plan on getting the gear, I'll get set up and go bow hunting with you next year."

"Now that sounds like a sport," Adam exclaimed. "I don't know how anyone can manage to get within range." Adam and Drew looked over toward the front door as the group of resort employees was walking away. Drew gave a slight waive as the stoner dude looked back at him. "Drew, those elk steaks, that the resort dining service was selling at their tent during jazz fest last August, were so good."

"I missed it," Drew mumbled as he looked down at a small pile of dead aspen leaves that had blown all the way to the back of the coffee shop. Drew sat up. "Dammit, why won't you go hunting with me on Saturday? What's with this archery talk? It's not some cockamamie gun control bent, is it?"

"No!" Adam replied. Adam paused for a couple seconds and then quietly said, "Drew, nothing's going to happen with gun control.

You can relax. This country has too much history with personal gun ownership that goes back to the frontier days. Gun rights and the use of guns for sport are so ingrained in such a wide swath of the population."

"Damn straight," Drew said. Adam looked over at Britt as she walked down to check on the family at the next table. "I will tell you this," Drew said, "I got plenty of ammunition. You just stay close to me."

Adam, with an inquisitive look on his face, turned his head toward Drew. "What are you talking about?" he asked.

"I'm just saying, I'll be ready."

"Ready for what?"

Drew didn't reply but was looking right at Adam, nodding. Adam rolled his eyes and shook his head. "Well, this issue," Adam said, "might be the best example of how so many people in different parts of the country are at such different places in their lives and with their politics." Adam started chuckling as he went on, "There is no way that someone living in urban Philadelphia can appreciate what this issue means to someone living on a five hundred acre ranch in Wyoming just like there is no way somebody living in a small community in the Alaskan wilderness can appreciate what this issue means to people living in south Los Angeles. Folks in the country can't understand how troubling it is for city dwellers to have to worry about their safety and the safety of their family due to all the guns circulating among the crooks while people in crime infested cities have trouble appreciating just what a heady experience it is for gun owners in rural American to be able to play with their guns in the woods."

Drew nodded firmly in agreement and then turned his head to ogle Britt as she walked by. Drew looked back at Adam, smiling and wiggling his eyebrows. "I really believe," Adam continued, "that all that the liberals want to do is try to stem the senseless violence, even if it's just by a little, that is killing so many of the urban youth and try to do something to keep guns out of the hands of the complete nut jobs. Why couldn't there be some small, basic background check completed when a gun is purchased and a requirement for purchasers to produce certification that they completed a two-hour gun training course?"

Drew suddenly leaned forward and looked over at Adam with his eyes wide open. "What?" he blurted out.

"Look," Adam continued, "if it prevents one catastrophe, if it saves one life, that would be worth it. There are mothers that are scared to send their kids to school. Little boys are accidentally shooting their little sisters with loaded guns they find under their parents' beds. People are committing suicide, in sudden, rash moments of hysteria with guns they find way too quickly before they come to their senses. Is a requirement for gun buyers to complete a two-hour training class too much to ask?"

"Yes!" Drew said. "Gun owners will take care of their own training. There's a very important principle involved." Drew took a sip of his coffee and quietly added, "Look, these isolated cases you mentioned are indeed horrible, but things will happen anyway. The nut jobs will get their weapons one way or another and accidents will happen, but responsible, law abiding gun owners cannot be punished."

"Well," Adam said, "nothing's going to happen anyway, primarily because I don't believe Democrats really want to change much. I actually see it as a smaller issue."

Drew chuckled. "Well," he said, "there are a lot of folks who would disagree with you on that."

"I will say this," Adam said. "I do think gun advocates need to be a little careful about putting too much focus on protecting rights for automatic weapons and this open carry nonsense. Public sentiment can shift fast. If mothers, collectively and suddenly, start feeling like they can't feel comfortable sending their kids to school or if people start feeling like they can't go to a pizza buffet without seeing a bunch of fellas walking around the buffet with gats openly visible in their holsters, general sentiment can shift quickly."

"Ah, it's their right!"

Britt started walking down the steps. "Can I get you boys anything?" she asked before she reached the table.

Drew looked up and asked, "Britt, what's your position on gay marriage?"

Britt furrowed her brow, bemused. "Uh, who cares?" she muttered.

"Ah," Drew said as he shrugged with a smile, "as long as the deviants stay away from me."

Adam dropped his head abruptly and started shaking his head. He looked back up toward Britt and rolled his eyes.

Britt smiled at Drew and said, "You sound like my grandpa." Seizing the opportunity to take a break for a few seconds, Britt sat down in a chair at Justin's table, opposite Adam and Drew. "I don't think you need to worry. You do know there's not going to be some sudden, huge swath of society that goes gay if people become a little more accepting? Trust me, you can count on essentially everyone remaining a dyed-in-the-wool hetero." Britt paused and looked down at Adam's boots. "My grandmother shrugs it off with a laugh. She says that my grandpa used to be so open minded and idealistic, compassionate." Britt paused for a couple seconds as she was still looking at Adam's boots, clean from where he had walked in the snow. She then quietly asked, "What happens to people as they get older?" Justin was hearing every word of the discussion, though he never gossips or hardly ever talks to anyone, so there is no reason why anyone would be concerned about discussing political issues or anything in front of him.

"Who are you going to vote for?" Drew asked.

Britt suddenly became uncomfortable and responded with a nervous laugh. "I don't even know who the candidates are."

"The election's four days away," Drew exclaimed.

"I know. I know. I'm registered to vote." Britt stood up and briskly walked back to the front of the shop without further comment.

"It's understandable that she not engaged," Adam said. "There are a lot of people that are just at a place in their life where they're simply more focused on other things. It's not a value judgment, whether they care or even know the issues. Actually, how can everyone be engaged. The real core underlying issues are not coming out in the televised debates, campaign ads, or news reporting. So many of the current details of the day are just a distraction from the platforms that ultimately drive all the prolonged major debates of the day. All we see is candidates criticizing each other, and other such froth, as opposed to any discussion about new ideas and solutions to the real problems."

"That's why your vote is so important," Drew said. "You know how I'm going to vote. You know how Josh and Hannah are going to vote. And we know that your little Icelandic princess here is probably not going to vote, so it all comes down to you! You're going to swing this election."

"Well, I'm glad you've been willing to talk about it. Hey, by the way, I'm sorry for running my mouth on the lift the other day." Drew shrugged and gave a slight wave. "I was just having fun, getting you all worked up," Adam added. "I hope you're not getting too annoyed."

"Ugh," Drew said as he leaned forward about to get up. "I'm so over it. Actually, you did get me thinking about it all, but I'll be glad when it's all over on Tuesday. We'll make it." Drew looked right at Adam, "So, you're really going to vote for her, aren't you?"

"I don't know!"

"You got that grand plan all figured out yet?"

"No."

Drew stood up. "Well, I got go check on a job."

"Where's that?"

"Oh, your old buddy, Sam Cooper, with the place up on Valley View Drive."

"Yeah, yeah, the guy from Houston. I helped design that place."

"Yeah, I know. He wants to pay me to deck out that entire seven thousand square-foot house with lights and all sorts of Christmas decorations before he gets here with his family for

Thanksgiving." Adam was chuckling. "I really don't want to do it," Drew continued. "We'll have to take it all down too, but he's willing to pay big, so I'm going to go check it out." Drew threw a couple bucks down on the table. "Watchin' the Broncos game at the Tavern?"

"Likely," Adam said as he shrugged.

"Cool," Drew said as he walked out. "You'll have it all figured out by then, right? You can lay it all out for me then."

"Uh, okay."

## *Chapter 6 - Financial Literacy for Dixie*

Adam stopped by Josh's place that Friday evening, uninvited. Josh's home was a modest two bedroom place down the valley from the resort. It had a wood burning stove, which was definitely the best feature; although, all the photographs Josh had blown up, framed, and hung throughout his place made his modest condominium seem like a gallery. Josh had a fire going in the stove, even though it was a bit warm for a fire. A college football game was on the living room television – two teams neither Josh or Adam cared to watch, but hey, it was football. Josh rented out one of the bedrooms but rarely saw his roommate as he worked nights and weekends at a restaurant and basically had the complete opposite work schedule from Josh's. Adam plopped down on the old couch immediately after entering.

"Want a beer?" Josh asked.

"Oh, I guess I'll have one," Adam replied. "Make it a light; I don't want to get a gut." Adam chuckled as he looked at the massive pile of chopped wood on the patio. "It looks like you have plenty of wood for the winter."

"It goes fast," Josh said, handing Adam a bottle of Colorado microbrew. "Sorry, no light beer in this house." Josh sat down in his old recliner that was covered with Dixie's dog hair.

Dixie was lying on the floor next to the sliding glass door, her eyes following Josh's every move. Dixie was a medium sized mutt with speckled fur, but mostly black. As with Hannah's dog, it would be difficult to identify the mixture of dog breeds, definitely some black lab and maybe some spaniel and terrier of some sort. Dixie's demeanor was very timid since the incident a couple years ago. She had a run-in with a bull moose way up Wallace Gulch. She took a hard swipe from the bull's antlers and also got kicked a couple times before Josh could scare the moose away. Dixie's never been the same ever since. It had only been within the past few months that she had finally become comfortable around humans again, but she would be incredibly skittish, forever. Josh may have actually had a rougher time with it than Dixie.

"What are you doing this weekend?" Adam asked.

"I don't know," Josh said. "Was it muddy on your hike up North Ridge?"

"Yeah, we only made it to the Eagles Nest Lookout."

Josh sighed. "Is the mountain open for uphill access yet?" he asked, somewhat sarcastically.

Josh was an avid skinner. Skinning involves attaching climbing skins to the bottom of skis and the skins allow for a skier to maintain traction while gradually progressing uphill – fantastic exercise. Josh had become a fairly experienced backcountry skier over the past five years and had all the required gear including avalanche safety equipment, but during the last season, he primarily enjoyed skinning up the runs at the resort, which the resort allows early in the morning before the mountain officially opens. Adam furrowed his brow as the mountain was still nearly bare except for the couple runs hit by the snow guns.

"I don't think you're going to be doing any skinning for a little while," Adam said.

"Ah," Josh scoffed, "I may just watch football this weekend, lots and lots of football." Adam laughed though he knew Josh wasn't entirely joking.

Josh sat and quietly watched the football game as Adam looked around the room at the photographs, including a couple new ones he had never seen before. Josh's minimalism is most evident in his home as he indeed lived simply. If he sold his condominium turn-key, leaving all the furniture, dishes, electronics, and appliances, he could probably fit all his remaining belongings in his old Jeep Wrangler and could drive away with about everything he owns. He actually didn't drive his jeep much, for he used the local bus system to get to and from his job and he also rode his bike a good bit for transportation, even during the winter.

"What are you doing this weekend?" Josh asked and then somewhat flippantly added, "Watching political debates on those public affairs networks?"

"Heck no," Adam replied. "They never get into the real nuts and bolts of anything in those debates. They never touch on any of the key differences between the platforms." Adam scoffed. "They always end up bickering about some inconsequential news topic that just made the headlines."

Josh stood up and opened his sliding glass door as the room was becoming too hot from the fire in the wood stove. Josh pet Dixie for a couple seconds and then sat down again in his old recliner. Dixie continued to lie in the same spot, content to be near the open door as opposed to the wood stove. "I've been thinking quite a bit," Josh said, "about this obsession of yours over this election."

Adam looked over inquisitively. "Yeah?" he asked.

"And I really think voters just need to worry about their own situation and quit thinking that all their struggles will hopefully be resolved as a result of an election."

"You're sounding like a Republican," Adam said with a big smile.

"No, but it works both ways. Sure, conservatives can't stand it when people, that are struggling, look to the government to fix their situation, but there are so many conservatives that also blame the government for their own situation. Highly educated people, with great jobs, living with a nice steady incomes, for many years, end up living paycheck to paycheck and have no net worth and want to blame their lack of progress on the government. If people would just make some slight adjustments in the way they live their lives, their entire situation would improve dramatically, much more than it would as a result of some little middle class tax cut loudly pushed by

Republicans, while they continue, on the side, to give massive bailouts and huge tax breaks to the uber-rich and oil companies and big investment banks that pay for their campaigns."

Adam had his eyes opened real big, feeling somewhat blindsided by the rant. "I don't know. I don't think what you talking about is a political issue," Adam said as he edged forward on the sofa. "I've heard this from you before and I know what you're thinking, but people have that right to consume and live however they please. If they want to sign up for hour-long commutes so they can live in their ultimate dream, massive, money-pit homes and drive large, gas guzzling vehicles, miles and miles every day, they have that right. If they insist on having all the latest new technologies; if they want to wear brand new clothes every other day; if they want a garage full of boats, motorcycles, and ATVs, and other toys they never use because they're always working to pay for them; or if they want to throw expensive parties for their spoiled kids' sixteenth birthdays, that's their right."

Josh was now rocking somewhat vigorously in his recliner. "Okay, okay, I know," he said. "But so many people can't really afford it and when they end up wracked with debt, they want to blame taxes or blame congress or blame the president directly. It really has so little to do with any implemented liberal or conservative ideology or anything the government is doing. It wouldn't matter how much they make or pay in taxes, they're headed down the same road. People just keep making decisions, throughout their entire lives, based on feelings and emotions as opposed to analyzing what they're doing, just a little."

"I think that's it. People become inured by the their fiscal struggles, and believe it's just part of life."

"If people would direct their attention on their own financial situation and be smarter with their own daily decisions and actions, they would all be so much better off. If they would think a little about the impacts of what they're doing to their own bank accounts, it would be so significant." Josh scoffed and rolled his eyes as he leaned back in his recliner to try to relax. "Look," he went on, "this applies to all people at all extents of political conviction and all socioeconomic conditions." Josh paused for a few seconds to try to calm down. He then quietly said, "Also, if a person has made several bad decisions in their life, blaming politicians is not going to fix it. Some little adjustment to tax policy is not going to fix it. They just need to identify the problems, start making better decisions, and right the ship to see the real results in their life that they hope to see someday."

"Josh, this sounds like what conservatives would say to a person looking to the social safety net for assistance." Adam was chuckling as Josh was still rocking vigorously in his chair. Adam added, "Okay, they may be confused over what really is causing their struggle and what their vote will really do for them, but that's not going to affect how they vote." Adam then started to laugh, having difficulty getting out his next comment. "Josh, you do realize that the entire world economy would come to a grinding halt if everyone lived like you. If people hardly ever bought ...anything ...ever, it would be worse than the Great Depression!"

Josh smiled and said, "Well, don't worry because it will never happen anyway." Josh grabbed his remote and turned down the volume on the television and then turned on some music. Josh and Adam sat quietly for a couple minutes, watching the game and listening to music.

Adam looked over at Dixie, and she immediately began wagging her bobtail. "The real problem," Adam said, "is the lack of education about personal finance. Even the most basic principles seem to elude so many people. Everyone should have to take a semester course before they graduate high school on all the rudimentary aspects of personal finance." Adam took a couple sips of his beverage. "They would learn the basics of household budgeting and all about the different expenses associated with maintaining a home. They would learn about credit cards, interest, inflation, compounding interest- "

"I believe it was Einstein," Josh interjected, "who referred to compounding interest as the Eighth Wonder of the World."

"Yeah," Adam continued, "and they would learn about the significant difference, over time, from paying interest versus earning interest. They would do simple calculations that would show the impact of miles driven per day and fuel economy on their entire household budget. The curriculum would include a section on mortgages and the process for getting a mortgage and some basics on what it takes for an individual to start a business." Adam was quickly getting excited over the idea. He stood up and started to pace slowly in front of the television. "They would learn the basics about different types of insurance, student loan and grant options, annuities, and all the retirement saving options. It would include a review of the facts about tax brackets–"

"The difference in the tax brackets for married people versus single people," Josh blurted out.

"Sure, and the differences between tax credits versus tax deductions," Adam yelled, "and taxes on capital gains versus wage income."

"The mortgage interest deduction," Josh quickly added, leaning back in his recliner.

"Yep, and they would learn about setting tax withholdings and exactly what it means when somebody receives a tax refund. It would include facts about just what Social Security is ...and how the formulas work. Heck, it could include a section to teach people about payday loans, gambling, and the lotteries." Adam stopped, playfully looked at Dixie as if he was seeking some approbation from her. He then slowly moved back over to the couch and sat down. Josh watched the game for several seconds as Adam was staring over at the wood stove. Adam leaned back on the couch, took a sip of beer, and said, "I don't know. I guess it's not a brand new concept. I think some other states offer something similar, but it sure seems like it could have a huge difference for so many people if it became universal." A loud pop from the fire in the wood stove startled Dixie, but she quickly recognized the sound and lay back down. Josh was watching the game but thinking about the idea. Adam continued, "It would need to be part of the core curriculum but taught during the last semester of high school. I guess it would be about the easiest course anyone would take and obviously not have any impact on their college applications but would have a huge impact on so many peoples' lives, right after they leave high school, have turned eighteen, and head out to take on the world."

"Okay," Josh said, "actually, this very well may be the best idea that has come out of this whole annoying discussion we've been having." He got up from his recliner and went over to close the sliding glass door but accidentally closed the door fairly hard, causing Dixie to shudder. She went scurrying into the kitchen. As Josh walked back to his recliner, he continued, "This could actually have far reaching impacts. If you have a better educated society on all these basic personal finance concepts, you would see many more people keeping their heads above water and maintaining more consistent, financially healthy lifestyles that ultimately keep them in better long-term situations."

"It might be the best way to keep more people free and clear of the social safety net," Adam said. Dixie, still in the kitchen, sat down, clearly confused over the excitement.

"There would be less personal bankruptcies filed," Josh said, "and it would maybe help reverse the current trend toward greater income inequality. The crime rate would be lower. There would be less domestic violence." Josh was lying back, looking at the ceiling, and rocking in his recliner. "There would be fewer divorces, with disagreements over finances maybe being the biggest factor in the divorce rate. There would be a resurgence in couples staying married and children growing up with both parents, which everyone agrees would be great for the long-term health of society, right?"

With the path clear, Dixie warily walked around the coffee table and sat down beside Adam. Adam leaned forward to pet Dixie for a few seconds. "I don't know," Adam said. "Maybe we shouldn't get too excited. Heck, they've been teaching physical fitness and personal health in schools for time immemorial, but we still have problems there." Adam quietly gestured for Dixie to go lie down.

"It would certainly help though," Josh said as he sat up. "You're not going to get through to every person, but I think you're right. After several years, the information would be assimilated into broad swaths of society. These high school kids would be going home and talking about the subject matter with their families. I imagine there are many affluent people, who are well educated and gainfully employed, that really wish they would have been inculcated with some basics about personal finance at a young age, and if people really understood the quantitative impacts of their life decisions, they would make adjustments that would have huge impacts on their lives. Wealthy people can now afford to pay for financial advice and get instructions as to how to navigate the maze of laws that affect their finances and utilize all the complex financial vehicles to ultimately accumulate wealth, and some people have the opportunity to learn about it in their households when they're growing up or they had an interest in financial topics at an early age, but with this important education, others would also learn, up front as opposed to having to learn from their mistakes. It would level the playing field." Josh took a couple sips of his beer and looked over at the football game for a few seconds.

"This basic course could alone have such a positive influence on everyone," Josh continued, "from all socio-economic backgrounds. While many people may be able to afford the sweet sixteen birthday parties they throw for their kids, there are so many that end up just wallowing in debt from such extravagance and end up beholden to the big banks and having to do the grind for the rest of their life to pay off all the debt, and for some others, ...it's much worse. Some people learn, in a tough way, about the significance of what seem like small life decisions, and they end up living with the impacts of their financial decisions for the rest of their life. Consider also that there were so many that were doing fine with their extravagant lifestyles until they were suddenly hit by the Great Recession. They took a much harder hit than others simply due to their approach to personal fiscal management, and after that impact, they still aren't looking to make the key, needed changes in their lives. They're still looking to blame somebody else, to blame the politicians."

Adam's excitement had waned. He was leaning back, more focused on the football game than Josh's continued discussion. "Of course," Josh added, "such an education will never prevent people from trying to keep up with the Jones. It's human nature. They will always, always, always want to be able to show off their cooler television that covers an entire wall or their more awesome man cave or the better treehouse their kids will never actually use."

"Well," Adam muttered, "you can try to impart to people about the differences between needs and wants and about how peer pressure can affect adults when it comes to decisions about spending, but yeah, it takes a unique personality to be comfortable with the notion of not *spending* their time at every moment and being able to live simply, in some regard, but you can't expect everyone to live like that. It requires people to eschew a natural human instinct. We know what others are up against when they try to get young people to completely ignore another very strong, natural instinct."

Josh furrowed his brow. "Oh man, please don't go there," he mumbled.

"Actually," Adam said, "it might be very difficult to find the instructors to teach these personal finance classes that would be taught in every high school. You remember how it was with our out-of-shape gym teacher trying to teach us about physical fitness."

Josh busted out laughing. "Mr. Wheeler?" he asked. Josh and Adam were laughing loudly. As Josh was leaning down in his chair laughing, he continued, "Are you talking about Eighteen Wheeler?"

"Oh man, who started that nickname?" Adam asked. "That was awful."

"I don't know."

"But really," Adam went on, "for teaching personal finance, how many teachers could be found that are the living embodiment, themselves, of strong, personal, fiscal responsibility? How can you rely on someone to adequately convey important, key pillars of personal finance if they have a mountain of debt themselves and all kinds of stuff on layaway?"

"Well," Josh said as he leaned back in his recliner, "you have to start somewhere, and I think you're right on. There has been a reduction in the number of people that smoke as a result of health education classes, right? Many people do eat much healthier, avoid fast food, and exercise more. Americans are living so much longer as a result of all the gains made there." Josh started chuckling. "We have politicians who could probably improve their own financial literacy. Also, it would really help to educate so many people about just how complicated some of the topics have become as a result of public policy. The education would result in more support for your grand plan, that's for sure."

Adam looked up, smiled, and gave a firm head nod. He then got up to toss his bottle in Josh's recycling bucket in the kitchen pantry. Josh turned the television over to the hockey game. "Older folks already get it," Josh then said.

Adam walked back over and kneeled down to pet Dixie. "Yep," he said, "I think they would actually be the first to see the benefit of everyone learning early, but they still wouldn't support any initiative and the extra resources required to actually implement a mandatory course." Adam stood up and stepped back over to the couch to sit down. Looking at Dixie, he said, "Hey, she's doing great."

"Yeah."

"That's one of the frustrating things about this election," Adam said, "well, all elections." Josh looked over curiously as Adam continued. "Candidates should be looking to represent the interests of the full range of ages in the electorate."

"Well," Josh said, "many more older people vote than younger people. Why do you think those over sixty-five have health care under a single payer system while younger people are not included, ...yet when polled, somehow the majority of those, sixty-five and over, say they're foursquare opposed to a government health care system?"

"Ugh," Adam mumbled as he grimaced. "Well, that's another topic. I don't want to go there right now."

"No, but I get it," Josh said. "Some voters are simply at an incredibly different place than other voters. Older voters don't have anything to gain from a new program to improve personal finance education for young adults. Heck, they are probably watching their kids, making the same mistakes they made themselves, but they're not going to go for this idea. I don't know. It's as if some older voters, long ago, fully grasped that they won't live forever, and thereafter, their youthful compassion and concern for assuring that the greater good of society is maintained for posterity just dwindled to nothing."

"Oh, I don't know about that," Adam said. "That's a significant allegation to place on an entire generation. I certainly don't believe that there's some general transition in sentiment that people go through as they age."

"Okay, but you do see a greater lack of concern and lack of sentiment, among older voters, for those caught in more disadvantaged circumstances. Rather than see, macroscopically, what a key component the social safety net is, or how beneficial personal finance education would be, they just think, to heck with them."

"Wow," Adam said. "You're sounding cynical, even for you." Josh shrugged and turned to watch the hockey game, rocking slightly in his chair. They sat quietly for a few seconds and then Adam said, "I will agree that it's not just people that move up the income ladder and people that are making more money that transition to become so conservative. There are so many people that worked so hard for decades, didn't really make much money, and maybe don't have much to show from all their hard work but some worn out old hands, and they just can't stomach seeing others getting public assistance after what they went through themselves."

Josh stopped rocking, sat up, and looked down at his feet, pensive. After a slight pause, he said, "Younger voters, alternatively, have their entire careers ahead of them – potential entrepreneurial endeavors. They haven't started a family yet. They have such a different view about investment in society."

"I think it comes back to human nature," Adam said. "I'm sorry, but I do believe the overwhelming majority of older voters do have a great sense of compassion and concern for what will happen after they're gone and want to know society will thrive and be safe and clean for their grandkids ...versus having a system that focuses only on allowing people to thrive in the moment without too much concern for anything beyond that moment."

Josh started laughing as he leaned forward in his chair. "Hey," he said, "do you remember, Jack Simmons, when we were kids, when he would put slugs in baggies full of salt and laugh while he watched them dissolve? I wonder how he votes today."

"Ugh," Adam groaned. "Why would you bring that up?"

"Human nature, like you said. Some people are just vicious by nature and just don't care about anything but their current moment of enjoyment."

"Wow, your sounding like a card-carrying misanthrope tonight."

"Okay, okay," Josh said, "I'm sorry. Maybe it is indeed a very small portion of the electorate that thinks that way, but it's out there. I really just worry that people aren't thinking, but ...ah, ...what are you going to do?"

"I was actually talking to Hannah about this some during our hike, demographics. The concerns of older voters are so much different than younger voters, and it significantly impacts how they'll vote. Gosh, it must drive candidates out of their minds when they try to mold their message to an electorate that contains voters at such different places in their lives, regardless of whether they lean left or right."

"Again," Josh said, "older people vote and younger people don't, so that makes it much easier for them. Anyway, I assure you that the politicians won't be pushing for a new, required, personal finance class for all high school seniors." Adam sighed as Josh turned the television back to the football game. Josh asked, "Who do the Broncos play on Sunday?"

Adam replied very slowly, "The Oak...land ...Raid ...ers."

"So how's Hannah?" Josh asked.

"Fine," Adam said, curtly.

"All this focus on political issues and the election is clearly just a distraction so you can avoid confronting that situation."

"There's no situation. We've been hanging out a bit. That's it. Anyway, she's moving to North Carolina."

"What?" Josh yelled as he leaned forward in his chair.

"She's going to go help her uncle do tax returns or something."

"What are going to do about it?"

"It's fine."

Josh sighed. "Look," he said, "it's perfectly understandable that you would harbor some resentment, but what do think's been going on? Why do you think she's been going on hikes with you in the mud and sitting around drinking beers, watching football? You don't think that's indicative of something? How many baseball games did she watch with you over the summer. Chics don't sit around watching baseball games!"

"She likes watching baseball."

Josh busted out laughing. "You really are at a loss. You're adrift." Josh leaned back in his chair. "Look, Emily said Hannah was doting on you all morning before her wedding. Why do you think she bolted? She couldn't go through with it."

"She should have thought about that before she rode off with Lane."

"Well, she's not with Lane now. He's long gone."

"Are you done?"

"Fine," Josh said, mockingly. "We'll talk politics."

"Where's Emily anyway?" Adam asked.

"She went to Vegas for a weekend conference for hospitality workers, something or other," Josh mumbled. He rocked in his chair for several seconds, watching the football game. "Adam, do you know how unique it is to find someone who is perfectly fine just doing your thing?" He looked over at Adam, waiting for a response. Adam shrugged. Josh and Adam sat quietly for a minute. Josh then quietly said, "That really is the sign of a dream union. If you can find someone who is perfectly content, just tagging along with you while you enjoy and pursue your interests, you got a keeper. The overwhelming majority of people out there are the exact opposite. They are so focused on their own world and their own interests, they can't even take the time to listen, for one minute, to hear about the book their significant other read, the movie they saw, or the trip they took."

"Wow, the misanthrope is entrenched tonight," Adam said.

"They can't be happy to hear about somebody's good news: their job promotion or their championship in the community basketball league or whatever. And they can't be the least bit sympathetic when someone else has some misfortune." Josh sighed and said, "It's very unique, what you have there. It's different."

"She wasn't showing a lot of empathy for me when she was riding the Eurail with Lane."

"Well, she's watching football and baseball games with you now." Josh looked up at the football game for a bit. He then said, "It's actually the secret to all relationships, to friendships, and to maintaining a good working relationship with any cohort. As soon as somebody refuses to show the least bit of concern for somebody else's area of interest or be the least bit empathic to another person's situation, the relationship is doomed."

They sat quietly for a few seconds, and then Adam said, "Everyone just wants to be respected. It even applies to politics. Many people have had some tremendous accomplishments in their career but don't get any follow-up respect, while many others that come from more unfortunate circumstances are trudging through life, just fine with their vocations, and just want to be respected. Really, the vast majority of the population, from a wide range of socio-economic conditions, is perfectly content except when they're not being treated with respect by the rest of society. That's it. Yet, it seems like so many politicians and special interest groups, from both sides can't appreciate that." Josh was focused on the hockey game. Adam muttered, "People also just want to be treated with respect in their relationships, in their friendships, and by their work associates."

"Alright, alright, I hear you," Josh said. "I'm not defending her, but please don't mess this up ...and don't mess up at the voting booth on Tuesday!"

"Do you have your votes figured out yet for all the amendments and propositions?" Adam asked.

"I mailed in my ballot a few days ago," Josh said.

Adam nodded. They sat quietly watching the game for several minutes. Adam picked up an outdoors magazine Josh had on his coffee table and was perusing through the pages, and Josh opened a couple pieces of mail he had on his end table. Dixie had closed her eyes. After a couple more minutes, Josh looked over at Adam. "Hey? So, how old is Lane?" he asked.

Adam shook his head for a couple seconds. He then peered over at Josh with a wicked stare. "Fifty," Adam said.

Josh started laughing loudly. Still laughing, he asked, "Does that qualify as a May-December romance or is that just a May-September romance?"

"You know what really burns me up?" Adam sputtered. "He's probably fine with the way everything turned out. He got to travel and have a good fling with a much younger woman, but he never really wanted anything more. Now he has the memories. He's happy." Adam scoffed and stood up. "I'm going to go."

"Hey, I'm sorry," Josh said. He was chuckling while trying to be genuinely conciliatory. "Hey, come on, we can talk about politics some more. Come on, what's your solution to health care? Seriously, I'm sorry."

"Nah, it's too hot in here anyway" Adam said, grimacing over the heat from the wood stove. "So, we're watching the Raiders game at the North Fork if you want to join us."

"Alright," Josh said, "hey, do you want to ride the bike path up to Porcupine Notch Monday after work?"

Adam stopped, very interested. "What's the forecast?"

"It's supposed to be clear."

"Sure. I'll meet you here at 3:30?"

"Cool. And you can then tell me your solution for health care reform." Adam was out the door with no response.

## *Chapter 7 - After Laundry, Finally*

Adam was emptying laundry from the dryers in his building while Hannah sat on one of the washers, watching him. Adam was moving with urgency that Sunday afternoon as kickoff for the Broncos-Raiders game was only minutes away. He was yanking clothes out of two adjacent dryers, popping his shirts, and folding them quicker than usual. Hannah, swinging her legs and clanging her lightweight hiking shoes against the washer, was happy to see that Adam was not being overly obsessed, on that particular day, about how perfectly his shirts were folded as he certainly had exhibited slight symptoms of obsessive compulsive disorder in the past when folding laundry.

"When are you going to buy a place?" Hannah asked. Adam suddenly came to a complete stop and slumped his shoulders. He was holding a clean shirt off to his side, barely off the floor, as he partially turned his head to glare at Hannah. "Uh, never mind," she stuttered. Adam and Hannah had talked about buying a place together shortly before Hannah left him to be with Lane. Hannah should also know to never broach delicate topics with anyone when they're already dealing with the always agonizing task of laundry. Adam continued folding his clothes slowly as he shook his head.

The room was warm from the multiple dryers that had been running, but the temperature was comfortable. Cody was sitting by the door, anxiously waiting for Adam to finish. He had no interest in lying down on the hard, concrete floor. Adam looked up at Hannah and asked, "Would you have done Lane's laundry for him if you two had gotten married?"

Hannah rolled her eyes, popped off the dryer, and took a few steps over to grab a pair of jeans to fold. "Come on," she said, "kickoff's in twenty minutes."

Cody suddenly bellowed a loud, impatient whimper and shifted his weight to try to find a more comfortable sitting position. Adam, with his back to Cody, smiled. "Even Cody hates laundry day," he said. "You know, the only times I've ever considered committing suicide have been on laundry days."

Hannah furrowed her brow as she lay a pair of folded jeans on a stack of clean clothes. "You considered committing suicide to get out of doing laundry?" she asked. Adam shrugged and grinned. "Well, I'm glad you're still with us, Adam. I hope you'll call me if you ever have such thoughts again."

"Wait, you mean all I have to do is call you and say. 'I think I'm going to end it all so I don't have to fold these clothes,' and you would come over and help me do laundry."

"Yep, except I'll be in North Carolina." Adam froze again, loosely holding a pair of socks. He turned toward Hannah, scrunched his nose, and stuck out his tongue at her, like a child would do.

Hannah finished folding a second pair of jeans, trying to deftly meet Adam's folding standards. She lay the jeans on the dryer and grabbed a pair of socks. "Did you enjoy the extra hour of sleep last night?" she asked.

"I woke up at the same time," he said. "Ugh, I dread it getting dark so early." Adam reached over and snatched the socks away from Hannah as she was folding them incorrectly. Hannah sighed, walked back over to the same washer, and hopped back up to sit down.

Hannah was kicking her shoes against the washer again. Cody watched as Hannah clanged her feet for a few seconds, and then Cody whimpered again. "So, did you mail in your ballot yet?" Hannah asked.

"Heck no, I'm going to the polls in person," Adam replied, quickly folding a pair of gym shorts. "I think that might be the most glorious aspect of the whole election."

A lady from the building suddenly burst through the door to the laundry room, startling Cody. She gave a stern look at Cody as she quickly went over to a dryer beside Adam and pulled out a load of clothes and stuffed all the clothes into her laundry basket. "Hi," Adam mumbled. She smiled, nodded, and then slammed the dryer door before quickly walking out of the room.

Adam continued with his previous thought, "To be able to walk into the polling place, fill out my own personal ballot, and walk out knowing I voted. A vote that counts the same as a vote cast by any actual candidate or anyone else in the country." Adam had completely stopped folding his laundry. He was now leaning slightly against the dryer and holding an orange, fleece pullover. "To be able to take in that entire scene of democracy in action is just too beautiful to miss. Regardless of the results, regardless of what does or does not happen afterwards, you have to love democracy." Adam put on the orange, fleece pullover over his blue t-shirt. "Hannah," he continued, "how fantastic is it that I get to vote and that my vote counts the exact same as everyone else's vote. They may make more money, make less money, or even have a whole lot more money, or have a powerful position at their work, but my vote counts the exact same as their vote."

"It's pretty cool," Hannah said. "Although, I'm afraid the few uber-rich in the country still have way more influence than the rest of us. They are the primary contributors to campaigns and control the propaganda, broadcast through the airwaves during election season, that does effectively swing how the disengaged vote. The uber-rich subsequently set the agenda for what policy makers do after they're elected, and they can completely derail much needed reforms with a single phone call if an effort goes against their interests. But yes, ideally, you have to love the intent – one person, one vote."

"Okay, sure, the system's broken and campaign finance rules need to be reformed, but the best opportunity to fix it is for every single American to vote. Voting should feel great to everyone, knowing that there are still so many people in this world that have to live their lives under the rule of some ruthless, authoritarian regime or even a flat-out totalitarian dictator. The citizens of those countries live in squalid, disease ridden societies with no schools, no clean water, no food, and no health care while their leaders enjoy the spoils of all their countries' natural resources and do nothing for their people."

"Some countries have no economic market at all," Hannah interjected. She shifted back on the washer. "Some countries have no system in place for private industry to flourish and create jobs for their citizens or for their citizens to be part of the global economy or even be a part of their own nation's economy." Adam was pensive, slowly folding his clothes. "You know what I really don't understand?" Hannah continued. "The leaders of some countries, even some developed countries, refuse to put some sort of capitalist system in place. How can a leader of a country continue to restrict such economic growth and extraordinary opportunity for their own people."

"Pride," Adam quickly said. "Of course it's cultural, or tradition, for some cases, but it sure seems like so many leaders just have too much pride to give in." Cody suddenly lay down with a thud, his collar clanging against the concrete floor, sparking Adam to move more swiftly with his folding.

"If our new leaders to be elected on Tuesday were to develop and implement your grand plan," Hannah started as Adam peered over at her, "I guess it could serve as a model government system and economic system for the rest of the world, but what makes you think any other country would adopt it?"

"Oh, I would never expect any country to just adopt it, but it could serve as an incredibly valuable reference, especially for countries that are now in a position to structure a new system that would allow them to be a part of the global economy, for the good of their people." Adam stopped folding his clothes and looked right at Hannah. "Hey, so you've never said. Do you think it would be possible for a new system to be developed for everything – the entire tax code, regulations, entitlements, policy on social issues – that would be bi-partisan, meet current needs and obligations, gradually pay off the nation's debt, and operate simply and effectively for decades, while left to its own devices? All the politicians would then be ennobled, for years to come, as they watch American families prosper – including those from more disadvantaged circumstances. They could watch the economy thrive and feel good about what they've done for all citizens. They could enjoy their own lives more, spend less time in Washington, and enjoy more time in their home districts – actually enjoy the holidays and their vacation time."

"Sure," Hannah said. "Of course it could be done, ...but it won't."

"Future legislators, of course, could subsequently continue to look to make small tweaks, or even major changes, and could continue to fight hard for their causes and issues that are important to their base, but a new starting point would be in place, and while much simpler, it would still closely represents the current state of policy."

"Nope, not gonna happen."

"Why? You're saying there's not even a sliver of hope?"

"All the special interest groups and their lobbyists – I wouldn't even know where to start – but they would balk and jawbone as soon as the simplification process resulted in even the slightest impact to their direct interests. Politicians, beyond reproach, would immediately respond to them and stop all work on refining the system."

"Nah, it can be done."

"And you think that guy can get it done?" Hannah asked.

"I don't know about that," he said. "Hannah, I really don't know who I'm going to vote for."

"Hurry up, it's almost time for kickoff." Hannah suddenly paused for a couple seconds. "Wait, did you just say, 'pay off the nation's debt?'" she asked. "So, you're not looking for a system that will reduce the annual deficit between annual revenues and annual spending, you want to see all the nation's debt paid off?" Adam nodded, stifling his laughter. Hannah then started nodding with a big sardonic smile. "Alright, alright," she said.

"Actually," Adam said, "an implemented grand plan may not eliminate the debt on its own, but it would address significant issues with entitlements, spending, and the tax code, and it would then be much easier to identify subsequent tweaks, if needed, to attain annual surpluses and pay down the debt."

Adam quickly finished folding his clothes, stacked the clean folded clothes in his laundry basket, and picked up the basket. They left the laundry room, walked down the hall, and up some stairs. Cody was running ahead of them. When they reached Adam's rental condo, Adam opened the door, dropped the basket on the floor, and closed the door without entering.

"Are you going to leave Cody in your car?" Adam asked as they walked down the hallway.

"Nah, we'll take him and I'll tie him up outside for a while."

They exited the building and began walking toward the North Fork tavern. They slowed down their pace to allow Cody some time to frolic and do his business before they would have him lie down outside the tavern. It was quite cool and smelled like winter. Hannah had put on her ski coat, but Adam was only wearing his fleece pullover. They ambled across the parking lot to take a path between a couple adjacent townhomes. The path led downhill to a pedestrian bridge over Spruce Creek. When they got to the bridge, Cody started rummaging around in the willows around the creek. Adam and Hannah stopped in the middle of the bridge and were standing close to each other, looking down into the water off the west side of the bridge. Only a bit of ice had built up around the edges of the stream, and they watched the river for a bit, listening to the light gurgle of the flowing water.

"Do they stock this section of the creek?" Hannah asked.

"Yep, rainbow trout," Adam said as they both looked around in the water to see if they could see any fish but neither of them saw anything. "Josh goes fly fishing further down the valley," Adam said as Hannah nodded, still staring down into the stream. "I don't think his fly fishing skills match his prowess with a camera, but he goes."

"Does he ever go ice fishing on the lake?"

Adam shook his head, but then said, "He will go out there immediately after the ice breaks. He says that's a great time to hit the lake." They quietly watched the river for another minute. Adam then spun around and leaned against the railing. He rested their quietly for a few seconds, looking up at the peaks to the east. "Hannah, I need to create more memories."

Hannah spun around too and was leaning up against him. "Nah," she said, "Adam, it's the person who dies with the most stuff that wins." She chuckled and looked for a response from Adam, but he was still quiet, introspective, looking up at the peaks.

"When I think back," Adam said, "on college, friends, and trips I've taken, it's very specific moments and specific events that I always remember the most – some good, some bad." Adam dropped his head and was now looking down at Hannah's shoes. "We can control whether we have a lot of memories or not," he continued. "We can create good memories. Or we could just get caught up in a daily grind of repetition that yields no lasting memories at all." Hannah had her head leaned back toward the sky and closed her eyes. Adam looked up toward the resort where snow guns were lined up on the next run they planned to open. It was cold enough that afternoon that the resort had kept three snow guns blowing that day. The roar of the guns was echoing throughout the valley, partially drowning out the sound of the river. "You know," Adam said, "many of my best memories are from being places with you." Hannah quickly turned her head toward Adam and with a slight smile, she looked right at him. Adam then scrunched his nose and stuck out his tongue at her. Hannah rolled her eyes and dropped her head. She was kicking around a small pile of slush for several seconds as Adam was looking up at the snow guns.

"Look I messed up okay," Hannah suddenly mumbled. "I grant you that. Is that what you want to hear?" Adam shrugged as if he didn't know what she was talking about. "People make mistakes," she continued. "It's not only about you and Lane." Hannah paused and then started slowly shaking her head. She then muttered, "If only I knew when I was younger what I know now." Adam turned and was looking right at Hannah. She was still looking down, kicking together a bigger pile of slush. She then picked her head up. She was aware that Adam was looking right at her but her focus remained up river. Adam then started to slowly lean toward her, but Hannah then abruptly stood up, away from the railing. "Oh gosh," she said. "Is that a porcupine?"

Adam turned and looked up river for a few seconds and said, "Yep." It was a good two hundred feet up the stream, waddling on a bar in the middle of the creek. They quickly started moving across the bridge.

"Cody!" Hannah yelled very loudly. Cody popped his head up from the willows, startled at the tone of her scream. Cody was only about thirty feet away. They quickly started moving across the bridge and up the path, away from the creek and toward the highway. Cody was swiftly in front of them. Of course porcupines are harmless, but even the best trained untethered dogs can't resist the furry-looking creatures. They wanted to get Cody out of there as fast as they could before he saw the porcupine and ended up, at the vet, with a snout full of quills.

They walked the quarter mile up to the highway. There wasn't a car in sight on the road, a pleasant scene compared to the bustle that would be evident all around the highway in a few weeks. They moved across the road to the North Fork Tavern. The parking lot at the tavern was nearly full. Hannah tied Cody up to a post outside the tavern. The serenity of the valley was suddenly replaced with the hoopla in the tavern, many people already in place, watching the Broncos game.

## *Chapter 8 - Stewardship Rewarded*

Adam and Hannah walked into the North Fork Tavern and sat down at the only remaining available table, next to the entrance. Drew was already there, standing at the edge of the bar and talking to the owner, Jake. The televised football game was in a commercial break, so conversations had picked up and patrons were shifting around to order food or check in with friends at other tables. It was so crowded that several people were standing behind chairs at the bar. Adam and Hannah were sitting with their backs to the front door and facing the large television behind the bar. Drew walked over and in signature fashion said, "Mr. Turner. Ms. Nelson."

"Hey Drew! Is Amy here?" Hannah asked with a smarmy smile.

"She should be here in a little bit with the kids."

"Did you get one?" Adam asked, referring to his Saturday hunting trip.

"No," Drew mumbled. "I didn't see anything."

"Are you now on the hook to watch the kids tonight?" Hannah asked, still smiling.

"Yeah," Drew said, "we're going to hang out here until the end of the game." This was the first time Drew had seen Hannah in a while, and they didn't have too good a rapport since she left Adam to be with Lane. Drew took off his coat and hung it on the back of the chair closest to the bar. "So Hannah, are you going to vote for her too?"

Hannah looked over at Adam but didn't respond. "Hey now," Adam said, "I don't know who I'm voting for?"

"Alright, alright," Drew said, "let's watch football." The game was back on and the Broncos had the ball. There were no obvious Raiders fans in the tavern, but there were plenty of people wearing apparel for other teams including the Packers, Seahawks, and Patriots. Adam, Hannah, and Drew were all looking at the television behind the bar.

"Hey Hannah," Drew suddenly blurted out, "whatever happened to that home, a couple down from my place, that your office was listing? The sign had indicated Under Contract for quite a while, but it obviously never sold."

"The buyers didn't qualify for the mortgage. It was a young couple. They absolutely loved the house." Hannah sighed. "The sellers waited for about two months."

Josh walked in with a group of four other random people. They had all just gotten off the bus at the shuttle stop in front of the tavern. Josh slapped Adam on the shoulder as he walked by, proceeded to another table, and began talking to three other guys. "Who is that?" Hannah asked, motioning in their direction.

"I don't know, just some random dudes." Adam then perked up. "Actually those are the guys he joined last spring on that trip to Lake Powell." Hannah nodded.

Adam, Hannah, and Drew quietly watched the game for several minutes, and Josh eventually came over and sat down. Hannah smiled and gave him a slight nod. Drew quietly muttered, "Mr. Carpenter."

Josh mocked Drew and firmly said, "Mr. Erickson."

Their table was small and round and provided barely enough room for all four of them to sit. Adam had his legs extended under the table. Hannah and Josh were sitting about a foot or so away from the table on each side of Adam, and Drew had now turned his chair around so he could see the television between the patrons standing at the bar.

After another minute, the server came by and dropped off four small glass mugs and a pitcher of light beer, unsolicited. She walked away without comment. "I don't know how you can drink this crap," Josh said as he looked over at Adam but then immediately moved toward the table, poured himself a full glass, and then filled the other three mugs.

"Hey Josh," Hannah said, "can I see your latest pictures?"

"I don't have anything with me." Josh took a sip of beer. "I do have a few new ones though. We'll check them out one of these days."

Josh looked at Adam and said, "Did you know Eric, over there, is an ex-Navy Seal?" Josh was gesturing toward the table he visited after he first arrived.

"Really? Wow." Adam said.

"Hey Drew, how long were you in the Army?" Josh asked.

"Two years," Drew said, still looking at the televised football game.

"You never talk about it," Josh said. Drew shrugged.

Adam was looking over at Eric at the other table as he said, "I don't think I could do it."

"You could do it," Drew said as he perked up and turned around to face Adam. "You wouldn't think about it; you would just do it." The game just went back to commercial break, so Hannah and Josh were looking right at Drew. "In the moment," Drew continued, "you're not in a position to over-analyze what you're up against. Actually, you would be fine soldier, Adam. Heck, I've seen how you motor up those fourteeners and just laugh with joy every time we reach another false peak."

"I don't think that means anything," Adam said. "That's different. I'm in heaven up there."

Colorado has more than fifty peaks that are over 14,000 feet above mean sea level, and the peaks, referred to as fourteeners, are very popular hikes among all adventure seekers in Colorado and visitors from out-of-state. Adam, Josh, Hannah, and Drew had hiked most of the fourteeners around Spruce Creek, but many avid hikers set out to hike every fourteener in Colorado.

"Did you ever see combat?" Adam asked Drew.

"Nothing too hot. I guess I kind of lucked out compared to some places I could have ended up."

"I just don't think I have the mentality for it," Adam said. "When that commanding officer yelled, 'Charge!', I just don't know what I would do."

"I'm telling you," Drew said firmly, "you wouldn't think about it. You would just go." Adam gave an incredulous shrug. Drew shifted back around to watch the game.

Adam looked right at Hannah and said, "Do you realize how lucky we are? Not just because of people like Eric and Drew but because of all of them …over decades. All those guys fighting down in the trenches in World War I, with their feet all gangrene." Josh grimaced as Adam continued, "All those guys marching all over Europe and Japan in World War II. And what about Vietnam?" Adam looked at Josh, "Can you imagine if we had to go to Vietnam?" Josh raised his eyebrows and shook his head. "We now get to go to Colorado Rockies baseball games on those beautiful seventy-five degree summer days. We get to enjoy our weekends and the peace and tranquility of Spruce Creek. We get to enjoy this great country under a sound, solid government and robust economy." Hannah, Josh, and Drew were all looking at the television but listening to Adam. "I know we sing God Bless America in the seventh inning at the Sunday games, but during those moments, do you think people really stop to think about what some of our forefathers went through?"

Hannah said, "My grandfather fought in World War II."

Drew quickly turned around. "Really? Where?" he asked.

"Gosh, I don't know for sure. I know he was fighting the Japanese, …so the Pacific …somewhere." Hannah gritted her teeth, admittedly embarrassed for not knowing the details. "Actually, he usually refused to talk about it."

Drew sat back in his chair and looked at Adam. "You are in rare form these days," he said.

"Hey, that doesn't mean I'm all for some ridiculously endless defense budget," Adam said. At that particular moment, Adam clearly wasn't looking to fawn all over Drew for his military service.

Drew quickly turned back toward the television, even though the broadcast was still in commercial break. "Two more days," he blurted out in the direction of nobody. Adam had a big grin on his face as he looked over at Josh and then over at Hannah.

Josh and Hannah were chuckling and shaking their heads. "I'm going to go say hi to Jess," Hannah said. Josh also got up and walked away without saying anything.

Drew moved over to Josh's seat. "See," Drew said, "your left-wing, liberal friends don't even agree with you."

"Are you saying there's not room for some improved efficiency with the entire national defense system?" Adam asked. "Updates and modernization ...to more efficiently deal with the new threats of the twenty-first century?"

"Adam, you're not as smart as you think you are." Drew took another swig of his libation.

"Ah, I don't think I'm smart," Adam muttered. "I wish I had it all figured out."

"Sure, there's plenty of room for improved efficiency," Drew said, "but I don't think you want to start there to get to a balanced budget. What about all those lazy government workers going on junkets and working on their endless boondoggle projects year after year?"

Adam sighed, closed his eyes, and leaned his head back. "Are you really going to impugn an entire workforce based on a few isolated bad stories? I doubt you even have any actual stories!" Adam pulled his legs up and shifted his chair up under the table. He leaned down on his elbows as he looked over at Drew. "Nobody would argue that there's some room for improved efficiency within all government agencies and room for changes to the way the budget is set for all the departments, but all the government workers, that you despise so, are just getting up and going to work every day, keeping a huge, vital segment of our economy and our society operating, week after week, month after month, year after year." Drew waved his hand at Adam and looked up at the football game as Adam continued, "That rhetoric, that they're all somehow a burden on our society, is so fallacious and ridiculous and downright mean." Adam shifted in his seat, looked over at the game for a few seconds, and said, "What about your neighbors that work for the Forest Service? They're working to manage millions and millions of acres for resource development and provide fantastic recreational opportunities for every American. Fighting wildfires on a minuscule budget. You take it all for granted! You think the forest is just *there* for you when you're ready to go hunting and camping." Adam paused, sat up, and quickly took a swig of his beverage. "The real examples are endless. There are so many valuable workers that are working hard to thwart terrorist plots, assure the massive bustling commerce system keeps cranking around the clock, and make sure you will always have a safe, clean food supply. Heck, if there's a foodborne illness outbreak, they'll track it down to a specific fruit farm within a matter of days!"

"Alright, alright, would you just chill?" Drew said. "There just need to be more performance reviews and accountability."

"You want more bureaucracy?" Adam leaned back in his chair. He continued in a muted tone. "Plus, they already do performance reviews. Look, they show up to work every day and take care of so much. They deal with politics that we couldn't even begin to fathom. The politics are not their problem. They are trying to take care of things while working within the constraints of so many different strict authorizations set years, maybe decades ago. Working with budgets established many months ago that may not even include any funding for the latest emergencies, which almost entirely dominate their time."

"The budgeting approach needs to be reformed," Drew said, still looking directly at the football game.

"Well," Adam muttered, "I won't argue with that." Several people in the tavern were now looking over at Adam and Drew. Adam was talking loud enough that everyone could hear him over the television audio.

"Taking care of projects," Drew said, "isn't just about setting spending. It's about proper administration, efficiency, and accountability."

"Adam! Drew!" yelled Jake, the owner of the North Fork Tavern, after he stepped up on something so he could be seen behind the bar. "If you boys don't pipe down, I'm going to have to eighty-six you. You think anyone else wants to listen to this crap?"

"Sorry," Adam said as he grimaced. Adam looked genuinely embarrassed.

Drew wasn't too affected. He sat up in his chair and looked right at Adam. In a hushed tone, he said, "Look, all these extraneous projects set up as favors from all the horse trading–"

"Oh, yeah, the Republicans don't have anything to do with that," Adam sarcastically interjected.

"Okay!" Drew yelled. "But how do you fix it?"

"Drew!" Jake yelled from behind the bar. Jake, with both his hands out, was looking right at Drew. "What the–"

"Sorry," Drew said with somewhat dubious concern.

Adam and Drew paused and watched the game for a minute. Adam was still looking at the game when he said, "A new approach for setting the budget for individual departments and agencies needs to be developed." Adam leaned slightly toward Drew. "The new approach has to be established based on a bi-partisan agreement that allows for all current projects to continue."

"There needs to be some protocol," Drew whispered, "for how the budgets are set for the different agencies and departments and for how the priorities are reviewed between the President and Congress to reach a final, reasonable amount of spending."

"Actually, I think that's exactly how the process works now, ideally." Adam shifted in his seat and looked down at the table for a few seconds. "Okay, so, departments make requests – those boring hearings you see on C-SPAN, the President references those requests, along with other established priorities of the Administration, to develop and present a full budget to Congress, the House and Senate have committees that ultimately work up their own funding bills for the departments considering the President's requests, the full bodies pass the individual funding bills, the House and Senate meet to reconcile differences and then pass final budgets. The agreed final products are sent to the President to sign and finalize. I think that's basically how it works. We could get into more of the details and all the non-binding resolutions and other formalities of the whole rigmarole."

"No!" Drew yelled.

Adam shifted his chair slightly, leaned back, and watched the game for a minute. Drew was now looking down at the table pondering the topic. "But your right," Adam said, "the process doesn't allow for everything to be reviewed each year without all the horse trading."

"Well, you can't cut projects in one politician's district and not another," Drew said before he took a sip of beer.

"Exactly," Adam quietly blurted out. "Even the biggest budget hawks in Congress celebrate big windfalls for their districts that come out of the appropriations process." Drew sighed and rolled his eyes as Adam reached over and poured the remaining few ounces of beer from the pitcher into his and Drew's mugs. "There's obviously something amiss with the entire approach," Adam went on, shifting his chair up under the table. "First, the new approach has to be set up to allow for current projects and current programs to continue as authorized through current laws on the books, but it should inherently allow for improved efficiencies to take effect gradually as current projects are completed, future priorities continue to be evaluated, and new important projects and programs are added under all those previously established authorizations."

"Okay, I'm with you," Drew said, as he almost seemed to be conceding defeat and agreeing to take a different tone over the subject. "But how do you restrain spending?" Drew asked. "How do you keep the budget process from continuing to have old items year after year or new unnecessary stuff added that hasn't been properly vetted?"

"Many of these old items aren't going away. Department of Energy laboratories, Army bases, and Corps of Engineers dams aren't going anywhere. Natural disasters are going to happen. The National Parks and the forest aren't going anywhere. The courts, VA hospitals, and railroads aren't going anywhere. Basic missions, such as supporting agricultural resources, maintaining the country's infrastructure, and disease control, aren't going away. There will always be a required budget to continue to administer and operate all such important facilities and vital programs year after year. We could go on and on and certainly quibble over some aspects, but that's what's being funded."

"Fine," Drew said, "actually, we could definitely discuss some details. There's plenty of spending on handouts and social programs and some artsy-fartsy nonsense that could be flat out cut, and there's certainly some specific line items that could be viewed as complete waste, but okay, I see you're trying to look at the overall process, so I'll agree to digress for now." Drew cleared his throat and added, "I will say this: it all has to be balanced with revenues."

"Okay," Adam said and then he paused. "Well, actually, I think the whole notion of a perfectly balanced budget – trying to perfectly balance revenues and expenses every year – would ultimately kill any new process because inevitably, someday, the economy is going to turn sour and revenues will decline. Suddenly making cuts to all those critical projects and programs, to balance the budget in a year when the economy is down, would result in job cuts at the absolute worst time and likely include cuts to many projects that are indeed vital." Drew was furrowing his brow, staring down at the floor behind the bar. The floor was mucked up and littered with crumbs and several napkins. "Imagine," Adam continued, "if a third party intervened in your family finances and told you that you can't have a debt in any calendar year. When you're setting up a nice home for your family and dealing with widely varying needs as your kids grow up, of course the needs vary. Also, your income may have a hiccup at some point. Or, one year, you may be suddenly faced with several emergency expenses at one time." The server stopped by the table and dropped off a new pitcher of light beer and a basket of chips with some salsa. She picked up the empty pitcher and walked away without comment.

"Okay," Drew said, "but you could still implement a formula to set some sort of a spending cap for each year."

Adam paused and looked at the football game. Drew leaned back in his seat. Josh walked over to the table and filled up his glass using the fresh pitcher. "You really can't stomach that stuff, can you?" Adam asked, smiling at Josh. Josh finish filling his glass, gave Adam a playful but firm smack on the chest, and walked away. Adam and Drew watched the game for several minutes without saying anything.

Hannah walked back over and sat down opposite Drew. She said, "You just made a lot of people happy by finally shutting up." Adam and Drew had no response and then Hannah slowly passed her hand over Adam's face as he gazed at the television. Adam smiled and peered over at Hannah without moving his head. Hannah then mocked Adam, playfully scrunching her nose and sticking out her tongue at him. Adam couldn't resist smiling. Drew got up and went to the restroom. "Where did you learn about that budget stuff?" Hannah asked.

Adam scoffed and said, "That old, radical, conservative buddy of yours, Lane." Hannah sat back in her chair and turned toward the game. "Did you ever talk about politics with him?" Adam asked. Hannah was shaking her head vigorously, still looking at the television. Lane was very conservative. Another odd aspect of his relationship with Hannah. He was actually more of Libertarian than a Republican and he used to speak his mind often around Adam and Hannah.

Drew returned and sat down, not saying anything. Hannah began picking at the chips on the table. Then, while chewing, she asked Drew, "Did you get a permit yet, from the Forest Service, to cut a Christmas tree?"

"No, I don't think they're issuing them yet, but yeah, we'll do that again."

"Where do you do that?" Adam asked.

"I don't know, wherever. I'll admit; it's actually really fun. The kids sure love it." Hannah was smiling real big at Drew.

After a couple minutes, Hannah got up and said, "I'm going to go check on Cody."

Adam and Drew were quietly watching the game but clearly still thinking about their latest discussion topic. Adam suddenly started laughing. "Seriously, how do you fix this?" he asked.

Drew smiled and chuckled. "I don't know. I'll give you credit; you've piqued my interest here."

"Okay, you could potentially set a cap," Adam said. "Fine, but that results in painful across the board cuts to all the good with any bad, or even worse, leads to even more horse trading among congressional committee members with their friends in the full Congress. Plus, again, many of these projects are army bases or laboratories or other significant efforts that can't operate correctly and work toward finishing their long-term missions with a sudden big cut." Adam took a sip of beverage and leaned forward on the table looking at Drew. "Seriously, imagine if a third party told you that your family budget would be cut and every line item would be cut by the same percentage." Drew shrugged as Adam went on, "You would be trying to deal with cuts to your auto and grocery budget when maybe you would already know that you could easily cut out some premium movie channels, that you never watch any more, or you could stop buying those nice bottles of wine that you simply don't enjoy like you used to." Drew was looking at the game as Adam starting digging into the chips and salsa. "It's almost like you need a non-partisan, appointed, budget cutting czar to ultimately make the final cuts based on an external, sound, solid review and investigation."

Adam paused and looked out the window at Hannah, along with the bar owner's kids, playing with Cody. "You can't hand that final effort over to the President," Adam continued. "The system will not allow them to make decisions without the influence of basic politics. Maybe they would weigh cuts toward states they don't expect to win in the next election or states with fewer votes in the electoral college. It would be politics at its worst. Then, when a new election effects a shift in the ruling party, old projects and programs would be restarted that were maybe inappropriately cut during the previous administration or just be restarted to hew to the ideals of that new ruling party's base supporters. The cuts would then shift to other projects that may be very important."

Drew suddenly turned toward Adam and yelled, "I'll be the czar! I'll fix it!" Drew then laughed, acknowledging he wasn't helping.

Adam continued, unaffected by Drew's outburst. "You can't just allot portions of the cap between political districts because the needs are not distributed that way. All the government facilities and programs, all the nation's resources and the important areas for resource development, and all the public lands aren't evenly distributed between political districts."

"Seriously, I want to be the federal budget cutting czar," Drew said. He wasn't laughing this time.

Adam started chuckling. "There wouldn't be enough Secret Service agents available to protect you," he said.

Drew sighed and leaned back in his chair again. "If you implement a cap," Drew said, "it would force the President and Congress to work together to make the tough decisions."

"Yeah but it doesn't really solve the core problem and is by no means a long-term solution. The President and members of Congress aren't realistically in a position to dicker over funding for individual projects and programs for individual agencies."

Adam and Drew focused on the game for a moment as the Broncos were about to score again. After a couple minutes of watching the game, Adam, Drew, and all the patrons erupted as the

Broncos scored a touchdown. "He caught that with one hand," Adam yelled. After the extra point, the broadcast shifted to a commercial break and people were shuffling around the tavern again. Adam and Drew sat quietly eating chips.

"Wait," Adam suddenly blurted out. He leaned forward in his chair. "So you know how agencies sometimes have trouble finishing previously planned work for a project within a specific fiscal year." Drew grunted and rolled his eyes. "I don't think it's waste when that happens," Adam added. "It's often that the timeline for completing work doesn't end up falling in line with the fiscal year or with the project's original schedule, as of when the budget requests were made. Budget requests may be prepared years in advance."

Drew leaned his head back and grunted. "Okay?" he mumbled.

"What if a system was created to encourage your favorite government employees to work to find efficiencies and potential savings each year, when such situations arise, and see that a portion of the savings carries over to the project funds for the following year. Government workers could also be rewarded with a small bonus that comes directly from the savings, and the remaining portion of the savings would be returned to the Federal government's total operating budget – that is, contributing to a total annual surplus, or to reduce an annual deficit. New appropriations for that specific project, for the one following year, could also be reduced slightly from the original budgeted amount, yet still leaving more funds in place for that following year after the portion of savings from the previous year is added."

"Dude," Drew said. "You're giving me a headache."

Adam was looking down at the floor as he continued, "The bonus amount would be smaller to prevent workers from neglecting important missions simply to pad a bonus, but the bonus amounts would be enough to encourage all workers, on the ground, to find savings." Adam paused and took a swig of beer. Drew was looking at the football game but listening. "Actually," Adam continued, "the resulting bonus pool for an agency or department could be split. A portion could be distributed evenly to all employees based on pay grade and the remaining pool could be distributed, by the higher pay grade, supervisory personnel to lower pay grade employees as performance awards. The lower pay grade employees would be getting a smaller portion of the evenly distributed amount. Bonuses for each individual employee would be capped at some specific, legislated amount or as a percentage of their annual pay ...or both."

"Dude, what are you talking about?" Drew asked.

"I don't know," Adam mumbled. "What's your solution? Other than making Drew the budget cutting czar?"

"Look," Adam continued, "with such an approach, you remove much of the onus off the politicians that simply cannot find reasonable savings without the enormous influence of politics. Your favorite government workers would suddenly have an incentive based system, that encourages them to look for ways to complete projects more efficiently and potentially find the most appropriate ways of finding savings from individual projects. Plus, these are the people that really know, week in, week out, where savings are possible and what needs to be done at a specific time. The bigger benefit may be that it would provide a means for workers to use annual appropriations for multi-year projects more efficiently by allowing some flexibility in how the final appropriations are used from fiscal year to fiscal year since exact funding needs can shift so easily, long after budget requests are made." Adam watched the game for several seconds. Drew was primarily focused on the game at this point. "There's something else," Adam said, "the government workforce is aging. Newer employees are not part of the older, federal pension system that worked well to lure and retain good talent in the past. This new approach would create a rewarding, incentive based system that would help to encourage younger people to join and remain in the federal workforce."

"I don't know about that," Drew said, "but what if the annual funding for a project continued to grow with carryover?"

"Well," Adam said, "that's an interesting point." Adam looked around and noticed several tavern patrons around them had started listening to their discussion. He leaned forward and continued in a more hushed tone. "The formulas or percentages for designating how savings are distributed would be set to assure reasonable bonuses, reasonable carryover to the next year's funding, and healthy returns back to the general coffer." Adam paused as Hannah entered the tavern after playing with Cody. He watched her walk through the pub as she went back over to sit down with her friend, Jess. "Actually, a carryover cap could be defined to assure no more than a set fraction of the original budgeted amount can carry over to the next year. After that maximum carryover amount is in place for the subsequent year, all other savings are returned to the total operating budget." Adam looked at Drew and smiled real big. Adam started laughing. "There you go. All fixed." Adam then started shaking his head, visibly dubious himself over whether there was any value to the idea.

Drew was smiling. He then hemmed and hawed a bit and said, "I don't know. It's just not that simple. Even after appropriations are set, money may be moved around by agencies and departments to deal with whatever fires that may flare up."

"Well, that's fine," Adam said. "If an agency is in that position, there won't be any savings for that agency. The bonus system won't be so significant that personnel would ever neglect fires or basic core missions or neglect facilities or important research and development efforts. Congress wouldn't let them do that. There would be a basic, simple filing required whenever savings are identified, and the savings would be reviewed by the corresponding appropriations committees in Congress. Also, the system could be set up such that a portion of the collective savings from all departments is evenly spread across the entire government workforce. Workers that are in situations where there simply is much less room for savings, through no fault of their own, would not be left out of this new small part of the federal pay system. Supervisory personnel would only be eligible for individual bonuses from the agency-wide pool to prevent managers from attempting to act, themselves, as budget cutting czars and to prevent them from neglecting important efforts and missions just to increase their bonus."

"What about contractors?" Drew asked.

"They wouldn't be included," Adam quickly replied. "Contractors are already working on an incentive based system to reduce costs by bidding against other contractors to complete important scoped tasks as efficiently as possible. Any savings from the use of contractors would go back into the pool of savings that affects the potential bonuses for government workers. Also, those working directly for the government would have a greater incentive to more efficiently issue contracts and utilize the private sector for additional savings, when pertinent."

"I don't know man," Drew said.

Adam was chuckling. "I really don't know either," he said.

Josh came over and sat down. "Got it figured out?" he asked.

Adam dropped his head and dejectedly said, "No." Drew chuckled. Adam looked at Drew and started laughing. He was still laughing as he said, "You do realize we're only talking about discretionary spending for the departments and agencies. Entitlement spending is a completely different issue ...and a much, much bigger component of federal spending that far outpaces discretionary spending. Quibbling over discretionary spending line items doesn't really do anything to solve the bigger problem."

Drew dropped his head. He was obviously enervated and worn down from the discussion and had no interest in starting another discussion. Drew leaned over on the table and was eating the chips and salsa. "Not now. You can give me your solution to that some other day. It's debilitating, talking to you."

"But the election's on Tuesday," Adam exclaimed. Drew sighed as Adam chuckled. Adam got up and went to the restroom.

As soon as Adam returned from the restroom, Hannah walked over and sat down in the chair with her back to the bar. She said, "You guys haven't even been paying any attention to the game."

"Hannah," Drew said, "I'm from New Hampshire – Patriots fan."

"Oh," Hannah muttered.

Josh looked at Hannah. "Browns fan," he said.

Jess walked over and sat down, off to the side of Hannah. They all quietly watched the game for a couple minutes. During a commercial break, Drew and Adam started throwing tortilla chips at each other, like little kids would do.

"Adam," Jess said "where's your office having their holiday party this year?"

"I guess we're going on a dinner sleigh ride." Adam said as he flung another chip at Drew without looking, hitting Drew square in the cheek.

"Oh wow, those sleigh rides are fun," Jess said.

"Yeah, I think we have two sleighs reserved. There's supposed to be live music out at the dinner tent. The bosses are paying for transportation out to the stable, or wherever we start." Jess didn't ask who Adam would take as a date, but she was looking at Hannah and smiling, jealous of her likely inclusion in the party.

"Are you doing a Christmas party?" Adam asked Drew.

"No, most of my crew is gone for the winter."

Adam then looked at Josh without saying anything. Josh chuckled and said, "We'll probably do a potluck lunch or something. Not much budget for holiday parties at the paper."

"Alright," Hannah blurted out as she started to stand up, "Jess and I are going to take off to hit the spa for her birthday. This is the last week the Lodge is running their off-season spa special."

Drew quickly looked at Jess. "Is it your birthday?" he asked, enthusiastically.

Jess nodded and gritted her teeth. "Twenty-eight," she muttered.

Josh nodded playfully with a big smile. "Well, happy birthday Jessica," he said. "We'll buy you a drink."

"No, no, I'm good. You guys can join us at the spa if you like." Drew, Josh, and Adam all dropped their heads, groaned, and rolled their eyes as they looked at each other. Jess asked, "Adam, do you ever exfoliate?"

Adam quickly replied, "When I go to the beach." Hannah dropped her head, embarrassed, as Jess busted out laughing. Adam was chuckling as he wiggled around in his chair, imitating himself writhing in the sand at the beach, as Josh and Drew furrowed their brows at him.

"Alright, we're out of here," Hannah said, still shaking her head at Adam. As she started to walk away, she leaned down toward Adam and somewhat flirtatiously asked, "You got Cody?" Adam nodded in confirmation. Hannah and Jess walked off. As they walked away, Jess was still laughing at the notion of Adam wiggling around with his entire body at the beach.

Drew, Adam, and Josh quietly watched the game for several minutes. During the next commercial break, Josh asked Adam, "So did any of that discussion help you figure out who you're going to vote for?"

"No," Adam groaned.

"You're not going to really vote for her, are you?" Drew asked.

"I don't know," Adam exclaimed.

Josh scoffed. "No, no" he said, "I think you got him, Drew. He's all in for your boy."

"I don't know who I'm voting for," Adam yelled.

They watched the game quietly for another minute and then turned as they heard somebody enter the tavern. It was Britt. Drew immediately smiled real big and wiggled his eyebrows at Adam. Adam just smiled and turned to focus on the football game. Britt walked over to another table by the windows. As they quietly watched the game, Drew and Adam were occasionally looking over at Britt. Drew kept wiggling his eyebrows at Adam as Adam just shook his head. After another minute, Britt suddenly walked over. "Hey Adam," she said, very chipper.

"Hey, what's up?"

Britt shrugged and looked at the game. She was standing right beside Adam, facing the bar. "So, what's the score?" she asked.

"Twenty-eight to six, Broncos," Adam said. He raised his arm, clenched a fist, and gave a single, feverish shake.

"Cool. Hey, so, do you want to go skiing with me on Wednesday? I still haven't been up on the mountain yet."

"Uh, …yeah, …I just need to check on work, but yeah, that shouldn't be a problem."

"Cool, want to meet by the ganjala at 9:30?" Josh turned and smiled at the intentional, sensational reference to the gondola.

"Sure," Adam said. Josh then looked right at Adam with an evil stare.

"I think the U.S. Ski Team will be practicing on the mountain this week," Britt said.

"Really?" Adam said as he shifted in his seat and turned toward Britt.

"Yeah, they were all in the coffee shop on Friday. I believe they have another week of training before their first race in Canada."

Adam stuttered, "Was, uh, what's-her-name there, that won– "

"Yeah, she was there. They were all there! It was fun."

"Cool."

"Well, alright, I'll see you Wednesday morning. That is, if I don't see you sooner for coffee cake."

"Sounds good."

Britt smiled at Drew and Josh and then dragged her hand over Adam's shoulder as she walked away, exactly as she did at the Java Alley Thursday morning.

Josh was shaking his head and as soon as Britt was away from the table, he blurted out, "Adam, what are you doing?"

"What?"

Drew chuckled and said, "Adam's got a date with Britt."

"We're going skiing," Adam exclaimed.

Josh leaned back, shook his head, and put his left hand against the side of his forehead. Drew continued to laugh. Adam and Drew continued watching the game for a few minutes as Josh was staring at Adam and shaking his head.

Drew's wife, Amy, walked in with their kids. Drew stood up instantaneously, without saying anything, and as soon as his six-year-old daughter saw him, she started screaming, "Daddy, daddy, daddy!" The entire tavern was distracted as he picked her up. His son was a bit shell-shocked by all the commotion in the tavern and was clinging to Amy's leg.

"Alright, I'm going to take off," Josh said. "I need to go let Dixie out. So are we still riding the bike path up to Porcupine Notch after work tomorrow."

"Sure," Adam said.

"With the time change, we need to be moving by 3:45."

"It only takes like thirty minutes to get up there," Adam said.

"Nevertheless."

"I'll be there," Adam said with a firm nod.

"Health care reform," Josh said.

Adam furrowed his brow and turned toward Josh as he was walking away. "What?" Adam asked, but Josh was already walking out the door. Drew, Amy, and their kids all sat down around the table to watch the remainder of the game. Drew's son was clamoring to be held by Adam, so Adam went ahead and grabbed him and immediately messed up his hair. Amy, happy enough to be free and clear of her son's clinging, didn't seem to care.

The Broncos ended up beating the Raiders by a score of thirty-five to twenty.

## *Chapter 9 - Pipe Dream Exfoliated*

Jess and Hannah were wearing robes and reclining in chairs at the resort spa, enjoying glasses of white wine they received with their spa packages. They had gotten massages and facials and were relaxing in a lounge area, enjoying the aromas. They were seated, Jess to the left of Hannah, along the back wall opposite a few windows facing the parking lot. A hallway to the left led to the entrance and a stylist area. The hallway to the right led to different rooms used by the massage therapists and aestheticians. It was dead silence throughout the spa other than the light New Age music being piped in to the different rooms. Hannah was leaning back with her eyes closed as Jess was perusing a travel magazine.

Jessica Murphy worked at the conference center for the resort and moved to Spruce Creek from Florida two years ago. She and Hannah only started hanging out together since Hannah ended her relationship with Lane, but Jess had been a great friend to Hannah over the past several months. Jess, a graduate from the University of Central Florida, had brown hair, dark eyes, and olive skin, she already looked like she just walked out of a spa as soon as she woke up every morning.

"Does Adam have any plans to take you to the Caribbean again?" Jess asked.

Hannah chuckled, still leaning back with her eyes closed. "No, not that I know of." When Adam and Hannah were dating, they went to Saint Thomas in the U.S. Virgin Islands for five days. It was most certainly the best trip they ever took together.

"It's so cute, you two being together again."

"Oh, I wouldn't say that."

"He'll come around," Jess said. She closed her magazine and slapped it down on a small glass table between their chairs. One of the massage therapists walked through the room and smiled at them as she passed the windows.

"Did you ever straight up apologize?" Jess asked.

"No!" Hannah yelled. "It wasn't all on me."

"Okay, I know," Jess said. "I'm sorry." Hannah slightly wiggled in her seat as if she was trying to regain her serene comfort following the distraction from Jess. Jess sighed as she leaned her head back and closed her eyes. "Why are boys like that?" she said. "They just want to hang out and avoid any kind of commitment and then when a girl bolts, they're all confused." Hannah moaned and shrugged, her eyes still closed. "Did you and Adam ever have candlelight dinners or do anything romantic like that?" Hannah turned her head toward Jess, opened one eye, and shook her head vigorously. "Flowers?" Jess asked, peering over at Hannah. Hannah furrowed her brow and shook her head again. Jess scoffed and mumbled, "Boys." Jess took a sip of her wine and leaned her head back again. "Hear from Lane?" she asked.

"No," Hannah droned.

"You did the right thing, girlfriend. I can't believe he sprang that bomb on you a week before your wedding." Hannah sighed and shook her head slowly. Lane had always indicated he wanted to start a family with Hannah, but the week before their wedding, he told Hannah, flat out, that he didn't want to have kids. "That cretin," Jess went on. "I don't know. I think I've resolved you have to be careful with the romantics. It's so nice to be pursued. I do love that. But those guys are all about the thrill of the hunt. As soon as they have their prey, they get bored and start pining for another hunt."

"Lane definitely got bored," Hannah said. "He wasn't into the wedding preparations at all. Our relationship changed so much during those last few weeks. I had my misgivings weeks before the wedding, but I was in denial."

"Did you and Adam ever talk about kids?"

Hannah shook her head vigorously. She then shrugged and said, "I assume he will eventually want kids. I don't have any reason to think otherwise. He definitely heard about Lane's position though. Actually, it kind of came up, for some reason, when we were hiking up North Ridge the other night."

"Well, you did the right thing, girlfriend. I'm sorry but there just wasn't much real about Lane. Did you give the ring back?"

"Yes, of course. He's alright. He's fine. I just didn't love him." Hannah opened her eyes, leaned her head forward, and took a sip of wine. "I don't know. I fell for the idea of this guy that I formulated in my head, but he wasn't actually that guy. And then, I got so caught up in all the wedding preparations and the beautiful party that I lost track of what I was doing. Jess, I still feel so horrible. Actually, I woke up in the middle of the night last Tuesday, all emotional about it all, thinking about my parents and all my family. I still haven't talked to some of my relatives since that day. Jess, I've been so lonely since that day. I'm a mess."

"Hannah," Jess softly said as she reached over and lightly massaged Hannah's shoulder.

"Can I confide in you?" Hannah asked. Jess immediately nodded with her curiosity aroused. "You know where I find comfort, find my escape? When I'm with Adam – and with you. You and he are the only people I've been able to relax around." Jess turned her head right toward Hannah and was looking at her with a sad face, sticking out her lower lip slightly. Hannah leaned back again and closed her eyes. Jess was still looking right at Hannah.

After a few seconds, Hannah said, "Adam wasn't good at being a romantic, but he did try, on occasion, but I was definitely his gal pal. I will say this: he cared for me. He does have so many endearing qualities. Jess, whenever I was sick, he would take care of me." Hannah leaned forward and took another sip of her wine. "Also, he never tried to change me. When I wanted to watch my trashy, gossipy celebrity television shows or sack out and watch a chic flic, he would get out of the way. He always let me live my life how I wanted and was always so encouraging and positive about anything." Jess was smiling real big, still looking right at Hannah. Hannah started chuckling. "Jess, he used to walk around the grocery store with me. He would tag along, not needing to buy anything himself, and push the buggy for me."

"Are you sure he wasn't following you around hoping–"

"No! No. Really, it wasn't anything like that."

"How did you two meet?" Jess asked.

Hannah started giggling and was shaking her head. She then froze for a couple seconds. "He saved my life," she said. Jess's eyes got real big. "Well, not really," Hannah continued, "but he sure helped me out. Did you ever hear about that epic snowfall we had in March, five years ago, that day when the interstate was closed for two days?"

"Yeah, yeah," Jess said, "when the resort reported like four feet within seventy two hours or whatever it was."

"Yeah, so, I was skiing in the trees on the back side of the mountain with some other guys – unbelievable day. Later in the afternoon, I was so tired but still ripping through the powder. Well, I went head first, right into a tree well."

"Hannah!" Jess yelled.

A tree well is the area around the trunk of a tree where the snow is not as deep as the surrounding area due to the shelter from the branches, common for pine trees with low hanging branches. If a person falls into a tree well surrounded by very deep snow, all the surrounding snow can tumble in on the person as they try to extricate themselves. All the snow collected on the branches can also fall on the person as they're moving around. Tree wells can be extremely dangerous after extended periods of heavy snowfall, and if somebody falls into a tree well, they can suddenly find themselves in serious peril.

"It was bad," Hannah said. "Every time I moved, more snow kept tumbling in on top of me. I couldn't even get turned around. I couldn't get my skis to pop off. I was panicking and became even more exhausted as I struggled. After a minute or so, I started screaming, but the guys that I was skiing with were already way down the hill. They never even heard me. Also, I was basically just yelling into the ground and my screams were muffled by all the snow on the ground and on the trees." Hannah shifted in her seat. "Anyway, Adam comes zipping in out of nowhere! 'You're alright, you're alright, you're alright' he's yelling. I think it took him about twenty minutes to help me get my skis off, get turned around, and get out of there. The snow was so deep."

"Hannah," Jess said softly.

"I'm sure somebody else would have been around to help me soon enough, but I was sure glad to see him show up so quickly. I don't think I would have suffocated, but it was bad. Adam never told anybody either. I was so embarrassed that I let it happen and I was crying the whole time he was helping me. I really didn't want to share it with anyone. The whole event was our little secret for quite a while. A few folks know now."

"Wow, I wouldn't have dubbed Adam to be so gallant. Wait, so, what about the other guys you were skiing with that day? You mean they just moved on, without trying to find you, while you were marooned in that tree well."

"Oh, they supposedly did a couple laps through the trees to look for me, but they never saw me. They didn't think much of it. They just assumed we got split up and kept enjoying the absolutely ridiculous powder day." Hannah took a sip of her wine. "Of course, I would see Adam around the valley all the time after that. We had that moment together, so we always talked. Well, we gradually started hanging out together more and more."

"Hannah, you love Adam," Jess said as she leaned back and closed her eyes.

"I do?"

"He'll come around. Hannah, you have to give him credit. He's clearly had abiding, unwavering feelings for you, through it all."

Hannah was rendered speechless. She was now staring down at the floor. After a few seconds, she softly said, "I don't know. I don't know what I want Jess. Are you a hundred percent sure you want to be with your beau, Daniel?"

Jess was rolling her eyes real big. "No, no, no. You know what he said the other day?" Jess said as she leaned forward and looked right at Hannah. "He said, 'We make a good team.'"

"Ugh," Hannah groaned.

"Is anyone ever a hundred percent sure?" Jess asked

"Well, actually, I put in my two weeks' notice at the office."

"What?" Jess yelled as she popped up and turned toward Hannah.

"I can't keep doing that job. I need to use my degree. My lease is up at the end of November. I'm broke and I need to pay down my student loans. I'm going to take that offer to work with my uncle in North Carolina."

Jess sighed and looked down at the floor for a few seconds. "Well, ...okay, ...does Adam know?"

"Yeah, I told him when we were hiking the other day." Hannah and Jess both leaned back and relaxed quietly for a minute. The receptionist walked in from the left and began watering several large potted plants in the room. Hannah and Jess watched her, but they were both clearly thinking about their discussion. The receptionist smiled as she left the room and walked down the hallway to the right.

Hannah looked over at Jess with a smile and somewhat sarcastically asked, "Does Daniel want kids?"

Jess turned her head quickly toward Hannah and gave her a dirty look. "Hannah, Daniel can't make a pot of coffee."

"Oh, stop it."

"Okay, I know. He's fine, but he's just such an ineffectual ...I don't know, but he's sure not there yet." Jess was shaking her head for a few seconds and then took a sip of wine. Then she blurted out, "So, what the heck does Lane think he's going to do with the rest of his life? Is he content with being all alone?"

Hannah rolled her eyes. "He'll meet somebody else," she mumbled. "I'm not worried about that." Hannah then suddenly started smiling and said, "So, I have a friend from high school. She got pregnant and her husband didn't have much to say at all for months during the entire pregnancy. He wasn't too compassionate at all over her daily struggles through the pregnancy, but you know what? As soon as he saw that little tyke at the hospital, he was done. She says he's been smiling ear-to-ear ever since."

Jess looked over at Hannah. "Hannah, are you brooding?!"

"No," Hannah exclaimed. "I'm just saying, you could have a kid with Daniel and he may be the best dad ever – better than you would ever imagine."

"Oh gosh!" Jess said. "Please, let's change the subject right now."

"Okay, sorry," Hannah murmured. "You started it." Hannah turned sideways, facing Jess, and sat with her feet on the tile floor. Jess had picked up her travel magazine again. "Jess, I'm not sure of this notion that people go out there, find the love of their life, and live happily, in love, forever. But I definitely believe strongly in pairing, living a life with someone, caring for someone that will care for you." Hannah looked down at the floor. "Then again, maybe that's how I got into that mess with Lane. I didn't think it mattered that I didn't love him."

Jess put down her magazine and looked at Hannah. "Hannah, you're in love with Adam. You're lucky. And he's right there!"

Hannah and Jess sat quietly for a minute. Hannah was still sitting sideways on the chair as they both finished their last sips of wine. All of a sudden, they heard a banging on the window on the other side of the room. It was Adam.

Hannah raised up slightly and yelled, "Yeah?"

"Cody's tied up to the bike rack," Adam yelled back through the glass, his voice muffled.

"Thank you so much," Hannah said and gave a flirtatious wave. Jess gave a big wave, using her right arm. Adam playfully scrunched his nose and stuck out his tongue before he walked away.

Jess was smiling real big at Hannah and pointed toward the window. "You see, he's right there." Hannah sighed and leaned back. "So, is he driving you nuts with all this election talk?" Jess asked.

"Yes and no. I've been okay with it for the most part. The discourse has actually helped me to not think about my own life. I will admit that he's got me thinking about a lot, and I feel like I've learned a few things over the past week. I really do appreciate his focus on all the important bigger topics as opposed to all the trifles we hear about on television – in the commercials, debates, and news – and all the rubbish we get in the mail."

"Maybe I should have been listening in with you. So does Adam have it all figured out?"

"No," Hannah exclaimed, "but I do think he is thinking about the right things and is not distracted by all the other froth."

"My roommate is all about the National Endowment for the Arts," Jess said. "I think I know more about those grants than any other issue these days."

Jess's roommate had an administrative job for a local non-profit orchestra that puts on concerts in the valley. It's a big part of the local arts scene. Several fundraisers are held throughout the year to raise funds to help support the orchestra, but they also rely on small grants from the NEA.

"Heck yeah!" Hannah said. "It's all so ridiculous. Admittedly, no program can be looked at as completely irrelevant, but the NEA is such a microscopic drop in the bucket compared to all the stuff Adam's been discussing."

"My roommate's always talking about it over and over. How people need to realize that it's not just insipid paintings that people don't understand and ugly sculptures in city parks. Art is music, dancing, singing, books, movies, plays, and comedy, and it's all been so pivotal for centuries to breakdown cultural barriers and help resolve conflicts."

"I actually see athletes as artists," Hannah said. "It helps me to enjoy watching games with Adam. He goes nuts when he sees some football receiver make some spectacular one handed catch. As he's talking about how awesome the guy is, I'm seeing the whole performance as this incredible work of art." Jess was squinting, not quite agreeing.

Hannah chuckled to herself and said, "So, you know how people are always looking for the secret to happiness? Well, can you imagine life without art? How would people get through bouts of unrequited love, the loss of a loved one, or even the loss of a family pet without the catharsis that various forms of art play in everyday life. Gosh, if the philistines want to see the government's miniscule role shut down, well, …that would be sad. I just don't think they understand the vital role it actually serves in society."

Jess was nodding. "You know what else I think about?" Jess said as Hannah looked up at her. "There needs to be more focus on working mothers."

"Oh my gosh! They're super heroes!" Hannah yelled, her voice echoed throughout the entire spa. There were only a couple other patrons in the spa that late Sunday afternoon, so they didn't worry too much about disturbing other guests.

"Alright," Jess said, "here's my contribution to Adam's debate. Times have changed, right?" Hannah was nodding whimsically with her eyes opened real big. "The days of one income households, where the woman stays home and cooks and cleans and does laundry, are over."

"Oh," Hannah interjected, "and there's so much more room in business for women to contribute more of their strengths."

"Yes," Jess exclaimed. "And it is so hard to have two working parents raising kids. It agonizes me to watch my boss and her husband get through each day with their three young children."

Hannah paused. She was still turned sideways, facing Jess. "I don't know an easy solution to that."

"A thirty-two hour work week," Jess blurted out. Hannah squinted and looked skeptically over at Jess. "I'm not saying people should be paid the same. Pay and benefits would be adjusted accordingly, but with a transition to more two-income households in the country, both parents would get the extraordinary life benefits of having their own careers along with adequate time to raise a family in a safe, clean, pleasant home." Jess leaned forward in her chair and looked right into Hannah's eyes. "Okay, there's a lot of focus on how corporations could create more family friendly policies for their employees, right? And we know the importance of parents being able to spend more time with their children, especially when they're younger." Hannah was nodding but still had an incredulous look on her face. Jess continued, "There's all this discussion about expanding tele-commuting opportunities for employees, expanding maternity leave and paternity leave, and workplace daycare. A thirty-two hour work week would, on its own, significantly address all the same needs without direct contributions from employers."

"I don't know. Don't hold your breath for that," Hannah said.

"Think about it though, each parent could work four days a week. Or there may even be an option for workers in some situations to get their hours in three long days. Each parent could stagger their schedules to increase their own personal time with their kids and to look after the home. Actually, it would really help single mothers too. It would sure make life easier for single mothers if they could drop their kids off at school and also be there when they get out of school. Single mothers could maintain a job and develop a career all while still caring for their children. Gosh, it would sure be positive for the children." Jess sighed for a couple seconds and then yelled, "Hannah, gosh darn it, what about exhausted mothers?" Hannah raised her eyebrows and nodded slightly but still had a skeptical look on her face. "Also," Jess went on, "it would even be an extraordinary relief on rush hours and the country's aging infrastructure that is overwhelming insufficient, right? Suddenly, the highways and public transportation networks are better serving employees, all working on more flexible, different schedules as opposed to the exact same grind, five days a week. Just the simplified commutes would add time to people's busy schedules and improve worker productivity."

"Jess, people aren't going to want to have anything to do with a twenty percent cut in their pay."

"Sure," Jess mumbled, "they would get less pay, less vacation time, and may have to chip in slightly more for other, potential employee benefits, but it would sure make it easier for working parents. Employees would still have plenty of options to work overtime, under new overtime rules, but at thirty-two hours a week, they could occasionally take three or four-day weekends together to effectively get more vacation time with their kids."

"You would make a good union boss," Hannah said, chuckling.

"No, no, but also, younger employees would have better opportunities to go back to school while still working. Older employees, well everyone, could live healthier lives with the extra personal time – adjust to healthier sleep schedules and exercise more. The health care costs for the entire nation would come down! Here's the real kicker: companies would use all the payroll savings to hire more employees. The unemployment rate would tank!"

"Okay, I'm sorry Jess. I don't see this happening. So many tech companies and other employers already have difficulty finding highly skilled employees. For so many positions, employers have to invest to train every new employee. They would have to suddenly find and train more skilled employees to make up for the sudden reduction in production. Heck, many companies already have their employees working well over forty hours a week. Maybe the return of the forty-hour work week should be the priority."

"Another thing," Jess exclaimed. "Many employers would see a significant increase in productivity for workers laboring at thirty-two hours a week. Employers would see less fatigue, workers performing with improved cognitive function, and increases to overall productivity. I understand that businesses think they get a better bang for their buck from employees working their lives away, but if a company is requiring employees to burn the midnight oil, either tacitly or through stern outspoken demands, there's a problem with the way that business is operating and the way it's managed."

Hannah was smiling at Jess and shaking her head. "Okay, okay, okay," Jess said as she plopped back in her chair with a scowl on her face. She reached over and grabbed her magazine and started flipping through pages very quickly.

"You're thinking though," Hannah said. Hannah reached over and patted Jess on the leg and looked right in her eyes. Jess threw the magazine back down on the table and closed her eyes. "I will tell you this," Hannah said, "I want a career and I don't want to put my career on hold for years to have a family. There have to be some improvements to work-life balance."

Hannah kept looking over at Jess for a few seconds and then turned and lay back in her chair. They relaxed quietly for a minute. With her left hand, Hannah started gently twirling her empty wine glass on the glass table. One of the therapists and a customer walked through the room toward the front desk. "So, that last year I was with Adam," Hannah said, "he was working all the time." Jess opened her eyes and turned her head toward Hannah. "He was never there," Hannah went on. "He was working every weekend and working until 7:30 every weeknight. He would stop by my place – maybe not until after going to the gym after work. We would start talking, and within fifteen minutes, I would look over and see him sound asleep." Jess furrowed her brow. "It's not just about families with young children. Work-life balance is important for every American."

"I bet there would be a lot less divorces if parents were working thirty-two hours a week," Jess added in a hushed tone.

Hannah looked out the window and noticed it was snowing and the wind was gusting. "I guess I better go get Cody."

Hannah and Jess stood up. Hannah put her arm around Jess and gave her a half hug, and Jess hugged her back. As they were walking out, Jess asked "Can I come visit you in North Carolina?"

"Heck yeah," Hannah said. She smiled and looked right at Jess. "We can go to the beach and exfoliate there the way Adam does it." Jess busted out laughing.

## *Chapter 10 - Care with Accountability at Porcupine Notch*

Adam and Josh started pedaling up the bike path to Porcupine Notch at a pretty good pace. The path starts at the highway, four miles down the valley from the ski resort, near the confluence of Wallace Gulch with Spruce Creek. Wallace Gulch drains a fairly large basin south of the highway. The path, which passes right behind the condominium complex where Josh lives, begins with a gradual climb along Wallace Gulch, through an open valley of sagebrush and grasses. Gunnison's prairie dogs, different from the white-tailed and black-tailed prairie dogs common in the high plains, were perched monitoring Adam's and Josh's progression. The path curves up to the west into a thin forest of lodgepole pines. Many dead trees, killed during the recent pine beetle epidemic, had been cleared by the Forest Service last summer, and with the thinned canopy, much of the path was exposed to sunlight and had dried earlier that Monday morning. Adam and Josh were able to ride through the few remaining patches of slush in the shady spots.

They didn't talk much on the seven mile ride up to Porcupine Notch as they wanted to make good time and reach the top in time to get back before dark. The weather was fair and calm, but it was still quite chilly for a bike ride, which helped motivate them to crank at a good rate. They made it to the top in about twenty-five minutes. Josh beat Adam, but only by about twenty yards. Josh quickly laid down his bike and walked around with his water bottle for a few minutes, getting his breath back. It was unspoken but he was trying to beat Adam to the top. Adam had pulled up, stopped, and leaned down on his handle bars. He stood over his bike for several seconds, looking down at the dirt, before laying his bike down and going over to sit on a large rock outcrop overlooking the valley. From Porcupine Notch, the entire Wallace Gulch valley can be seen along with most of the Spruce Creek valley to the east.

Adam turned his head around and looked at the next ridge that could be seen off to the west. "Wow," he said, "it's going to be a nice sunset tonight." Josh glanced off to the west. Sunsets are not always so spectacular in the mountains since the sun falls behind the mountains long before the sun completely sets further off to the west. Josh continued to stand, looking to the west, quickly getting his breath back from the ride.

Josh began walking over to sit down and then suddenly blurted out, "Hey, check out the alpenglow!" Adam summarily turned back to the east. Exactly as Adam and Hannah had seen from the Eagles Nest Lookout the previous Wednesday night, the sun had dropped below the mountains to the west but rays of sunlight were still shining on the snowy peaks to the east.

"It's still purple," Adam said. "Hannah and I got a good glimpse last Wednesday and it looked the same." Adam took a quick gulp of water from his bottle. "Too bad you don't have your work camera. Why is it purple like that?"

Josh shrugged and said, "Well, let's see, I guess it's a combination of the color of all the vegetation above tree line going dormant for the winter and the thin layer of early season snow, and with the angle of the sun and the different colors in the visual spectrum being absorbed or reflected, red and blue are being reflected, to combine into a beautiful purple glow." Josh, dubious over his own explanation, looked over at Adam with a grin. Adam rolled his eyes but then shrugged, not prepared to provide a counter explanation. Adam and Josh watched the alpenglow quietly for a couple minutes before it faded. Both now seated on the rock outcrop, they were still slightly damp from sweating on the short sprint up the hill and were starting to shiver. Josh started chuckling and said, "Did you see me nearly wipeout in the slush, going around that third switchback, in the aspen grove?"

Adam chuckled and said, "Yeah." Adam lay back on the rock and asked, "You have health insurance through the paper, don't you?"

"Yeah, do you have a good policy through your firm?"

"I guess so," Adam said. "Thankfully, I've never had to use it." Adam was looking up at the clouds as Josh stood up. Josh took a couple steps over and began picking up small rocks and throwing them over the slope below. Adam sat up and took a big gulp of water, the bottle gurgled as he squeezed it to get out the last bit of water. "Hannah doesn't have insurance right now," Adam said.

"What?! They don't offer anything at her real estate office?"

"She's part-time. I'm sure they would help her get set up, but it's not included as part of her employment package."

"She could blow out her knee skiing," Josh exclaimed. "She could have an appendicitis and have to get her appendix removed tomorrow! That kind of deal could happen to anyone at any time."

"Yep, she knows," Adam said as he stood up. He walked over and put his water bottle back on his bike. He then began to also pick up rocks and take turns with Josh, throwing small stones in the same direction. It quickly became a competition as to who could throw a rock furthest down the slope. They kept it up for a couple minutes before finally stopping with no clear winner.

Josh took a last swig from his water bottle and then pretended to squirt water on Adam, but the bottle was empty. They both stood quietly for several seconds. Adam, with his hands on his hips, looked out over the valley. Josh started kicking lightly at the dirt with his bike shoes. "So," Josh said, "if I was to start my own gallery– "

"Yeah," Adam brightly interjected.

"I would have to get my own health insurance."

"Yep."

Josh sighed and looked out over the valley. He then suddenly froze and took a few steps to the north, squinting to focus on a specific point off in the distance. Adam furrowed his brow and looked in the same general direction. "Coyote," Josh said. "It just went into the brush over there."

"Hey," Adam said, "have you ever seen a lynx during any of your backcountry photography expeditions?" Josh shook his head vigorously.

Canada lynx have been listed as threatened under the Endangered Species Act, and while the large, silvery-brown, furry cats were successfully reintroduced to the Colorado high country, they stealthily move about, often at night, in areas that are higher in elevation with deep snow and are thus rarely seen by humans.

Josh walked back over to the rock outcrop and sat down in the same place where he was sitting before. He picked up a couple rocks and threw them over the slope. "So, can you imagine," he said, "how much entrepreneurship it would encourage if every American paid into a Medicare system and received catastrophic health coverage."

Adam busted out laughing. "Oh man," he said, "it's a good thing Drew's not here. He'd whip your hide."

"I don't understand that though," Josh quickly interrupted. "With such a system, he wouldn't have to offer health insurance to any of his employees." Adam smiled and slowly sat down as Josh continued. "Just indulge me for a few minutes here. No small business would necessarily have to offer health insurance. For many, it would be up to individuals and families to either use savings in a Health Savings Account or acquire extra health insurance for coverage up to the bigger annual deductible before the government catastrophic program kicks in, but smaller companies would no longer need to provide health insurance to employees."

"You would still have to have some sort of Medicaid program for people who just can't afford any insurance or any of the costs before the deductible," Adam said. "What about children of poor families? What about veterans?"

"Yeah, yeah, we would still have the Veterans Affairs Administration working toward providing top notch care for veterans and people would still be covered by the Military Health

System. The government would also still work with the states to cost share for Medicaid and the Children's Health Insurance Programs, but those programs could be significantly reformed with catastrophic coverage set up for every American." Adam was lightly chuckling as Josh continued while stacking rocks in a small tower between him and Adam. "Most importantly, with the catastrophic program in place, you keep so many Americans from ending up on the streets or in bankruptcy due to medical bills from catastrophic health events."

Adam was shaking his head in disbelief and he quickly stood up and began lightly stretching his legs. "The problem with high deductible coverage," Adam said, "is there are so many people that just won't go to the doctor when they need to if they have to pay anything substantial. All-important preventive care would tumble under such a misbegotten system."

"Listen," Josh said, "many companies would not have to provide health insurance, specifically small businesses, but employers could then make small direct contributions to employees personal Health Savings Accounts as part of their pay package. Actually, the rules could be established where employers automatically contribute a portion of each employee's pay to their Health Savings Accounts if the employer is not offering health insurance. Employees could easily opt out, that is, if they don't have a negative balance from previously covered care, but the setup for automatic contributions would be simple – employers would submit contributions through a government system where the funds are then transferred to an identified account trustee or a default investment company for each employee. The funds would be transferred by the employer at the same time that payroll taxes and income tax withholdings are submitted for each employee. When an employee changes jobs, contributions would continue, seamlessly."

"Actually," Adam noted, "I guess they could set up a similar system for employee contributions to personal retirement savings to eliminate the need for employers to administer retirement savings plans."

"Okay, well, that's a different topic, but sure, that's fine. As for Health Savings Accounts, the accounts would be set up with rules, similar to tax advantaged retirement accounts, such that the savings could only be accessed for health care expenses before an individual turns sixty-eight, and say, even then, the balance below, say, three times the deductible could still only be used for health care expenses. Maybe the rules could also be configured such that employees do not have an option to opt out of contributions until they accrue enough to cover the deductible for one year. Basic beneficiary designations would be set up for transferring unused balances to patients' heirs where the balance is shifted tax free to a beneficiary's Health Savings Account or to a qualified charity. With potential employer contributions to Health Savings Accounts and with savings people add themselves, people would gradually accrue a balance in their Health Savings Accounts that would be there, ready for them to use as soon as they need to see a doctor, get a prescription filled, go to the dentist, or get eyeglasses. Even younger, low wage employees, working lower level jobs or under seasonal employment, could potentially begin accruing a balance in their Health Savings Account, starting when they're teenagers, and they would automatically accumulate funds needed to cover their basic, future health care costs not covered under the government catastrophic health coverage program."

Josh paused and looked out over the valley as Adam was now trying to stack a tower of small rocks, taller than Josh's tower. Adam then said, "Even if such a catastrophic program doesn't kick in until somebody is dealing with some significant health care costs, it would be so expensive. It would require a big increase to the Medicare payroll tax or something."

"Sure, but again, companies would no longer have to offer health insurance. Individuals could potentially go without supplemental insurance and focus solely on accruing savings to a Health Savings Account. Or if an individual or family decided to purchase insurance to cover their costs up to the deductible, such insurance options would be cheaper and very competitive due to the annual limit, where thereafter, costs are covered by the government catastrophic plan." Adam stood up and was shaking his head as he began throwing rocks over the slope again. Josh said, "It would be an incredible boon to companies as they would immediately see huge savings on their operating statements. Companies would immediately become more competitive in the global marketplace against foreign companies that also do not cover employee health insurance costs due to the government programs in their countries."

"I don't know. The hospitals and doctors don't want to deal with such a government bureaucracy and having to negotiate reimbursement rates. Doctors would be fighting the government on reimbursement rates to no end. It's already projected that there will be a shortage of doctors to meet future needs because of such problems."

"Okay," Josh said, "but advocacy groups would work with the government to assure regional reimbursement rates for all procedures under the new system are competitive to control costs but also be updated to appropriately compensate hospital staff and nurses along with doctors that work so hard and see their youth devoured in college, medical school, residency, specializing, and subspecializing." The skeptical look on Adam's face was unabated. "Also," Josh continued, "with such a new program, alternate reimbursement approaches to fee-for-service could potentially be used that allow for providers to be compensated by episode of illness. When patients are treated for more serious conditions, patients, or insurance companies, would only be on the hook for the deductible portion of the cost, so their cost would likely not be affected by such alternate reimbursement approaches. And, with a single billing system, alternate approaches for reimbursing doctors that provide basic preventive care could also be considered where the reimbursement approach may not be the same as the way patients are billed but it would allow for services to be provided more efficiently, possibly utilizing home health care options or better using twenty-first century options. Costs for preventive care would still be evenly offset with patients' contributions, but doctors could focus on quality of care as opposed to quantity of care."

"I'll admit," Adam said, "that all sounds interesting."

"Also," Josh continued, "administrative costs would plummet! Hospitals would no longer have to cover unpaid bills for Emergency Room visits by uninsured people caught in catastrophic circumstances. Billing for every patient would go through one government system." Adam busted out laughing and dropped his hands down on his knees as Josh continued, "The amount of charity care, or uncompensated care, by hospitals would immediately drop to zero."

"Look," Josh went on, "clinics and hospitals would send billing for every patient, using a simplified form, to one location, and the government would track costs, verify that the billing is correct, and pay the bill upfront. Hospitals and clinics are not involved in bill collection from patients or insurance companies. The government would then forward all billing, up to the annual deductible, to the insurance provider for the patient; the trustee for the patient's Health Savings Account; any pertinent state Medicaid program, the Military Health System, or other government program; or directly to the patient, based on the specifics identified on the original bill and information about the patient on record in the government's billing system. Clinics would have some low level responsibility to inquire with patients to get updated information about whether a patient's insurance, health savings, or some other government program should be billed for the deductible portion, but the details of those options for a patient should be set up in advance, by the patient, through the government billing system. I guess some simple defaults could be used if no information is provided in billing."

"Actually, I just thought of something," Adam said. "With a catastrophic program, the burden for a good portion of the more socially controversial health care needs would not likely be covered by the government since many of those costs would more likely fall within the annual deductible; that is, unless they're enrolled in another government program. Those costs would more likely be covered with a patient's personal insurance or health savings."

Josh continued, undistracted by Adam's note. "Patients who have to pay directly, themselves, for all or some portion of a bill and don't pay would have liens imposed, similar to a basic tax lien." Josh was pacing back and forth, looking down at his bike shoes, and making a lot of arm movements as he stated his case. "Also," he blurted out, "a new, single, central repository for patient records would be initiated as part of this process and maintained through the central billing system allowing any health provider to easily access a patient's medical record from one location."

"How do you prevent fraud?" Adam asked. "How do you assure that the government is being billed for services that are warranted?"

"Patients would have to sign a billing form as services are rendered or up front acknowledging that they are receiving treatment. Insurance companies could also still challenge bills as a means to audit the process and prevent fraud to protect themselves," Josh said. "Also, patients would receive follow up copies of all billing and a simple statement on the status of the year-to-date charges." Josh looked right at Adam. "If their personal Health Savings Accounts are being tapped, I promise you they would make sure they're only being billed for the services they receive. They can challenge a bill if it's flat-out fraud. Also, insurance companies would be able to increase premiums as a result of claims, like car insurance companies do after somebody has a claim, so patients will want to check any billing that is passed on to their insurance companies to assure there are no fraudulent charges against their policy that would result in an increased premium. There would indeed have to be a fraud investigation unit as part of the government's catastrophic program."

"I'm sorry! It's a single payer system," Adam yelled as he threw his arms up in the air. "It's not going to fly!"

"No! It's only a single payer system after a large annual deductible is covered by each patient ...or their insurance ...or some other program ...or a scaled down state Medicaid system."

"Republicans will never agree to an expensive, catastrophic government program for everyone," Adam said, "and Democrats will never agree to scale down Medicaid."

"Let me finish!" Josh yelled back. "You're the one that's been focused on being open minded, believing that some sort of grand compromise could actually be reached. Why the abject negativity all of sudden?" Adam, throwing up his right arm up, waved at Josh and turned his head. Josh asked, "The whole system needs attention, right?" Adam dropped his head and nodded. "Medicare is incredibly expensive. So many people are already currently covered by the government through Medicaid, the Children's Health Insurance Programs, the Veterans Health Administration, the Military Health System, or through health care plans for federal employees. There's overlap between programs, and the administrative costs for health care are through the roof, right?" Adam was looking down and nodding slightly. "Here me out!" Josh yelled.

"Okay, okay, sorry," Adam said with a smug smile.

"There would be no net cuts to coverage for the military and veterans," Josh said as he looked over at Adam, looking for confirmation that Adam was paying attention. Adam gave a firm nod. "And while all the baby boomers would continue to get Medicare in its current form, this new system would eventually replace Medicare for current younger generations. So, it would be grandfathered in as the Medicare program for the current younger generation." Josh paused and looked over at Adam again to make sure he was paying attention. "Everyone born after a certain date would, alternatively, know that they would have this catastrophic coverage as opposed to the current Medicare program when they're older, but that younger generation would know, years in advance, and could save money into their tax deductible Health Savings Accounts. Everyone would have to immediately start paying more to the Medicare payroll tax, but they would promptly have catastrophic coverage. Also, many younger Americans won't actually need care and won't burden the system, so their increased tax payments would help to assure the current Medicare system is solvent for the baby boomer generation and until the new catastrophic program is phased in for the current younger generations."

"Some would rather just see it all end, forever," Adam said as he leaned back on his hands.

"Well, I dare any politician to promise to end Medicare for all those over age sixty five as part of their campaign," Josh said. "That's not a realistic option. They'll never do that. This solution is realistic."

"What about insurance companies? Do you think the health insurance lobby would ever let this idea even come up for debate?" Adam asked.

"Insurance companies would still serve a huge role in the system," Josh exclaimed. "They would still be offering policies to every American to cover costs up to the annual deductible and the costs for preventive care, basic dental and vision, and cosmetic procedures that would not be covered under a catastrophic program. Insurance companies could set higher premiums to high risk patients, but at the same time, premiums would still remain competitive for everyone since all insurance companies would know that they'll never be on the hook for much more than the annual maximum not covered by the government catastrophic program. Also, administrative costs would plummet for insurance companies because they would no longer be involved with developing complex coverage plans and establishing networks of doctors and facilities covered by their plans. They would simply cover preventive care and costs up to the annual deductible for the governments catastrophic plan. The costs to insurers would be covered based on the same final billing rates negotiated for the federal billing system and the insurance can be used for any health care provider registered to be part of the new government system, in any state! The entire system with the government catastrophic program and a patient's Health Savings Account, or any personally acquired insurance, would be completely portable to anywhere in the country. Also, providers would have to provide a quality product because patients would be able to switch to a different provider."

"The transitional period would be a nightmare!" Adam yelled.

"No, here's the thing," Josh said. "A patient would be able to use any doctor at any time and would be able to pay for any doctor using their supplemental insurance or with their Health Savings Account funds, again, as long as the doctor is registered to be part of the new government system. That is, the provider agrees to the reimbursement rates, negotiated with involvement of the health lobby and the advocacy groups for their industry, which again must be updated to control costs but assure doctors are appropriately compensated and the market of available professionals is strong. Also, if a patient goes to the Emergency Room when they should be going to a general practitioner, the patient would be on the hook for the higher cost. Insurance providers could maybe charge a higher co-pay for covering Emergency Room visits. People would very quickly learn to stop going to the Emergency Room when they should be going to a regular physician."

"What about the unions? They've fought for decades to assure their members are set up with good health insurance. Do you think they want to have anything to do with a big change at this point?"

"It will be important, as part of a bi-partisan deal, for union rights to be maintained such that unions can negotiate cost efficient group health insurance options to cover the non-deductible portion or see that additional compensation is made in the form of direct contributions to members Health Savings Accounts. They can also negotiate pay raises: one, to offset for the reduced employer costs with the switch to such a program and two, to offset for any higher tax on employees that would be implemented to cover the cost for such a government catastrophic program. These negotiations would be important for workers, and thus, unions would still have power, but all the implemented changes would go a long way to simplifying the negotiations between different industries and labor unions for decades to come and significantly ameliorate the rift between industry and unions."

Adam picked up his tower of rocks and threw them all on Josh. Josh smiled and started laughing at himself as he looked over at Adam. "There you go," he said. "All fixed."

"Nope," Adam said with a grin. "I'm afraid you can go ahead and write that whole discussion off as a bunch of useless guff."

"Okay, okay, well look," Josh said as he stood up to get all the rocks off him, "here's why I really think it would be great. The economy has changed. The work environment has changed. There's been a transformation in the labor force in the new post-industrial twenty-first century economy from the days when such a high percentage of Americans used to work in manufacturing, right?" Adam was looking down but listening intently. "Companies are looking to outsource so much more to people working as freelance specialists. These days, it's different from the way so many people worked decades ago or even just a few years ago. Now, people don't get a job with a company, get their family set up with a good health plan, and work there until they're sixty five. With all the technological advances and with a greater segment of the American population with a broadened education, there's an opportunity for this country to lead the world in research and development of new innovative solutions to all the world's problems and develop new technologies to improve business and economic efficiency. The truth is that the technological revolution is just getting started and the economic system needs to foster entrepreneurship and encourage all the young workers with bright ideas to initiate start-ups and lead the way. All these new small businesses would create jobs. For this development and this new opportunity in the Smart Age to flourish, workers need to be able to pursue these endeavors without having to worry about basic health care under the unfortunate scenario that they, or a member of their family, gets seriously injured or very sick. Health care needs to be more individual and portable."

Josh was still standing up and looking out over the valley as he continued, "Or, the rationale may be as simple as seeing that a system is set up to provide Americans with a better situation to run their own corner businesses or work on their farms or run their ranches while not having to worry about the potential costs should they, or a member of their family, have an unfortunate catastrophic health event."

Adam stood up and said, "Josh, do you understand the power of the health care and insurance lobby in Washington?"

"No."

"Well," Adam said, "uh, ..neither do I, but I don't think we could even begin to fathom their opposition to such an approach. Any effort to enact such significant reforms would be nothing but an exercise in futility."

"Okay, but something needs to be done, right?"

"Yeah."

"Well, there's a solution that would not affect all those on Medicare, or about to go on Medicare, and would assure Medicare will remain solvent for the baby boomer generation. The long-term costs of Medicare would eventually be reduced, but the younger generation would know, in advance, and be able to prepare for that day. At the same time, catastrophic health care would be immediately provided to everyone removing a key restriction on economic prosperity. Big business would suddenly have a big burden removed that would allow corporations to better compete against foreign companies. Yes, it would involve a tax increase, but it would also dramatically reduce health insurance costs for individuals and businesses. Health insurers would thrive while providing a wide range of coverage to individuals and families for preventive care, dental, vision, cosmetic treatments and the costs up to the annual deductible under the government catastrophic program, and the insurers could operate more soundly knowing they would no longer have to cover costs for catastrophic cases. A new central repository for health records would be created significantly improving the efficiency and quality of care. Administrative costs would plummet, thus reducing health care costs for everyone along with the cost of the new program in government."

"You're vamping. I heard you the first time. How big would the deductible be?"

"I don't know, fairly big. Reasonable but big. It would be painful for a family or individual to cover an annual deductible without health insurance or some accrued savings in a Health Savings Account. A bigger deductible would be key to keeping expenses under the government program in check, to a certain extent."

"People would start playing games with their care to have multiple needed procedures completed in the same year, so they're only hit with the annual deductible once."

"Oh gosh," Josh groaned, "okay, if needed, the deductible could maybe be configured differently as a rolling three year maximum on out of pocket expenses and in a manner that maintains the same out of pocket expenses regardless of when procedures are completed over a three year period. Maybe a second tier could be defined where a percentage co-pay must be covered by the patient until a second threshold is reached. Also, note that the program would be configured such that some routine care would never be covered by the program to prevent people from trying to time when they go to the doctor, dentist, or optometrist for basic checkups. Actually, I don't know that it needs to get too complicated though. If somebody needs care at a level that requires resources beyond the deductible, I don't know that there's a need to over-analyze how the program is being used for someone that has fallen into such unfortunate circumstances that their medical bills exceed the deductible. They're still paying the deductible. The important consideration is that so much of the health care costs for the nation, specifically for younger and middle age people, are for small ailments, and the costs for those services would never be a burden on the government program due to the higher deductible. This would keep costs for the government program way down."

"If it's not a bipartisan plan," Adam said, "it's dead on arrival."

"Agreed. Republicans wouldn't like the increase to the Medicare tax, but they would agree with a scale down to Medicaid.

They would agree with seeing small businesses and entrepreneurs relieved from the burden of providing health care coverage to employees. They would also favor the significant role of individuals, and insurance companies, in the new setup to effectively help control overall health care costs. Democrats wouldn't like scaling back Medicaid or the eventual changes to Medicare for those born after the baby boom generation, but they would strongly favor catastrophic coverage for every American. You would also have to think that every politician would take pride in seeing the implementation of a program that would assure every American would get the care they need and not have to unduly suffer should they become horribly injured or very sick."

"Actually," Adam muttered, "I guess auto insurance premiums might go down for everyone if coverage for bodily injury and medical costs from automobile accidents were suddenly partially covered by such a new catastrophic government health insurance program." Josh raised his eyebrows and looked off to the side, having not thought of that consideration. "Workers compensation insurance may be a bit cheaper too," Adam added.

Adam and Josh stood quietly for a few seconds before they were suddenly distracted by a cacophony of loud yipping and howling sounds that could be heard from multiple coyotes in the valley. Josh pointed across the valley at one coyote that could be seen, on the edge of a rock outcrop. Adam gestured to the north, up the valley, where the silhouette of another coyote, on a treeless point, could be seen against the twilight. Within seconds, the coyotes were collectively making an absolute racket.

"They're getting started early tonight," Josh said.

"Actually, it is getting dark," Adam said. "I don't have any lights on my bike and we don't have any moonlight tonight. We should go."

"Yeah, yeah," Josh said. Josh and Adam quickly went over and picked up their bikes. The loud yipping and howling from the coyotes continued for several seconds as they immediately began cruising down the bike path.

As Josh rode into the aspen grove, Adam yelled, "Easy on that switchback ahead." Josh gave a little sarcastic yet acknowledging wave. It only took them a few minutes to get down the hill to Josh's place. They went a bit slower than they normally would to cut down on the wind chill.

When they got to Josh's place, Adam rode around the building to the parking lot, took the front wheel off his bike, and put his bike in his car. He then walked back to Josh's place. Josh had already begun starting a fire in the wood stove, and Dixie was moving around ecstatically. Adam sat on the floor and played with Dixie for a couple minutes using one of her chew toys. He then got up and grabbed a banana off Josh's counter. He sat on a stool in the kitchen and said, "So, you mentioned up there how there are so many bright young people in our country that are ready to solve the world's problems?"

Josh shrugged. "Ah, what do I know?" he muttered.

"No, I agree, but our education system needs some work."

Josh dropped his head and froze, holding a log that he was about to lay in the wood stove. He turned his head slightly toward Adam and started chuckling. "One more day," Josh whispered to himself.

## *Chapter 11 - Respect and Education for Opportunity*

While the path to Porcupine Notch makes for a short bike ride, it was enough that Adam and Josh were a bit spent but now warm and dry, watching the pre-game broadcast for Monday Night Football. Adam had plopped down in his normal spot on Josh's couch and Josh was sitting in his old recliner. Dixie had finally calmed down from her excitement following their return and was lying next to the woodstove, which was not hot yet. During a commercial break, a loud political advertisement came on and Josh and Drew couldn't help but laugh.

"One more day," Josh mumbled. Josh leaned forward in his chair and looked right at Adam. "So, who's it going to be?" he asked.

Adam smiled and started shaking his head. "I don't know," he said softly. "I really don't know."

"Oh, come on, man," Josh yelled. "You're really going to vote for that guy? How could you even consider it?"

"That's not even how I'm thinking here," Adam said. "Look, I don't have a huge stake in anything. I feel like an outsider looking in on this debate, and I just see the big problems and the road the country will head down if nothing's done." Adam sat up on the sofa. "Let me ask you something. Okay, so both sides are playing the process in anticipation of someday, maybe someday, having complete control of all the branches of government with a super-majority. That's never going to happen, right?" Josh leaned back in his recliner and subtly shook his head. "So, who's going to get it done?"

Josh rolled his eyes and sneered, "What? You're grand plan?"

"I'm looking at it entirely from the perspective of a problem solver. Not who's right and who's wrong, but there's this inevitable division. Who's going to get both sides together for that final, much needed grand compromise. I just know we need a solution, and we need it now. Next year!"

"You'll have to forgive me for my misgivings," Josh said. He then got up real quick and went over to his refrigerator and grabbed a couple sports drinks. He threw one at Adam, fairly firmly, but Adam caught it. Josh plopped back down in his recliner and the chair creaked as it continued to rock for a few seconds.

Adam looked over at Josh and said, "Do you really think my one vote matters?"

"This election might come down to the Colorado electoral votes," Josh said. He then started laughing as he continued. "And what if Colorado comes down to one vote? That will be your vote!" Josh and Adam were both laughing at the ridiculous notion, but it made the whole discussion more interesting. They quietly watched the pregame broadcast for a bit before Josh quietly muttered, "Did you see they had another one of those videotaped police brutality cases back east?"

"Yeah, I saw it," Adam said. "You can't get too focused on those, man. You can't judge the job of the entire country's police workforce based on a few dumbasses."

"I know that," Josh said. "You think I don't know that? Of course, I know that."

Adam sighed. "Gosh," he said, "there's another job I couldn't do. Those guys don't get paid much and have to deal with so many punks and operate in so many scary situations all within the constraints of so much protocol."

"The protocol is critical," Josh said. Josh was lying back in his recliner and rocking, holding his drink on his belly. "There's definitely a racial component to some of the mistakes made by the few bad examples," Josh said, "but I also know we have to appreciate what nearly all of them are doing for us. I know that." Josh took a few sips of his sports drink and started rocking rather vigorously in his recliner. "You know what people need to understand about the race relations problem?" Adam's eyes got real big as he peered over at Josh. "So many African Americans are still having a tough time. The days of racial segregation, or the even the more horrific events of long before, indeed occurred a long time ago, but many African Americans are still only a few generations removed from those days. That said, all they want is to be respected. You summed it up yourself the other night. And it's free! It doesn't cost anyone anything to just treat other Americans with proper respect. It takes no extra time out of their day."

"Uh, yeah," Adam said somewhat nervously. "I'm respectful."

Josh looked over at Adam. "I'm not talking about you," Josh said, chuckling.

Adam started awkwardly gulping his sports drink and then said, "I agree. I agree. Yeah, and again, people can't get so focused on the actions of a few specific individuals in these run down communities or a few specific events or what they see on television. They have to look at it macroscopically. That's key to seeing some important needed changes in this country." Adam set his drink on the coffee table, and he and Josh quietly watched the analysts on television making their picks for the football game.

"Well, it's a cycle," Josh suddenly blurted out. "It doesn't even have anything to do with race, but people that grow up in these more dilapidated communities with high crime rates, high drug use, high unemployment, and underperforming schools are at such a disadvantage. And they're children! We're talking about children, Adam."

"Hey look," Adam said, "I hear you. But you know politicians have to be careful about using children as pawns for pushing some political agenda. I'm not arguing with you, but it really can be a trite, hackneyed approach for making a political argument. It's used in the same way to support child tax credits and so many other ideas, but yeah, I hear you. I definitely agree that it's the cycle that needs to be fixed."

"Okay, but it's so easy to get focused on blaming their parents while so many of these parents didn't have any foundation when they were children. How could anyone look at these children and not want to see them afforded better opportunities?" Dixie sat up and whimpered. Josh watched as she slowly walked into the kitchen and drank some water out of her bowl. "The social safety net is so important for these children," Josh continued, "to help them have clean shelter and nutrition, to help them live up to their potential. The solution is certainly not as easy as taking it away and expecting that people will thrive simply because they have no other option but to overcome the tougher obstacles they face. It's not that simple."

"I understand that," Adam said. Adam started chuckling lightly. "Drew about pushed me off the lift last week when I was talking to him about it, but he's also right. It can be crutch. Anyone would be remiss to not acknowledge that."

"Okay, so, what's your solution …for this grand plan?"

"They need opportunity, and it all comes with education. Education is without a doubt the one clear answer. Heck Josh, there are people in some of these communities that have never been on the internet."

"Oh, I know," Josh said. "I agree, but the investment in education needs to come from everyone. And when I say that, I understand that local communities need to provide matching funds, but so many people in this country have benefitted from the great education systems in their communities and it's simply a matter of paying it forward, to help children in these tumbledown communities, with reduced class sizes, improved facilities, and good, appropriately compensated teachers."

"Also," Adam chimed in, "the economy is so much more knowledge-based now than it was in the twentieth century, and if America is going to lead the world in the Smart Age, there needs to be more opportunities for higher education for those that can't afford it."

"Everyone should want to see that," Josh interjected. "When significant portions of the population can't afford higher education, it undermines economic growth. Everyone suffers. It promotes greater income inequality which simply is not good for the overall economy. Those that are well off will see their investments suffer, their businesses flounder, and the entire economy contract."

Adam started laughing. Josh turned and gave him a dirty look. "No, no, it's fine," Adam said. "I just realized I'm feeding the beast." Josh didn't smile, but he turned his head back to the telecast of the Monday Night Football game that had kicked off.

"There has been so much investment in tax breaks and loopholes for big business – corporate welfare," Josh said, "all in the interest of bolstering the economy and creating jobs, but it only resulted in greater income inequality. You're dead on, the key to promoting the American Dream for the middle class is investing in schools and education. Education is the key to self-reliance and changes are also needed to assure more people have the necessary problem solving skills for the new Smart Age economy. You read how employers can't find qualified talent. Creating a more educated society would result in a thriving economy that benefits everyone. Those that are well off would then see their businesses grow and investments appreciate."

Adam got up and took his sports drink bottle to the recycling bin in Josh's pantry. He walked back over and stood on the stone platform by the wood stove, that was now getting warm. Dixie moved over and sat right in front of Adam. Adam squatted down, and in a completely different manner from the way he treats Cody, he pet Dixie very gently for several seconds. "So how do we get more kids properly educated in science, technology, engineering, and math?" Adam asked.

"I don't know," Josh groaned. "Yeah, it starts right there though." Josh started rocking vigorously in his chair again. "I wish I knew how to code. Did you ever program much?"

"A little, but not really," Adam said. "All the high schools in the country should now require every student to take one class in basic coding. It doesn't matter what programming language they use as long as every kid is introduced to the rudimentary aspects of programming. You would have to think that there would be so many who would take that initial introduction and run with it to become excellent programmers."

Josh and Adam both suddenly yelled, "Oh!" as they focused on the football game. Dixie was startled over their yelling and scurried into the kitchen. A wide receiver just got clocked while jumping up for an overthrown pass, and Josh and Adam both stood up, in front of the television, and grimaced as they watched the replay about eight times. After the injured receiver eventually got up and walked off the field, Josh stepped over and grabbed a football from under his end table and quickly threw it at Adam as they both sat back down.

"I think universities and professors need to do a better job of encouraging more students to pursue those STEM programs of study," Josh said, "rather than focusing so much on weeding out students that might be a little below some defined standard. They should be encouraging more new students to enroll and stick with STEM programs. There are too many students getting specifically directed into majors that have less value in today's economy. Those kids then get out of school with mounds of student loan debt and few valuable skills." Adam and Josh threw the football back and forth. Dixie was still sitting in the kitchen and now watching the football flying back and forth across the room. "I started in Engineering," Josh continued, "I could of done it. I should have done it." Adam knew this but they had never talked about it.

"Why did you change?"

"I didn't do that well to start?"

"Did you miss some GPA requirement or something?"

"No, but I got *the talk* from one of my professors." Mimicking his professor, Josh said, "'I should maybe consider pursuing another major that better suits my strengths and abilities.' Good grief, I was still a teenager. I could have continued or just taken a lighter load for a couple semesters. I don't know, maybe proceeded under a five year program."

"You never told me all that. Wait a second, I thought you got like a 30 on your ACT or something?"

"I just needed to get my act together a bit. It's all so stupid."

"You're going to be just fine with your new gallery." Adam then smiled and sarcastically said, "That place is going to be a cash cow."

"Yeah, I'm fine, but I'm just saying: schools, and more specifically all the professors and administrators, need to change their approach to get more kids in STEM programs. I understand that schools must protect and constantly improve and update academic standards, but I don't think that's even a problem. I think much of the future need, for more workers educated in STEM fields, could be met if professors and school administrators simply worked to encourage students that are getting started in those programs."

Adam got up, went into the kitchen, and poured a large glass of water. Dixie was now sitting in front of Adam in the kitchen, wagging her bobtail. Adam laughed and said, "I don't have anything for you." Dixie whimpered and lay down on the tile floor. Adam chuckled and walked back into the living room. Adam and Josh watched the game quietly for several minutes, occasionally making a rhetorical comment about the action. During the next commercial break, Josh blurted out, "Are you really going on that date with your little ingénue from the coffee shop?"

"Oh, stop it. She's fine. Plus, it's not a date! We're going skiing."

Josh was shaking his head. Adam was looking right at the television, not looking for additional discussion over the topic. Adam watched Dixie as she slowly walked back over to the wood stove and lay down. Josh was still chuckling. "Drew thinks Hannah is trying to get you back only so she can get in good graces with her parents. You don't buy that, do you?"

"Why do you say that? Did he say that?"

"He said something to that effect when you went to the restroom at the North Fork yesterday."

Adam was shaking his head. "She's moving to North Carolina anyway. What about you and Emily?" Adam sternly asked. "Are you two getting married soon?" Josh dropped his head and groaned. "By now," Adam continued, "you two should be married with 2.3 kids and all the signature family pets and the picket fence, all of it." Adam was smiling real big and enjoying that the tables had turned. "Does Emily want all that?" he asked.

"Yeah, she wants it," Josh said, looking over at Dixie, her eyes locked on Josh. "But she doesn't want it with me."

"What?" Adam said, inquisitively.

"Look, I've always known that she finds me to be a bit uncouth, but she always seemed so happy whenever we would go backpacking, camping, fishing, or whatever. I've never worried about it too much. Anyway, I think she really sees it all as passing time until somebody better comes along."

"She said that?"

"Kind of. But there's no need to mince words here. It has become so obvious that she thinks she can do so much better than me and treats me, accordingly, with indifference. I've gradually picked up on it, more and more, to where I've become bitter about it and it affects our time together."

"I don't know man. I don't see it."

"Yeah, there have been several times, where she slips, and says things to her friends, right in front of me, about how it will all be better when she meets a doctor and they have their big house with the pool, the boat, and the beach house." Josh growled and chucked his empty sports drink bottle into the kitchen. It bounced around in the sink and made a bunch of noise against a couple dirty dishes. Dixie sat up again, startled. Josh scoffed and quietly continued, "The maid and the nanny."

"She's joking! Come on, all chics joke about their celebrity exceptions and other such nonsense."

Josh turned and stared at Adam. Adam quickly dropped his head and turned back toward the television. "No," Josh said firmly. Josh turned his head back toward the television and continued, "She's gradually gotten so comfortable just talking about such stuff right in front of me. I used to think that we were taking it slow and not looking to get too serious too fast and that we both had this unspoken understanding that we wanted to focus on our careers and paying off our student loans. But I think she's dead set that's she's not going to settle for me. Actually, I think she's seriously considering moving back to Atlanta and has no interest in seeing me follow her."

"Grievous man. I'm sorry. I didn't know." Adam hadn't seen Emily for a while, but he hadn't inquired. Josh quickly popped up out of his chair and went to the restroom. Adam didn't know what else to say and was clearly relieved to be free of the topic. The broadcast had gone to commercials, and Adam got to watch three political ads during the break.

"So?" Josh said as he walked back into the room.

"So what?"

"Tomorrow's the big day. You got it figured out yet?"

"No," Adam said firmly. "I'll be voting though. I guess it will be a game-time decision. I still say you have to love the process." Adam stood up. "Alright, I'm going to go." Adam went over and softly pet Dixie for a several seconds and then walked over and opened the door. He then stopped with the door open, turned around, and looked at Josh. "Emily," he said.

"Yeah?" Josh quietly muttered.

"Break up with her, tonight. To heck with that nonsense."

## *Chapter 12 - Surely You Jest, Anchorman*

A mass of election signs greeted Adam as he drove up to the local elementary school, the designated polling place for all residents of the Spruce Creek valley. There were so many election signs that the overall mass distracted from any individual candidate's name or any references to particular ballot measures. It was the middle of the lunch hour, and the parking lot was bustling with voters. Adam proceeded to the back of the lot, and then he slowly followed the small *Vote Here* signs to the polling room while carefully avoiding several cars jockeying for close parking spots. Voters, from all demographics, hurried in and out of the voting center, frantically squeezing in their all-important vote within their already hectic, normal daily schedules.

Adam entered the voting room, which was hectic but quiet, with no conversation other than the occasional whisper by a volunteer poll worker. Four other individuals were ahead of Adam in line. He looked around the room, focusing on the intense concentration of each voter making their way through their ballots. With his identification in hand, Adam then stepped forward to the first volunteer. He took a deep breath and slowly muttered, "Ah, democracy." A taller, older gentleman – he was maybe around sixty years old with a beard that hadn't been trimmed in quite a while – heard his mumble and couldn't help but smile and nod. Adam signed his name and received a slip to take to the next volunteer. "Do I get a sticker?" he asked.

"When you submit your ballot," the volunteer whispered.

"You aren't going to run out, are you?"

"No, we have plenty."

All the electronic voting booths were occupied, so the next volunteer took his slip and handed him a paper ballot. A third volunteer was standing in the middle of the room, and she directed him to an available carrel in the back of the room, by the windows facing the parking lot. Adam sat down in one of the elementary school's rock solid chairs and was clearly fascinated by how unbelievably uncomfortable the chair was, but he quickly redirected his attention to the ballot.

Final decisions were now to be made for school board, county commissioners, judges, state representative, state senator, U.S. House representative, U.S. Senator, and the President. Measures were also included for two state constitutional amendments and two other propositions. Adam decided to start at the end, with the propositions, and work his way back to the beginning of the ballot. He was perfectly familiar with the questions at hand but read each in detail, shaking his head lightly, on occasion, while marveling at the specific language used for some of the measures and at the subtleties in the language that could easily affect how propositions are interpreted. He then moved up the ballot to the votes for several regional positions, including judges, county coroner, and county clerk, with some candidates running unopposed.

Votes were then to be cast for the more prominent positions. Adam slowly stopped at each one, gathered his thoughts, and made his final decision, taking pride in impeccably filling in the boxes for each selected candidate. Adam then made it up to the very first question on the ballot – the selection for President of the United States. Adam noticed the ordering of candidates' names for President and other positions on the ballot. For the different selections to be made, sometimes the Democratic candidate was listed first and sometimes the Republican was listed first. Final ballot positions are determined by separate drawings before the election, starting with major party candidates, minor party candidates, and then unaffiliated candidates. Adam then made his selection for President, chuckling softly over how quickly he ended up making a decision.

Adam looked over the entire ballot again and assured nothing was missed. As he shifted back his chair to depart, the chair made a loud roar against the hard, vinyl tile floor. He took the ballot, in the provided folder, to a fourth volunteer and slid the ballot into a ballot box as instructed. The volunteer handed him an *I Voted* sticker and Adam promptly peeled off the sticker and smacked it to his chest. Adam walked out of the voting room and began to slowly navigate his way through the parking lot, saying hello to a couple residents he recognized. As Adam walked up to his car, he stopped, turned around, and looked again at all the voters, shuffling in and out of the polling center and rushing to and from their cars.

"Well, I guess that's that," he muttered to himself.

Adam stayed at the office late that day, and while he was not particularly stressed about the final results, he was glad to have plenty of work to distract him from his anxiety and his excitement to watch the election night television coverage and witness democracy at work. Early results from the east coast aren't reported until well after 5:00 p.m. Mountain Standard Time, so Adam worked until 6:30.

Later, at his home, Adam was sitting in the middle of his sofa, eating leftover pasta and watching as results came in faster than the information could be disseminated, with the primary reporting focus on the Presidential race. For some states, where the results were not in question, the national media would tag electoral votes immediately after the polls closed and long before any results were actually available from precincts. Analysts provided commentary on past blunders or gaffes, during the campaign process, that specifically hurt some candidates for Congress, and the pundits also expounded on Presidential candidate's positions on specific topics that may have contributed to them losing a key swing state. Correspondents reported on the *Get Out the Vote* efforts and potential impacts of inclement weather in some key districts. There were definitely some surprises that made the coverage entertaining but nothing as significant as what was about to be reported.

When the polls closed in Colorado at 7:00 p.m. Mountain Standard Time, national media outlets soon thereafter reported that Colorado would be too close to call. Calls were continuing to be made for Virginia, North Carolina, Ohio, Florida, Pennsylvania, Iowa, Arkansas, Nevada, and Iowa. Time seem to fly by but there was no clarity yet as to the final outcome, and then the mostly unlikely scenario was posed.

As the situation seemed as cloudy as before any results were available, a lead news anchor reported, "We have Breaking News. With the call now made for Missouri, a potential historical scenario has become very possible. The Electoral College votes for the Presidential Race could end in a 269 to 269 tie, ...depending on the outcome in Colorado." Nobody was going to bed early that election night. Correspondents were scrambling to report the math and explain just how this scenario had become possible, but the key news was that ...it can happen and ...it very well may happen. All the media outlets were pushing out presentations to explain how the President would be determined under such a scenario. Adam was now standing in his living room, right in front of his television.

"First," a correspondent began explaining, on one of the twenty-four-hour news channels, "let's assume that state electors will indeed vote based on their pledge and based on the popular votes for their state, thus yielding a 269 to 269 tie in the electoral college votes." All the other commentators on the broadcast set were staring intently at the reporter. Nobody was smiling. "Then," the correspondent continued, "all the newly elected representatives to the U.S. House of Representatives would determine who would be President; however," she tittered a bit, "while we now know the party that will control the House of Representatives, that potential vote for president would not be based on a typical full House vote. For a possible vote for President, to break a tie in the Electoral College, all the representatives from each state would collectively vote to determine which candidate gets *one vote* for their state."

Graphics were used for the explanation. It was described that while Texas has thirty-six representatives in the U.S. House, they would all collectively determine who gets one vote for Texas, and likewise, California has fifty-three representatives who would select the candidate that gets the one vote for the Golden State. Wyoming only has one representative in the House who would solely determine who gets the one vote for that state. The candidate getting the majority of the 50 representative votes for each state, would win the Presidency. It was too early, and actually impossible, to try to do the math on which party would have the House majority under such a voting scheme, given that every House seat was up for re-election.

"Oh," the correspondent continued, "and the Vice President would be determined by a separate vote in the Senate." All the commentators and correspondents on the broadcast set broke out in rollicking laughter. They were all already fully knowledgeable of this system but couldn't help but enjoy the comedy associated with the scenario maybe coming to fruition. Two or three noted at the same time, "We could have a President and Vice President from different parties," as it was explained that every senator – two from each state – would vote to determine who is Vice President.

The broadcast had begun to take the air of late-night comedy skit on a variety show, with pandemonium ruling the set. The lead anchor then interrupted the brouhaha, and after quickly regaining control of the discussion, he reported, "America, this may be the closest election ever in this country, and every American should know now, more than ever, your vote matters."

Josh's phone had been ringing, but he wasn't answering. It had been Josh and Drew calling repeatedly. As the excitement of the possible scenario grew around the country and social media networks became overloaded, more and more results were coming in from Colorado. After another thirty minutes of excitement, a call for the state of Colorado was made, and the final tally for the Electoral College votes was 278 to 260. There would be no tie, and all the media outlets made their final projection for who would be President of the

United States. Victory and concession speeches were made shortly thereafter.

Adam knew he was supposed to meet with both Josh and Drew at the North Fork on Sunday, and somebody …was going to be very disappointed.

## *Chapter 13 - Road to Retirement at Two Peaks Lodge*

Adam arrived at the gondola about five minutes early on that sunny, pleasant Wednesday morning. He waited for several minutes, saying hello to a few locals he recognized. It wasn't nearly as busy on the mountain as compared to the hoopla he and Drew had experienced on Halloween. The novelty of being back on the hill, after the long summer break, was wearing off for many faithful riders that had become more interested in holding out for some natural snow and more open terrain. Just as Adam started to think that Britt might not show up, he saw her walking through the village.

"Hey, there she is," Adam said with a big grin as Britt walked up. Britt nodded with a cherubic smile. "Ready to go?" he asked. Britt nodded again, still smiling, and they began walking toward the gondola loading zone.

There was no line to get on the gondola. After getting their passes scanned, they stepped into one of the large six-passenger cabins for the ten minute ride up to the top of Spruce Creek Mountain. Britt talked most of the way, mainly about her work schedule and she told some stories about interactions with her co-workers and customers at the coffee shop. Adam listened and given that he already had some background information on the people involved, he genuinely enjoyed hearing the anecdotes. Upon reaching the top of the mountain, they stepped out of the gondola cabin and walked out to the top of the run to put their skis on.

"I'm slow," Britt said, somewhat anxiously.

"You're fine. There's no need for us to us to break any records today. We'll just enjoy the day."

They eased down the run, carving smooth turns into the fresh corduroy, left overnight by the snowcat groomers. After a fairly quick run, they skied into the lift line maze to get on the chairlift. There was no need to ride the gondola on such a beautiful day, and on that quiet weekday, they were able to ski right up to loading zone. They skied four more runs, with Britt leading the way fairly quickly, despite her request to take it easy. On the lift rides, Britt continued with her coffee shop talk and other light conversation. After their fifth run, the two open slopes were getting skied off from all the other riders packed on the same runs. They rode the chairlift up but decided to take a break at the Two Peaks Lodge, located just to the east of the lift's upper terminal.

After placing their skis on a ski rack, Adam went inside the Lodge to get a couple hot chocolates as Britt scoped out a couple chairs on the outside patio. The patio afforded a panoramic view of the entire valley to the north and distant mountain ranges in the next counties. Britt was turning two chairs to directly face the sun as Adam walked out of the building. Britt sat down and then Adam plopped down, to her right, in the low seats that resembled beach chairs. They took a couple sips of hot chocolate and quietly looked around for a minute. Four other groups were relaxing on the patio. Adam and Britt, both with their helmets on but their goggles pulled up over their helmets, closed their eyes as they leaned back to feel the warm sun on their faces.

Britt wiggled slightly in her seat to get more comfortable. "It sure is nice to carve up some early morning corduroy," she said without opening her eyes.

"Yeah," Adam said, somewhat chuckling at the trite comment, "the groomers did a great job last night; though, I'm ready for some powder days. But yes, it was nice."

"Have you checked out the park yet?" Britt asked, referring to the terrain park, eventually to be set up with boxes, rails, jumps, a half pipe, and numerous other features for snowboarders and skiers, many with twin tips, to perform all sorts of tricks.

"No," Adam said, "I don't hit the park too much these days." The average age of riders at the Spruce Creek terrain park isn't much over twenty, and there are rarely skiers over the age of thirty in the park. "Actually," Adam added, "they probably only have a few features set up so far."

"It sure is fun to watch all the kids hucking over those big tabletops," Britt said, "doing their backside double cork ten-eighties or whatever."

"Oh, they're insane!" Adam said. "Job security for ski patrol." Adam and Britt sat quietly for another minute. "Such a nice view," Adam suddenly slurred.

Britt opened her eyes, looked around at the peaks to the east, and smiled as she looked over at Adam. Britt started laughing as she said, "A little kid at the shop last weekend asked me, 'What's the Continental Divide?' I started to explain it, but then I stopped myself. What would you have said?"

"It's a drainage divide," Adam quickly replied. "Any water on the east side ultimately flows to the Atlantic Ocean. Any water on the west side flows to the Pacific Ocean. Any raindrop, or any flake of snow, that lands to the east, would ultimately contribute to the rivers flowing to the Atlantic. Likewise, any rain on the west side contributes to the flow to the Pacific Ocean, that is, if it doesn't evaporate or get consumed in some other way."

"Got it."

"It's indeed an impressive, very high ridge in Colorado," Adam said as Britt was still looking off to the east at a portion of the Divide, "but it's less noticeable along the high plains, where people often travel over the Divide without noticing." Britt nodded.

An employee for the Twin Peaks Lodge restaurant was preparing a large grill, in the corner of the patio, to cook up lunch options. Adam leaned back and with his head turned to the west, he watched a southbound commercial airliner flying overhead that had a persistent contrail holding for miles.

"Well, I voted," Britt suddenly blurted out. "You and Drew inspired me."

"Really?" Adam said. "That's awesome!"

"I really didn't know what to do. I'm embarrassed to say this, but I ended up voting for that guy my dad told me to vote for."

"Well," Adam said, "you voted. I'm not saying you went with the right person or the wrong person, but it is good to think for yourself. I would encourage you to figure out the issues and your positions on your own. But that's great. I do wish everyone would vote." Adam leaned forward in his chair and exclaimed, "The turnout should be one hundred percent!"

"One hundred percent?" Britt uttered as she let out a shrill laugh.

"Well, okay, how about ninety-nine point nine percent? I understand that there are some isolated cases where people might be caught in an unfortunate, unplanned quandary and just can't make it to the polls, but full voter turnout would make me happier than about anything else that comes out of an election."

Britt leaned forward and took a couple sips of hot chocolate. "The problem is that there are so many that are disenchanted with all of it," she said. "They really don't know what to make of it all. They don't trust any of the politicians."

"That's exactly why they should vote!"

Adam and Britt sat quietly for another minute. They both had their legs extended, tapping their ski boots together on occasion. Adam then stood up and looked to the north. He was assessing the progress of a new housing development, down the valley, where several homes he designed were located.

"I'll be honest with you," Britt said, "I really don't understand it all." Britt turned her head toward Adam as he was sitting back down. Britt then dropped her head and peered up at Adam as she quietly muttered, "Adam, can you give me a lucid explanation of Social Security?"

Adam paused for a few seconds. "Well," he said, "I guess I can try." Adam was clearly skeptical that Britt would actually want to hear more, but then Britt sat up, scooted her chair a bit toward Adam, and looked right at him. "Okay," Adam said, "you know how there's a separate tax that shows up on your pay stubs for FICA?"

"Yeah! What the-"

"It stands for Federal Insurance Contributions Act. You pay in a percentage of your total pay and the Java Alley also pays a matching portion for you. A significant portion of that is for Social Security. The Social Security portion is a flat percentage, regardless of your income, but the contributions are only paid up to an annual maximum." Adam sat up some. "That maximum corresponds to the tax for a higher threshold salary, that is way more than we make. In return for your contributions, you eventually become insured to receive checks when you're older and not in a position to work, or that is, you reach retirement age." Britt was nodding. "You could also potentially receive payments if you were to become disabled and unable to work. The Social Security payout is not too significant, but it really helps many older, or disabled, Americans to maintain shelter, pay utility bills, and buy food. It's – without a doubt – one of the most expensive federal programs, but it's viewed fairly positively by most, for the most part." Adam paused for a few seconds, looking down at the snow around their chairs. He shrugged. "Actually, that's pretty much it, in an attempt to be brief."

"I guess that all sounds reasonable enough," Britt said as she leaned back in her chair, closed her eyes again, and turned toward the sun.

"If we didn't have it," Adam continued, "there would be elderly people, unable to work, that literally may not be able to buy groceries. There would be older people that couldn't afford shelter and if they didn't have family to take them in, where would they go? Actually, before Social Security, older people would often move in with their grown children. Or, they may end up in poorhouses."

"Poorhouses?"

"Yeah," Adam said, chuckling, "there really were poorhouses. Anyway, none of that happens as much anymore. Britt, would you like to have your parents move in with you in a few years?"

Britt turned toward Adam and opened her eyes real big. "Okay," she said, "so what's the debate?"

"Well," Adam said, "the Republicans don't like the disability portion of the program; that's for sure. They feel it's abused and that some folks, who get disability benefits, could be working," Adam paused and shrugged, "which may very well be the case for some isolated cases. Many conservatives would also prefer for the old-age program to be run using individual accounts, but it really doesn't work that way now. The total payout, when you're old, of course largely depends on how long you live, but if a person makes more money and pays in more, they receive more back in each monthly check. Though, the checks increase by a smaller percentage with increases to the amount paid in by a worker – that's how the payout formulas work."

"Okay," Britt said, distinctly.

Adam took a couple sips of hot chocolate. "I guess the Democrats," he continued, "see it more as an insurance program for the entire society, and they would actually like to see the program expanded. The checks are indeed fairly small, and nobody argues that it's almost impossible for any elderly person to live on the checks alone." Britt was pensive, now looking down at the patio. "Here's a big problem with the ultimate objective," Adam said, "people of course have the ability to save money themselves, to support themselves when they're older, but they just ...aren't ...doing it. It's not just lower income people that aren't saving for when they're older. Many more affluent people aren't putting money into their personal retirement savings accounts. Also, the concept of a pension has faded for most. Many baby boomers are still getting pension checks in addition to their Social Security, but that won't be the case for most of our generation."

Britt perked up and said, "I have an aunt who worked at a factory, back in Virginia, for decades. She contributed to a pension fund the entire time, and they screwed her over. She still gets checks, but the checks are for much less than she had expected all along. She's been telling stories for years, about potential cuts to the payouts and how it was all in the courts for a long time. I think she's resolved that she's going to get much less than she was promised the entire time she was working."

"That's awful," Adam said. "Well, times have changed. Very few people will be getting pension checks when we're older. There are tax advantaged options for people to now save for themselves, but they don't do it. They just …don't …do it. I really don't think it has anything to do with how much money a person makes. It simply requires a unique personality to voluntarily utilize these retirement saving options to any significant level. Our brains are wired to survive and live for today and not worry so much about tomorrow or several years from now."

"Uh," Britt droned as she looked over at Adam and put her hand to her forehead to block the sun. "I don't have any retirement savings."

"Well, you still have a lot of time, but it would be good to get something set up now."

"My boss said she would help me get something set up."

"Do it! Yeah, get her to help you, this afternoon."

"My brother," Britt quietly said, "had a bit saved from his last job, but he cashed it out when he quit." Adam was shaking his head lightly. Britt added, "He said he needed the money."

"The rules need to be reformed to assure the programs are working as intended."

"How so?"

Adam shifted in his seat. "Britt, are you sure you want to talk about this?"

"Yes," Britt exclaimed.

"Okay, first, the approach for retirement savings needs to be simplified and consolidated into one consistent approach for every worker in America, regardless of their position, to level the playing field. Saving options now vary widely depending on somebody's work situation. A consistent system could be set up where everyone is automatically enrolled, at their jobs, to have a minimum percentage of their pay directed to their own personal retirement savings. Of course, they can opt out, but they would have to sign a carefully crafted form acknowledging that they understand the impact of that decision and acknowledging that they want to forgo the very important and valuable savings vehicle for their future. Everyone could also increase the percentage of their pay that goes into their savings, but contributions would cease each year after an established individual annual limit is reached. Employees would chose to make contributions to either a tax deferred account, where they won't pay income taxes on the contributions until they take the funds out of their accounts during retirement, or to an account with tax free growth, where they'll pay income taxes up front on their contributions but not on any withdrawals from the account during retirement. If an account type is not identified, a default approach would be automatically set based on an employee's age and pay rate."

Adam paused and looked at Britt. "Okay," Britt mumbled, "I'm with you."

"Employers would route employees contributions through a government system where the contributions are paid in at the same time that the employer submits employee FICA taxes and income withholdings. Contributions would then be routed by the government to the account trustee identified for each employee in the new government system. If an employee has not set up a trustee under the system, an account would be initiated with a default trustee and that investment company would be used thereafter, unless the employee transfers it to another investment company, but it would be very easy for people to select a preferred investment company for managing their retirement savings. All the numerous investment companies would simply get set up to be part of the system and receive contributions for account holders through the system. Employees would then, on their own, work with the trustee to designate investment choices for their savings and for future contributions. Default safe investments would be used if no choices have been made by an account holder."

"Okay," Britt said, looking right at Adam.

"The annual contribution limit would be the exact same for every single American – a big change from the current blend of different retirement savings vehicles. Rules for pulling money out of accounts before reaching retirement age would be very strict – even stricter than current rules. Here's a huge advantage to the approach: employers would no longer have any role in administering retirement savings plans, other than, again, routing employees contributions as a percentage of their pay through the new government system. When people change jobs, it would have no impact at all on the administration of their retirement savings. Contributions from future employers would simply be routed to their retirement accounts in the exact same manner without any extra steps required by employees or employers. Employees would have a much lower tendency to cash out their valuable retirement savings, and employers would no longer have to cover the cost of administering retirement savings plans for workers."

"So," Britt said, "if this program was set up, I would already have some money saved for my retirement from contributions taken out of the checks from my summer jobs? I wouldn't even have really noticed that it was happening?"

"Yep," Adam said as he sat back in his chair a bit. "Well, that's it. With that, you eliminate all the existing retirement savings vehicles. Of course, all existing retirement savings would be retained for all Americans and could be rolled over into their savings with the new system."

"Anyway, that partially addresses the issue of financial security for the elderly in society, but Social Security would still be very important." Adam took another sip of hot chocolate. Britt was still looking right at him. "There's a single big issue pertaining to Social Security," Adam said. "More has been paid into Social Security by employees since the program began, versus the amount that has been paid out to beneficiaries. Actually, that surplus has been spent to cover other past government expenses, but that's all more related to government deficits and politicians running amok and not assuring revenues and spending match for other priorities – a different topic.

But more importantly, benefit payments are projected to fairly soon use up the amount built up in the trust fund based on current payout rates and contribution rates. With people living longer and more and more people claiming benefits, as those in the baby boomer generation reach retirement age, the current approach cannot be sustained. So, Social Security will not be there, in its current form, when we're older, if there is not some sort of change. Also, there's technically a separate fund for disability benefits and it's dry."

Britt sat up again and turned toward Adam. "Okay, so what's the Social Security solution?" she asked.

"Well," Adam said, slowly, "one, they could raise the tax rate." Britt quickly took a gulp of hot chocolate, as their drinks were getting cold. She then looked right back at Adam. "Two," he continued, "they could raise the annual maximum contribution so those who are making over the current threshold, pay more. Third, they could increase the retirement age that people begin getting checks. Or some mixture of the three." Adam turned toward Britt, covering his eyes to block the sun. "I think reform to level the playing field for retirement savings is maybe most important. Some people think some retirement savings plans are being used just as a tax shelter, for the well-off, and not actually helping regular middle class Americans save for when they're older." Adam started chuckling. "It's good that Drew's not here, he would throw hot chocolate in my face."

Britt busted out laughing. "Oh, I like Drew," she said. "He's sweet. He always tips me well."

"Oh, I know! He's great," Adam said. Britt turned her head toward Adam to signal she was still listening and waiting for him to continue. "There are a whole lot of details and confounding rules for Social Security that could probably be refined to find some small savings and help the program be solvent. The rules could sure be simplified. Now, older folks almost need a lawyer, or a professional advisor, to help them figure out the best way to claim their Social Security benefits, depending on their health, marital status, current interest rates, and the age of their spouse."

Adam and Britt both suddenly looked over to the right as a local gal, crazy Kelsey, as she's known throughout the valley, walked on to the patio and was immediately dancing and cackling loudly with three guys sitting on the other side. Adam and Britt looked at each other and smiled, for they both knew her and there was no need to say anything – just watch. They both looked on quietly and giggled lightly as they watched her for several seconds.

"Social Security is not actually the calamity that it's sometimes made out to be," Adam continued, still watching Kelsey. "Social Security isn't nearly as big a problem as Medicare, the government health care program for the elderly, but everyone needs to realize that something, ...something has to be done with Social Security, very soon. Also, our generation will be paying to help maintain the Social Security trust fund and assure that payouts, based on current rules, continue to be made to the baby boomers for a while, which is fine, but our generation needs more than some offhanded, glib, verbal assurance, ...but action, right now, to guarantee that the program will still be there when we're older."

Music, piped out over the lodge patio, was suddenly changed to a reggae station and the volume was increased. More and more people were sitting down on the patio, and the barbecue aroma from the grill was drowning out the sweet smell of the forest.

"So," Brit said, "did you watch the election coverage last night? It sure got interesting there for a while."

"Yeah," Adam muttered while chuckling. "I watched it for hours, late. I just love the process. Just that people get to vote and their voices are heard. It's so fascinating to watch all the results come in so fast." Adam turned toward Britt. "Just think, after all that, after months and months of fundraisers, primaries, debates, campaign commercials, after all those countless, irrelevant topics that were analyzed into dust by the analysts and pundits, it all ended so fast." Adam leaned back in his chair again. "But it's great. Democracy."

Britt turned toward Adam and blocked the sun with her hand, "I get to eavesdrop on people at the coffee shop, and you know what

I sense? People want to be able to look back and know they voted for the winner. It's as if they're selecting the most dominant boxer to be their *favorite* boxer, so they can really cheer when that boxer wins with another knockout in the first round. Or as if they're selecting their favorite professional golfer and want to select the best as their favorite, so they can gloat after their favorite golfer wins yet another major tournament." Britt sighed. "Then, they feel that they, themselves, are 'oh so tremendous' for being on the side of the winning team."

Adam scoffed. "Just hopping on the bandwagon," he said.

"Yeah, but I never overheard a single person in the coffee shop talking about potential solutions to assure that the Social Security trust fund remains solvent." Britt leaned back and closed her eyes. "They just want to ride the biggest wave," she concluded.

A breeze had picked up, but it was a day with a full, dark blue, autumn sky in the Colorado high country – about as pleasant as they come. Adam looked over at Britt. With her eyes closed, Adam, clearly smitten, looked right at her in comfort. Her cheeks were all red from the cool air and the wind blowing in her face while skiing. "Hey, so, where's Brandon?" he asked. Brandon was Britt's boyfriend, the guy with the motorcycle and the tattoos.

"Brandon's a jerk," Britt said without opening her eyes.

"Oh," Adam stammered. He then sat up and started looking around the patio. "So, uh, he's not going to come by here and break my kneecaps for skiing with you, is he?"

"No, no. It's all so stupid."

"I'm sorry," Adam muttered. Britt shook her head slightly. Adam took one last big swig of his hot chocolate. "You want anything else?"

"No, I'm fine."

Adam and Britt sat quietly for several seconds. Adam now had his head back, turned toward Britt. He had his left eye open – the one shaded from the sun – looking right at Britt. There's no way she couldn't sense he was looking at her. "Have you ever heard," he said, "of older people, who got married, had kids, and lived their entire lives together …for decades, while maybe one of them was really in love with another person the entire time. For whatever reason, it didn't work out with the person they loved, when they were younger, but they never forgot them."

Britt smiled, opened her eyes, and turned toward Adam. She froze for a couple seconds and said, "I don't know. There are two different types of love in those scenarios. Young love is great, but I want to be loved. You know, like the use of the word as a verb. People's needs are different as they get older. It's all so different as people get older." Britt sat up slowly and looked down, in the direction of Adam's ski boots. "I've had some boys who were crushed on me." Britt got nervous and started stuttering, "I mean, well, I don't know for sure, maybe not–"

"It's alright Britt," Adam said, smiling. "You're a very pretty girl, and I'm sure you've had plenty of boys crushed on you. You can say it."

"I don't think I'm special or anything. It's all so stupid. My calves are fat."

"Your calves are fat?" Adam was laughing out loud. "Stop it. What were you going to say."

"Well, that's what I want. I want to be loved. For some boy to be in love with you is something completely different. Where will they be when they finally notice my calves are fat." Adam rolled his eyes but didn't comment further. Britt continued, "I know there's this perception among young people that having a life partner is no fun and that eventually choosing that kind of union is just giving in to convention and following the masses, filing in with the lemmings at the cliff or whatever, but I eventually want that. I want what's on the other side of that cliff: nirvana."

Adam chuckled. "I don't know about nirvana," he said.

Britt smiled and leaned back in her chair again. She looked over at a couple little boys scuffling in the snow, off the edge of the patio. Britt laughed, hit Adam on the leg, and pointed at the boys. The bigger boy had the smaller boy in a headlock and was down on the ground, pushing the smaller kid's head into the snow. The bigger boy was laughing as the smaller boy kept blindly wailing on the bigger boy. A man came over, who was obviously their father. He said, "Cut it out. Let's go." Britt reach over and put her hand on Adam's left knee as she continued to watch the boys scuffling.

The boys got up and just as the bigger boy was about to step into his ski bindings, the smaller boy pushed him over. The smaller boy then, very sprightly, shifted over, popped both his boots into his bindings, and pushed away from the bigger boy. The bigger boy then ran over and pushed the smaller boy over. The father stood there, saying nothing the entire time, as he now had his boots in his bindings. He was looking off in the direction of one of the open ski runs and waiting for the situation to resolve itself. The bigger boy then got his skis on as the smaller boy stood back up, and they finally scooted away.

Adam had his head turned toward the boys, but he hadn't been paying attention. He was focused on Britt's hand on his knee.

Adam suddenly leaned forward. "Britt, I got to go," he said.

"Oh," she mumbled, leaning forward. "Okay," she said, confused.

"I gotta, ...I have get back to work."

"Okay," she said, scrambling to grab her gloves.

Adam stood up and started putting on his gloves. "Do you want to ski down?" he asked.

"Actually, no, you go. I can barely keep up with you anyway. I'll ease on down. I'm going to stop by the coffee shop and see if my boss is there to help me set up that retirement account."

"Okay. Hey, this was great."

"Yeah, I assume I'll see you at the coffee shop later this week."

"That's very likely," Adam said, whimsically.

"Okay," Britt said with her signature, cherubic smile. She gave a slight wave and said, "See you, Adam."

Adam plodded off the patio in his ski boots, threw his hot chocolate cup in a trash can, and grabbed his skis off the ski rack. He popped into his bindings and was quickly blazing down the trail past everyone, digging his edges into the man-made snow, and carving hard around every turn. Adam was racing down the slope very rapidly, by anyone's standards. There weren't as many people on the run, versus what he and Drew contended with on Halloween, but then Adam came up on the third roller, right before the steepest section of the run, and as soon as he could see over the rise, all he saw was people everywhere, maybe thirty people scattered all over the run. A few skiers had fallen on the more difficult, steeper section of the slope, and a few beginners were very gingerly making their way back and forth across the full width of the slope. Adam quickly dug in his edges at the lip and turned to the right. He then tried to turn back to the left but was airborne. His arms were suddenly wailing to try to maintain some balance in the air while still avoiding a lady with a small child. He somehow managed to avoid hitting anyone, but he landed very awkwardly, his left knee buckling as he went off the right side of the strip of man-made snow and eventually came to a stop in the dirt, just at the edge of the trees.

After overcoming the initial shock from his wipeout, Adam tried to quickly get up but he slipped back on his rear. His left ski had popped off. As he continued to try to get up, a couple skied up beside him. "Hey buddy, you alright?" the man asked, with a southern accent. "I should yell at you," the man continued, "but I gather you probably learned your lesson. So, where's the fire, bud?"

Adam grunted and said, "I have to talk to Hannah."

"Well, I don't think Hannah, whoever she is, would want you to kill any kids today. You just about took that little girl's head off."

Adam finally conceded defeat and lay back on the dirt. He reached down and grabbed his left knee. He took off his gloves and slapped them down in the dirt. He looked up at the couple. "I'll be alright," he said. "I just need a minute. Thanks for stopping. I'm sorry; you're right. I'll slow down." They shook their heads and eased away.

It took Adam several minutes, but he finally managed to get up and step back onto the ski run. Another beneficent passer-by had thrown his ski back up to him. He locked back down into his ski but didn't move for several minutes. He had really hurt his left knee and could only hope that it wasn't too serious. It was now going to take him much longer to get down. There was no way he was going to ride down in a ski patrol sled – a taxi ride, as it's called by patrollers, so he began a very slow progression down the hill, stopping after every couple turns to assess the condition of his knee. It took him nearly an hour to ease down the slope. He then went straight to the resort clinic. He wouldn't be seeing Hannah that afternoon.

## *Chapter 14 - Not Gonna Quit*

Adam limped into Hannah's workplace around 11:45 a.m. on Thursday. She was sitting at the reception desk, to the left of the front door, and was obviously relieved to have a break from the monotony of the slow November day at the office. Cody had been lying at Hannah's feet, behind the desk. Even though Cody couldn't see Adam, Cody somehow was aware that it was Adam and he slowly got up and lumbered over, for he had been asleep when Adam arrived.

"Do you always bring him to work?" Adam asked.

Hannah peered down the office hallway and then shook her head vigorously. Only one other agent was in the office at that time. Hannah whispered, "Only when it's quiet like this." Adam reached down to pet Cody for a couple seconds and then stood up and began looking around the lobby. Adam, out of the office for lunch, was wearing a plaid, button down shirt tucked into his dark brown, twill pants and leather lace up shoes. He hadn't actually been by Hannah's office in months. He took a few steps around the room and stopped to review several real estate listings posted on a bulletin board, hung on the wall opposite the receptionist desk. Hannah sat quietly and watched Adam as he became focused for a moment on a posting for one of the homes he designed. Cody suddenly plopped down in the middle of the lobby, next to Adam's feet.

"What are you doing here?" Hannah asked, curiously. Adam didn't respond as he kept reviewing the real estate listings. Hannah then sighed, stood up, and walked over to the sofa aligned along the front wall to the right of the door. She had some mascara on and was dressed business casual with navy slacks, a white, button-down, ruffled blouse, and a lightweight, hunter green cardigan.

Hannah noticed Adam's limp as he took a couple steps away from the bulletin board. "Adam, stop it," she yelled. "You know I hate it when you joke like that."

"I'll be alright, …I think. I biffed blazing down the mountain yesterday." Adam shrugged and waved his hand as he looked around the lobby some more. "I'm fine. I went by the clinic and they did a quick check and said everything appears to be stable. I think it's just a sprain."

"What happened?" Hannah asked slowly.

"At the end, I was cruising down to …uh, get back to work, and I just lost it there on that one steeper section after the third roller." Hannah turned away from Adam and looked out the window. Her eyes glazed over as she slightly shook her head. She then slumped into the sofa and rolled her eyes.

"So, how was your date?" Hannah asked, exasperated.

Adam groaned, looked down at the floor, and froze for a couple seconds. "It wasn't a date," he said firmly. He plopped down in a chair under the real estate listings. After a couple seconds, he sighed and started shaking his head. "How did you hear about that anyway?"

"It's a small community, Adam."

"You should talk to her. She's funny, insightful."

They sat quietly. Hannah had shifted on the sofa and was looking out the window. Adam started nervously fidgeting in his seat as he looked at Cody. "Hannah, it was nothing," he said. "We went skiing." Hannah just shook her head lightly as she continued to gaze out the window. "Hannah," Adam quietly started before he heard the agent in the office walking down the hall, talking loudly as he rounded the corner.

"Hannah, can you prepare another packet on the Pino Pista lots for the Johnsons," the agent said, entering the room. Hannah quickly jumped up. "Oh, hi Adam," the agent said. "Hey, did you see we got the listing for your place up on Pika Court?"

"Yeah, I saw that. I wish it was my place," Adam said, chuckling.

The agent smiled and turned back toward Hannah, who was seated at the receptionist desk. "They'll be by after 3:00," he said, "so have the packet ready." Hannah nodded. Cody had been very good and was still lying, motionless, in the middle of the lobby floor. Hannah started hammering on her keyboard as Adam was now leaning forward, lightly feeling his left knee.

"So, what did you two talk about?" Hannah asked, still focused on her computer monitor.

"The election, Social Security."

"Oh gosh, you even tortured Britt over this obsession of yours?"

"She started it."

Hannah stopped typing and looked over at Adam. "Hey, so, I was thinking about something the other night. Drew was yammering all about cutting government spending, but didn't he work on several federal contracts to clear dead pine beetle trees in the valley?"

"Yep, but he's not worried about that kind of spending. He just wants to end the handouts and welfare spending."

"Well, okay, anyway, what was he doing again?"

The lodgepole pine forest in the Spruce Creek valley became infested with pine beetles years ago, and the problem has been one of the biggest issues for government officials in the valley for years. The infestation process starts when the small female beetles initiate attacks on individual trees and then attract males to each host tree. The beetles tunnel under the bark, lay eggs, and also introduce a fungus that protects the beetles and prevents the transport of water and nutrients in the trees. When the eggs hatch, the larvae winter in the trees, feeding on the inner bark, and then transform into pupae before emerging from the trees in the summer as adults, seeking new host trees. In recent years, the epidemic devastated the lodgepole pine forest throughout the Spruce Creek valley and much of the Colorado high country. The forest, which had reached the end of its life cycle, was particularly susceptible due to several factors including recent mild winters, drought conditions, and the overcrowding of trees in the forest.

While individual trees can be effectively protected with preventive spray, if applied before infestation, there is no feasible way to protect an entire forest. Once trees become infested, the introduced fungus causes trees to have a blue-stained appearance. The needles then become rust colored, indicating that a tree is dying or dead, and within a few years, all the needles fall off. Such mass destruction of the forest can have a devastating impact on water resources, which is significant with so many major river systems having headwaters in the Colorado mountains. The added wildfire danger is particularly troublesome for officials. As a result of the wildfire threat, some stands of dead trees are cleared around populated areas or other areas of particular importance to natural resources.

"Yeah," Adam replied, "Drew's crew cleared several stands of dead trees and worked with another contractor who transported the wood to a sawmill in Wyoming where it was converted to wood stove pellets." Hannah nodded and resumed hammering away at her keyboard. Adam slowly stood up, grimacing as he favored his left leg. "When's your lunch break?" he asked.

Looking up at a clock on the back wall, Hannah said, "I should get this packet ready first and then I could go somewhere."

"Alright, it's a nice day. I'm going to get us a couple steamer hoagies from that new Knoxville Subs place and we'll picnic at the Bugling Elk turnout. Is that cool?"

Hannah paused, tilted her head slightly, and then said, "I guess so." Hannah furrowed her brow as she watched Adam limp out the door without saying anything else.

Adam returned about twenty-five minutes later. Hannah already had her coat on and was ready to go. With the temperature around fifty degrees, Adam may have been more appropriately dressed for this occasion with his orange, fleece pullover. Hannah walked out with Cody and they both got in Adam's German front wheel drive sedan. As they rode down the highway to the picnic spot, Hannah kept adjusting the music selections, never completely satisfied. Cody, not sensing any reason to be overly excited about the journey, immediately lay down in the back seat.

Adam and Hannah didn't talk during the eight minute drive down the highway to the large, gravel turnout with four picnic tables, all overlooking a large, treeless area in the valley floor. The field, about fifty feet below the turnout, is defined by the highway on the east side of the valley, Spruce Creek about a half mile to the west, and a dense, mature aspen grove further down the valley to the north. The expansive meadow, a couple miles above Lake Labash, is a conservation area owned by the state parks and wildlife department and is a common location for elk herds to gather, especially during the fall. When the elk are in rut and bulls are bugling, throngs of gapers park in the turnout, sit in lawn chairs for hours, and watch the bulls as they tend to and defend their harems. The field was still covered by a thin layer of snow from the last storm and while no elk or other animals were currently visible, the field was crisscrossed with countless tracks from different animals that had moved about the meadow over the past few days.

Adam pulled into the turnout and eased to the back northwest corner. They quietly got out of the car and sat at the closest table, positioned off the gravel in a grassy area and partially shielded from the highway traffic by a thin stand of aspen. They were both facing the meadow with Adam seated to Hannah's left, and due to the highway and the wide open space, they kept Cody on his leash, which he reluctantly accepted. Noise from the highway would normally be a horrendous nuisance but there were few passing vehicles on that quiet afternoon. There was also little wind, which was rare for that spot in the valley. They began eating their steamed sandwiches. Hannah lifted the top bun on her sandwich and, without comment, was scrutinizing the contents.

"Uh, Hannah?" Adam mumbled, his voice trembling.

"Uh, Adam?"

"Look, I know," he said nervously as Hannah peered over, somewhat aware of Adam's anxiety, but she quickly refocused her attention on the makeup of her lunch. "I know I kept you at a distance and all that. I know it's my fault." Hannah froze, her mouth full of the first bite of her sandwich. She slumped down with a sorrowful look on her face and looked right at Adam. "It will be different," he went on. "You can't leave."

"Adam, I gotta do something different."

Adam turned and looked out over the field for a few seconds. He then sighed and looked down at Cody who was completely focused on Adam's sandwich, held loosely in his hand.

Hannah, very suddenly, sat up. "Hey, look," she quickly said, pointing off at a large cottonwood, about two hundred feet away to the northwest, in the middle of the meadow. There were two mature bald eagles resting in the leafless tree. Adam gave an unenthusiastic nod. "Would Josh have a lens powerful enough to take a picture of them from here?" Hannah asked. Adam wasn't looking anymore.

"Hannah, if there's anything I've figured out over the past couple weeks, it's that people have to relax, enjoy life, enjoy the passage of time. It's just not worth it to go through life with constant frustration and anger and end up missing out on some very important, pleasant aspects of our short time here."

Hannah slouched back down. "I could have told you that two weeks ago," she said. Hannah took another bite of her sandwich and looked back at the eagles. Cody was way too focused on the sandwiches to pick up on any uneasiness between Adam and Hannah.

"It is all so important. Of course, it's good and appropriate to discuss it, think about it," Adam said, "but there are other more important things." Hannah nodded as she took another bite of her sandwich, still looking at the eagles resting so peacefully on this pleasant overcast day. "Hannah, you really would, wouldn't you? You really would be good to me, always." Hannah froze. She stopped chewing and didn't move her head, which was pointed toward the eagles, as she slowly turned her eyes on Adam. Adam was looking down at his sandwich that was resting loosely in his hand on his lap. Cody could have reached it, but he seemed to sense that he would still have better luck with Hannah.

"Eat your hoagie," Hannah then blurted out with her mouth full. Adam was looking out over the field again. Hannah reached over and gave Adam a bite of her sandwich and then redirected her focus back on the eagles.

Adam then sat up, slowly wrapped up his sandwich, and set it on the table. He gingerly stood up, favoring his left knee. Hannah was unaffected by his movement and continued eating. Adam hobbled a couple steps over to Hannah's right. He stood right in front of her for a couple seconds and then slowly began to kneel down, wincing slightly from the pain in his knee. Hannah, with a mouth full of food, completely froze again and stared at Adam with her eyes real big.

"Adam! What are you doing?" Adam had finally gotten into position and looked up at her. Hannah quickly turned her head and spit her food out on the parking lot. "Adam, this isn't funny." Hannah then busted out laughing: laughing at Adam, laughing at herself, and laughing at Cody as he quickly picked at pieces of her sandwich on the ground. Adam was not laughing, his entire body trembling.

"Hannah," he said, almost inaudible.

"Adam, I'm eating a hoagie! We're sitting on the side of a highway!"

Adam wasn't laughing. He was still shaking, looking right into Hannah's green eyes. He was quivering so much he couldn't say anything more. Hannah squinted her eyes and stared right into Adam's eyes as if she was trying to identify an ulterior motive behind his actions. Without looking away from Adam, she reached over and set her sandwich down on the table. Cody quickly moved forward and put his nose right up to Hannah's sandwich. She instinctively pushed Cody firmly on the head, and Cody stepped back and sat down. Adam was still on one knee, shivering and looking right into

Hannah's eyes. Hannah looked down at Adam's hand and noticed he had a toy ring. She didn't laugh or smile, she just looked right back into his eyes. Adam was clearly prepared for any awkwardness, prepared for anything, and while very nervous, he was clearly prepared to hold firm. They kept staring at each other as if they were waiting for the other to blink, like poker players looking for some sort of tell to signify the other was bluffing. Suddenly, there was an incredible stillness – no wind, no traffic, and no awkwardness. Adam had stopped trembling. Hannah had relaxed. They were looking easily into each other's eyes.

"Yes," Hannah said. It wasn't an excited confirmation. There was no sense of relief or long anticipated closure. It was a definitive, unquestioning affirmative. Finally, Hannah cracked and had a huge smile on her face. She lunged toward Adam and they both fell back into the wet grass.

"Oh, my knee," Adam yelled.

"Sorry, sorry, sorry," Hannah said as she started petting Adam's head, as if that would help with the pain in his knee.

"Easy, easy" he said as he finally started giggling. They were now lying in the grass. Hannah kissed Adam as Cody came over and nuzzled them for a few seconds and got in a few licks on their faces before they could push him away. Cody then turned and redirected his attention back to the sandwiches on the table.

Hannah and Adam lay in the grass quietly. They didn't say a word as they rested there, holding each other. They didn't hear the trucks passing on the highway, couldn't feel the breeze that had picked up, and were unmindful of the wet grass below them.

After a couple minutes, Adam said, "Okay, help me up." They got up and sat back down at the table. "Sorry, I guess that wasn't the most romantic proposal."

Hannah was leaning toward Adam with her face about two inches away from his face. She then started talking but was talking right into his mouth, like three-year old kids sometimes do. "Actually, no, this is about right," she whispered with a whimsical nod. "A proposal over hoagies with a toy ring – I shouldn't be surprised by that. Where did you get this ring?"

"Toy machine at Knoxville Subs," Adam said with a chuckle. "It took me four quarters to get the one I wanted." Hannah laughed as she was putting the ring on her finger. "Oh, come on," Adam blurted out, "we'll get you a real ring. You're the one that's going to be wearing it. There's no way I would try to buy one without your help."

Hannah nodded in full agreement as she looked at the toy ring on her finger. She then looked back at Adam. Still positioned right in front of his face and talking into his mouth, she softly said, "Well, after we get it, I'll be wearing it *forever*." Hannah leaned over and hugged Adam again as he hugged her back. They didn't say anything for another minute. They just held each other. Cody eventually let out a little whimper, and they finally got up, grabbed their sandwiches, and Hannah helped Adam limp back to the car, even though he wasn't so bad off that he needed help.

As they drove back to Hannah's office. Hannah was holding up her left hand, cherishing the toy ring on her finger. Adam was leaning over on his armrest, smiling, admiring the ring with her.

"So, was that proposal better than Lane's proposal?" Adam asked. Hannah sighed, dropped her hands, and rolled her eyes with no response. "Where did he propose?"

"Venice."

Adam scoffed. "Well, I couldn't compete with that."

Hannah start laughing lightly. "Actually, it was bad. It was so hot – sweltering. I was being bit by three or four mosquitoes at that very moment. The water in those canals was putrid that evening. It smelled so bad. We were right outside of Piazza San Marco in the middle of the main shopping district. It felt like he was proposing to me in a mall. There were no Italians there. It was nothing but American tourists all around, watching it happen. I was so uncomfortable." Adam, no doubt, reveled over the discredit given to her previous experience. Hannah raised her hand again, admiring her toy ring. "I'm going to keep it forever," she quietly mumbled to herself. She then turned toward Adam and blurted out, "Did you tell Josh or Drew, yet?"

"You only said, 'yes,' a few minutes ago."

Hannah gave an acknowledging nod. "Oh," she said slowly, "have you talked to them since the election?"

"Uh, no." Adam raised his eyebrows and gritted his teeth as he looked over at Hannah.

"Well, *somebody's* going to be very disappointed in you."

Adam pulled up to Hannah's office. He got out, walked around the car, and hugged Hannah again, holding her for several seconds. "Well, I better get back to work," he finally said.

As Adam drove away, Hannah tied Cody up outside. She entered the office, and the agent was at the reception desk writing up some instructions for another task. "How was your lunch?" he asked, with an indifferent tone as he continued writing.

Hannah shrugged. "Ah, I got engaged," she said, coyly. The agent summarily stopped writing, looked at Hannah, and smiled. Hannah's attempt to be cool only lasted for a few seconds before she started giggling uncontrollably. She then showed off her toy ring.

The agent then asked, "So does this mean you're not quitting?"

## *Chapter 15 - Answer to the Grand Plan*

Drew walked into the North Fork Tavern on Saturday afternoon, looked around, and located Adam and Josh sitting near the foosball table and in front of the largest television. Drew walked right over with a big grin on his face. He leaned down right in front of Adam and smacked him hard on the chest as Adam giggled. Adam and Josh, sitting on opposite sides of the table, were facing the television. Drew sat down in front of them, with his back to the wall. Adam and Josh were laughing and in the middle of conversation.

"So, did you have your mouth full of food when you proposed?" Josh asked. His question was barely discernible since he was laughing so hard.

"No," Adam mumbled while giggling. "Hannah did." Josh and Drew busted out laughing even louder. "She spit out a whole bite of her sandwich as I was asking her," Adam added.

"Over hoagies? Really?" Drew said. Drew was shaking his head and rolling his eyes. "She's probably thinking she should have married Lane after all. Well, that will be the most memorable hoagie she's ever had. For your wedding gift, I'm going to get you one of those big, industrial sandwich steamers so you can have hoagies every day for the rest of your lives." The server stopped by and set a glass mug on the table for Drew. "Did you set a date yet?" Drew asked.

"No," Adam said as he relaxed and leaned back in his chair, slowly extending his legs while favoring his injured knee. "I assume it will be next summer. We got plane tickets to go and talk to her parents the weekend after Thanksgiving – she has to work at the real estate office over the holiday. She's going to stay on there, for a little while at least."

"That discussion with her parents could be rather interesting," Josh said, raising his eyebrows.

Hannah had been at the bar and began walking over to their table. She walked up behind Adam very slowly, smiling. She leaned down behind him and gave him a big, gentle hug.

"Hannah," Drew said, "you better show up."

Hannah ignored Drew and kept hugging Adam with a big smile on her face.

Josh slapped his knee. "I knew it!" he yelled loudly, startling a couple seated at the next table. Hannah kissed Adam on the cheek.

Hannah then looked at Josh for a couple seconds with her expression immediately shifting to a more sorrowful look. "Sorry about you and Emily," she muttered.

Josh did break up with Emily, and he seemed perfectly fine with it. Adam looked up at Hannah, searching for some more commentary from her on the situation, but she had nothing to add. Being a friend to Emily, she had witnessed and heard enough that she was perfectly in tune with the status of their relationship but she had never discussed it with Adam. Her expression did indicate sincere empathy for Josh. Hannah then stood up and walked away, patting Josh on the shoulder as she left. She strolled over to another table, close to the front door, where Jess was sitting with a couple friends. Hannah, Jess, and Jess's friends immediately started giggling as they looked at the toy ring on Hannah's finger. Adam and Drew watched and rolled their eyes.

"So, when are you going to do something about that ring?" Drew asked.

"We're going down to Denver on Friday to start looking."

Adam, Josh, and Drew sat quietly for several minutes watching football. Adam and Josh were monitoring the Ohio State-

Maryland game on the largest television, and Drew was checking out a couple other games on the televisions hung on the opposite wall. The tavern was not as crowded as it had been for the recent Broncos games. Some of the patrons were skiers from the Front Range, still decked out in their ski gear and enjoying a little après-ski following their early season Saturday on the mountain.

Drew suddenly looked over at Adam. "So," he said, "did you get that grand plan of yours all figured out?"

Adam smiled and then froze for a couple seconds. "Yep," he said. He sat up, expressing confidence and resolve. He whimsically looked around with a big smile, but after a couple seconds, he chuckled, slouched back down in his chair, and started shaking his head.

"No, come on," Josh said, "you're the one that insisted on embarking on this journey. Now let's hear it."

Adam smiled smugly, focusing on the football game. He said nothing as Drew and Josh stared right at him.

"We're waiting," Drew said slowly.

"With bated breath," Josh whispered with a smile.

"Okay, here's what we need in one fell swoop," Adam said. "First, it all has to be done together to assure the give-and-take from the deal balances as much as possible and assure bi-partisan support." He shifted his chair up and moved his legs under the table. "First, it must be recognized, before it can be put together, that it's now time for an end to the animosity and enmity and time for everyone to work together to get us out of this morass of sheer gridlock." Josh and Drew immediately started rolling their eyes. "So much has come together over the past seventy years, hundred years, whatever, and everyone has to realize that it's time for a grand plan to reform the system to better suit the needs of the rest of the twenty-first century. Our generation will soon be the biggest component of the economy and spending more money than the baby boomers and there needs to be an understanding that the current system is a product of the ethos of the baby boomer generation, but the system now needs to be updated accordingly for the new economy that we're going to be such a big part of. There needs to be an understanding that things are going to be so different from what previous generations experienced. That acknowledgement of a clear need for profound changes must not only come from all the elected politicians but also from all the lobbyists and advocacy groups ...and from all the voters – the whole gestalt. It must be recognized that it's time for all politicians to avail themselves the opportunity to make history and for everyone to come together and support the effort and to understand and agree to the bit of give-and-take that will be required from every American and appreciate that the net result, that will culminate from the effort, will be a much improved, reformed, laudable system that everyone can appreciate and look at with pride, knowing that they were part of the solution, even if it was by simply maintaining support for the effort."

"Oh, anyone could say all that," Drew yelled, contemptuously. "What's the plan?!"

"There are many components to a comprehensive plan," Adam said. "The social safety net would be reformed to continue to provide the key protections to the overall economy, to maintain that important insurance to everyone in society, and to help children from disadvantaged circumstances to become better educated in safe, healthy communities with adequate shelter and proper sustenance and under a system with key changes implemented to assure that those that benefit are prepared to participate in the new Smart Age economy. Reforms to the social safety net would be implemented to maintain that same basic level of insurance and assure important existing programs remain solvent for the twenty-first century but under a new design where the programs, on their own, would gradually result in less reliance on the social safety net in the future. The programs would be designed to specifically reduce the cycle of dependency, that is handed down to subsequent generations of people from the same communities, by focusing more on better education for all Americans." Drew was now leaning down, with his elbows on the table, resting his forehead in his hands.

"Massive reform to the Internal Revenue code would be included in the plan," Adam continued. "A revenue neutral, dramatic simplification to the tax code would be implemented to eliminate so many of the tax breaks and loopholes, that have complicated the tax code to no end, while lowering the corporate tax rate and all marginal tax rates for individuals and affected businesses."

"Revenue neutral," Drew blurted out.

"Look, after it's all done, there would be plenty of opportunity for both sides to fight for their base, to either cut taxes or to increase revenues for new investments in society. But to get the grand plan done, to get it all done, it has to be revenue neutral, overall. Listen, I'm talking about cutting the Internal Revenue Code down from thousands and thousands of pages to maybe a couple hundred pages." Drew started laughing uncontrollably. "While a progressive tax system would be maintained, all marginal tax rates for individuals and businesses would be reduced as a result of the elimination of all the tax breaks and loopholes that were added over decades to pander to special interests. After it's done, it would then be much easier to have follow-up debate on subsequent improvements and changes to the tax system."

Josh scoffed and rolled his eyes. "You know," he said, "it would all gradually become so convoluted again as countless amendments and adjustments are implemented thereafter."

"That's fine," Adam said. "Do you want me to finish?" Adam and Drew looked at each other with incredulous smiles. "The new tax code," Adam continued, "would allow individuals, businesses, and corporations to complete tax filings using a very simple worksheet. Heck, maybe it would only be one page!" Adam looked over at the game for a moment as an Ohio State running back had forty-yard run.

"The American education system," Adam went on, "would include a mandatory one semester course on personal finance for every high school senior and key changes to better introduce students to STEM subject matter. Needed changes to Social Security would be implemented to dramatically simplify the overall program while assuring the same basic level of benefits for older Americans and the disabled and ensuring the program, that an overwhelming majority supports, would be in place for generations. This would be done with a combination of changes: an increase to the maximum threshold for which the FICA taxes are applied while maintaining the same tax rate, a single retirement age of sixty-eight would be designated for when old age benefits can be received, and massive reform and simplification to the rules would be implemented to not eliminate but significantly simplify rules for how spousal and survivors benefits are received. Those changes would be gradually phased in but would be fully applied before our generation would receive old age benefits." Adam noticed Drew's face turning red.

The server came by the table. "You ready to order food yet?" she asked.

"Not yet," Adam said, "thanks, in a few minutes please."

Josh was looking at Drew with his hands up. "I'm famished," he said, turning toward Adam.

"Rules for tax advantaged retirement saving accounts," Adam went on, "would be refined to level the playing field for all Americans by creating a single system for every American. Every worker would be automatically enrolled, through their jobs, to have a small minimum percentage, say four percent, of their pay taken from their checks with the opportunity to increase the percentage, with contributions cut off when an annual maximum is reached. The contributions would be routed by the employer through a government system to an identified private trustee that manages the employee's retirement account. As a result of the system, savings would be seamlessly portable when employees change jobs."

Drew and Josh were both laughing and gibing Adam, but Adam was not distracted. "The budget process," Adam continued, "would be reformed and updated to reduce the impact of politics and campaign contributions on the appropriations process and see that funds are used much more efficiently while ensuring society and all the government lands and facilities receive even better attention. The process would allow for important research and investments to be initiated to assure all the basic missions of the government agencies and departments can continue to be achieved even more efficiently in the future. The budget would include new needed development of energy resources, including expansion of the use of renewables, and investments in the country's infrastructure – schools, roads, bridges, ports, dams, airports, waterways, railways, landfills, treatment plants, and distribution systems. Changes would also include a new means for individual agencies and departments to request for a portion of unused fiscal year funds, for any specific budget line item, to be pushed into a subsequent fiscal year when needed due to unforeseen scheduling issues. In return for seizing such opportunities, a portion of the savings would be used for small bonuses for the federal workforce and a portion would be used to slightly cut overall government spending with no direct penalty to the funding for the associated line item for future years. This process would be configured to assure that all projects would still be completed and all core missions would be achieved." Adam and Josh were both looking at each other, furrowing their brows.

"Federal regulations for businesses, including the banking sector and energy development companies, would be updated for the twenty-first century to protect the economy and also protect the environment and the planet while encouraging economic growth, entrepreneurship, and innovation."

"Wow, you made that sound so easy," Josh said, laughing. Drew was mocking Adam and repeating his last comment in a whiny, high pitched voice.

"Health care coverage by the government," Adam said as he looked at Josh to avoid being distracted by Drew, "would be set up to provide care, under catastrophic circumstances, for every American. Coverage for basic preventive care and cosmetic treatments along with all costs up to an established maximum out-of-pocket cost would be covered by individuals with supplemental insurance policies, acquired through a massive private market, or with funds individuals accrue to personal Health Savings Accounts. Contributions to Health Savings Accounts would be managed the same way that retirement accounts would be managed under the full plan. The new health care system would be completely portable when citizens change jobs or move to different states, and under the system, other government programs, such the Veterans Health Administration and Military Health System, would be retained to provide care for qualified participants before the catastrophic program would cover costs. Medicaid and the Children's Health Insurance Programs would be retained but could be significantly reformed through coordination with the states and could be scaled down with the catastrophic program in place. While Medicare, in its current form, would be retained for older generations, the new approach would eventually be phased in to cover all Americans and replace Medicare for current younger generations when they're older to ultimately deal with the unsustainable projected future cost of Medicare in its current form. With the burden of providing health insurance removed from so many employers, small businesses would prosper and corporations would be more competitive in the global marketplace, and while the new program would have a dramatic impact on reducing bankruptcies, keeping unfortunate individuals off the streets, and assuring families and households all over the country are secure, entrepreneurship would flourish. Administrative costs would plummet, a central repository for health care records would be created, and overall health care costs would decrease as adults take more responsibility for basic preventive care."

Adam, still completely ignoring Josh's and Drew's japes, took a deep breath as he looked down at the table. In a more hushed tone, he said, "The overall result of the grand plan would be a system that helps to stem the amount of unmitigated hate and anger over public policy and instill confidence, in every American, that a system is in place that will work better while maintaining the same current protections and preserving all the important investments in society. Conflicts between employers and unions would be simplified, resulting in even better working conditions and rights for workers while yielding more economic prosperity. The entire plan in operation would be sustainable and function efficiently, when left to its own devices."

"Sure," Drew said with a mocking nod. "So, how does this get done?" Drew asked.

"Well," Adam said, "it's not about one individual developing the final details of such a grand plan. Construction of the single bill in Congress would require listening to every member of the House and Senate and hearing the concerns of every lobbyist, every advocacy group, and every voter that can so easily steer representatives and senators. It requires listening to all the concerns to assure the perfect compromise is reached. It absolutely must be bi-partisan." Adam slowly leaned back in his chair. "There needs to be recognition," he said, "by politicians that the current approach of assuring gridlock and stalling everything until their party finally has a super majority and control of both the legislative and executive branches of government is not the way to solve major problems affecting every American." Adam looked right at Josh. "I mean, what really are the chances of such a super majority anyway?" He then looked at Drew. "And if it happened, there would be so much discord and infighting within the ruling party. Even if it happened, no standing, long-term solutions would ever result from such a case. It requires a majority of members from both parties to agree, to themselves, to put an end to the friction we've experienced for so long. Sure, there will be a few intractable senators and representatives that will make it their raison d'etre to sabotage such progress, so it will require some moxie from all those willing to put the needs of the country and all citizens closer to the heart and make a positive legacy of their time in Congress and their time on this planet to fight those forces, ...but it can be done! It also requires voting Americans to acknowledge that they are going to be the part of something big, take pride in the progress, and understand the give-and-take involved with the final product that is being sold. Then, it can get done."

Josh and Drew had continued to chuckle and mock Adam as he talked. "So," Josh said, "who did you vote for? Who did you decide would get this done?"

Adam pursed his lips and raised his eyebrows. He looked at Josh with a slight smile, and then he looked at Drew with the same coy smile. "That's personal," he muttered.

"Oh, come on!" Josh yelled.

Adam leaned his head to the side and peered over at Drew, "I'm afraid you would be disappointed."

"Are you kidding me?" Drew yelled.

"Yeah!" Josh yelled very loudly, as he started laughing and shaking his fist. Adam looked over at Josh and shrugged slightly. "I really think she could get it done."

Before Adam could finished his comment, he felt an incredible thumping blow right to his cheek and was sent reeling, immediately falling back in his chair, nearly bonking his head on the floor. His feet swung up and kicked the table and knocked over one of the beverages. Drew had flat-out cold cocked Adam right in the cheek! Josh was laughing even louder, with his laughter almost sounding fake. Josh was vigorously rocking back and forth in his chair, continuing his fake sounding laugh, absolutely giddy as he just looked over at Adam on the floor. Drew then quickly stood up and walked away as Adam slowly rolled to his side, with his right hand on his face and his left hand on his knee. He was still processing what happened. He lay there on his side as Hannah had rushed over to grab him, for she had been watching Adam out of the corner of her eye during the entire discussion and saw him get clocked.

"What the hell, Drew?!" Hannah yelled. The entire tavern had gotten quiet as everyone was looking over at Adam on the floor; although, nobody else actually saw him get punched. Cody had been sitting, untethered, outside the tavern and saw Adam and Hannah on the floor. He ran inside as some other patrons were walking out the door and quickly scurried over to nuzzle Adam on the floor.

The North Fork owner, Jake, walked over and yelled, "Adam would you get up off the floor? Hannah, get your dog out of here!" Hannah got up quickly, grabbed Cody by the collar, and pulled him back outside.

Josh was still rocking back and forth, and his raucous laughter sounded even louder as the rest of the patrons had gotten quiet. Josh finally stood up and gave Adam a hand up. He helped Adam sit back down in his chair as Adam still had one hand on his cheek and another hand on his knee. Hannah walked back in, dashed back over to Adam, and then stood right beside him with her hands on her hips. She was looking at his eye, that was already a little swollen. "Drew!" Hannah yelled very loudly, "I'm going to call the sheriff." Adam reached over and grabbed Hannah's pants and pulled her down into Drew's chair. Hannah leaned back in the chair, crossed her arms, and just stared at Adam as he covered his eye.

The server stopped by with a small ice pack that Drew had requested. She dropped it on the table and scoffed. "Boys," she mumbled as she walked away.

"Oh, Hannah," Josh said, "your betrothed, here, he'll be just fine. Drew has training in hand-to-hand combat. He knew what he was doing."

"You mean there's an okay way to punch somebody in the face?!"

"He's fine," Josh exclaimed. Josh was still having trouble talking as he couldn't stop chuckling. Josh looked at Adam and asked, "Adam, who's the President of the United States?" Adam tilted his head up and gave Josh a stern stare with his one good eye. Josh looked down at the floor and muttered to himself, "Well, now, that's interesting. We've gone from asking Adam who should be President of the United States to asking Adam who is the President of the United States."

Jess walked up to the table and looked at the icepack Adam was holding to his eye. "What the heck happened?!" she asked.

Hannah threw her arms up and said, "Drew just up and decked him."

"For going on that date with Britt?"

Josh started laughing loudly again. Hannah got up and grunted. She grabbed Jess by the arm, pulled her – almost causing her to stumble – and said, "Come walk Cody with me."

Adam sat quietly, slouched over, for several seconds. Drew eventually walked back over, stood behind Adam, and put his hands on his shoulders as he looked down at him. He then looked up at Josh and whispered, "Glass jaw." Josh was chuckling yet again. "Oh, you'll be alright," Drew said.

Adam lowered the icepack. His cheek was all red, more from the cold icepack than the punch, but his eye was indeed a bit swollen. "Hmm," Adam finally mumbled, "I think that's the first time I've ever been punched in the face." Drew moved over to the side, seeing this comment as some added confirmation that Adam was going to be fine. Adam looked up at Drew and yelled, "That was the biggest sucker punch ever!"

Drew laughed. "Oh relax," he said. Drew sat down and watched Adam, assessing his condition. "Okay," Drew eventually said as he lightly pounded his fist on the table, "you're alright. I got to get back home to the wife and kids. I already paid the tab." Drew leaned down and lightly pounded his fist on the table again as he stood up. "Your eye will be fine in time for the wedding," he said as he walked away.

Adam looked up at Josh, who was shaking his head slightly and unable to get rid of his smile. "You really did have that coming," Josh said.

"I don't guess I could call that a resounding vote of confidence in the plan," Adam said.

They both chuckled and turned their chairs slightly such that they could focus again on the Ohio State-Maryland game. Neither of them said much for several minutes, other than a couple light groans and mumbled comments about the football game.

Then Josh looked at Adam. "Hey," he said as Adam slowly looked over at him, "this is it. The election's over. It's now time. It really is. I certainly don't know that you got it figured out, but whatever it's going to look like, it's time to get it done. You're dead on about that. So now we sit back …and watch it happen."

"If they don't get it done," Adam slurred, "it will be wanton negligence."

## *Chapter 16 - Mistakes Mended*

A stiff breeze was blowing through the aspen at the Spruce Creek amphitheater on that beautiful mid-June day, and the noise from the rustling leaves was drowning out the sound of a rendition of Clair de lune, mellifluously emanating from string quartet that was seated to the audience's left of the stone stage. With the temperature around sixty-five degrees and only a few passing cumulus clouds overhead, it was about as beautiful a day as anyone could ever expect in June in the Spruce Creek valley. A small gathering of about forty people were seated in seven rows of white, wooden event chairs. The amphitheater, located to the west side of the resort's main village, is about an eighth of a mile from the resort's main parking lot and accessed by a well maintained, gravel walking trail.

Adam, Josh, and Drew, in standard black tuxedoes, were already standing at the front of the amphitheater, on the right side, opposite Emily and Jess to the left. Emily and Jess were in dark hunter green bridesmaid dresses, which were made with sleeves, for they did not know how warm it would be on Hannah's big day. Everyone's hair was messed up from the breeze, and they had all given up on trying to do anything about it.

"Nervous?" Drew whispered to Adam with a smile.

"Of course I'm nervous," Adam muttered back. "I'll be fine once Hannah's up here."

Josh then nudged Drew and motioned toward the back corner of the congregation. It was Lane, sitting in the far left seat. Lane, with a dark complexion and salt and pepper hair, was dressed nicely and had a date seated beside him who was much younger than he. Adam turned his head slightly toward Josh and whispered, "We invited him but didn't think he would actually show up. We both agreed it might help bring some closure to that chapter."

"Shush," Emily quietly mumbled with a stern look on her face. Josh furrowed his brow at Emily and quickly waved his hand back at her as a retort to her onomatopoeia. Emily was indeed there and Hannah's maid of honor, again. After Josh had broken up with her in November, she packed up her stuff, and moved back to Virginia for the winter, but in March, she drove back to Colorado and unexpectedly knocked on Josh's door one night. They spent several days talking and both working through several issues which they had never discussed before. Throughout their entire time apart, Hannah guilefully and craftily executed some delicate shuttle diplomacy, that turned out to be integral to their reconciliation.

So, Josh and Emily were back together and their relationship was indeed very different. Emily treated Josh differently and he treated her differently. It wasn't so much that they were working hard at their relationship but they both respected their relationship so much more, and as a result, they treated each other differently, better, and were committed to doing so. Emily was back in Spruce Creek full time, working at the conference center again and as happy ever. She was Josh's biggest fan and supporter – a role she never assumed previously.

The breeze had let up for a minute and the music from the string quartet could suddenly be heard clearly. The amphitheater had become imbued with a calm, peaceful stillness, and everyone, relishing the nice weather, had become quiet and relaxed. A small events tent was set up about thirty feet behind the amphitheater seating, and Adam abruptly stood up straight and pulled his shoulders back as he noticed some movement around the door flap to the tent. The event planner from the resort stepped out and motioned toward the string quartet. The two violin players, viola player, and cellist from the local non-profit orchestra smoothly wrapped up their current piece and adjusted their sheet music – the pages all tightly clipped to their music stands to remain firmly in place in the breeze. They then initiated a rendition of Pachelbel's Canon, and as prompted by the event planner, all the wedding attendees stood up and turned toward the middle aisle.

Adam looked over at Josh and gritted his teeth. Josh raised his eyebrows and responded, "Here we go." Hannah walked out of the tent with the event planner and her father right behind her. Hannah was clearly uncomfortable but looked as beautiful as ever. Drew's daughter, now seven years old, wearing a dress made with the same hunter green fabric used for the bridesmaid dresses, was walking behind Hannah and holding the train to her gown that had a high neckline and lace sleeves. Hannah, low maintenance as they come, had never been so dolled up in her entire life and was assuredly as happy now as ever that it was only a small gathering of family and close friends. She immediately looked up at Adam, didn't smile, but had a look of complete horror on her face, not because of the wedding or the marriage vows but due to the sheer anxiety from being the center of attention like never before. Her father was trying his best to help her relax as they slowly initiated the short walk to the front of the amphitheater.

The ordained chaplain that handles many of the weddings held by the resort was conducting the nuptials. He also conducted small Sunday services on the mountain, attended primarily by visitors to the valley. Hannah was holding her father's arm as they walked slowly up the aisle, temporarily covered by a strip of red, outdoor carpet. After she had reached her spot on the small, stone stage and became comfortably positioned, the resort minister began the service that consisted of a standard wedding homily with citations from the scripture and a few declarations that were directed specifically at Adam and Hannah about their pending responsibilities as husband and wife. Adam and Hannah stood nervously and were intently focused on every word. The rustling leaves in the breeze made it difficult for those in the back of the gallery to hear, even though they were only about fifty feet away. The minister reached the point in the service where Adam and Hannah were scheduled to exchange their own personal vows to each other, per their own interests. Hannah went first. She took a deep breath and exhaled. Adam was trembling as much as Hannah as he held her hand. Neither was able to help the other relax.

"Adam," Hannah quietly said.

"Speak up!" Hannah's uncle yelled from the left side of the gallery. Hannah's eyes got real big as she continued to stare right at Adam, mortified. Adam dropped his head laughing as he held tightly to Hannah's hands.

"Adam," Hannah said loudly, "there have been times when I thought, I really don't deserve this guy. I've certainly made my share of mistakes. We didn't get here the way we were supposed to or the way we should have, but I really can't put into words how happy I am that we got here, that we're here now, and that I'm standing with you at this very moment …and will be standing at your side forever." Hannah turned toward the audience and paused as she looked around at her parents, her relatives, and all of Adam's extended family, "I can't tell you all, how happy I am that you've been patient with me and stood with me through my missteps and supported me despite my mistakes." Hannah started crying, "I love you all so much." Emily stepped forward and gave Hannah a tissue. Hannah used her left hand to gently wipe her eyes as Adam still held her right hand. Hannah's mother, in the first row, started sobbing. Hannah turned back to Adam, "You noted one day that you had thought I would always be good to you, unconditionally. I haven't always been good to you, but I am giving you my word. I will now always, always be good to you, unconditionally, forever, and I love you so much, Adam." Adam, smiling real big, was shaking as he massaged Hannah's hands. Hannah looked over at the chaplain indicating she was done. The minister gave a subtle nod to Hannah and looked toward Adam.

Adam inhaled deeply, pursed his lips for a second, shifted his feet slightly, and then exhaled. He chuckled lightly. "I don't guess I can beat that," he said. He looked out at the attendees. "I didn't prepare anything for this, but I really wanted to do this …because I thought it would be such an important part to the ceremony to further assure we feel married after we step away from here." He looked back into Hannah's eyes and took another deep breath. "Hannah, I can't explain how it happened. I just knew, five years ago, when I first met you, when you were drowning in that snow pit." Several attendees laughed lightly as Adam had motioned his head in the direction of the back side of the resort where they met. "I've known all along." Adam paused and looked out toward the attendees again and spoke directly to them. "I used to really try to figure out my feelings. I used to be in the middle of meetings at work, thinking about Hannah, and I couldn't get her out of my mind. I would be sitting there having heart palpitations in the middle of a work meeting and thinking to myself, 'Adam, what are you doing? Would you stop thinking about Hannah and focus.'" The wedding attendees were now laughing loudly. Hannah dropped her head, embarrassed. Her face was red and her eyes glossy from her tears.

Emily stepped around and said, "Come here, sweetie," as she gently helped Hannah wipe the tears away from her eyes and then quickly got repositioned behind her.

"I went through a period there," Adam continued, still peering off at the seated guests, "where I had decided that love stinks, but I was fine with it. I really just wanted Hannah to be happy. If she was happy, I was going to be happy, …but today, …she has made me the happiest person in the world." He looked right into Hannah's eyes. "I am so happy to be here with you and can't wait for you to, now, always be there with me, forever." Hannah winced as she wanted to grab Adam and hug him, but it wasn't time for that. Adam looked up at the minister and gave a very slight nod.

The minister continued the service with the typical vows and exchange of rings. After the ceremony ended, Adam and Hannah quickly walked down the aisle as the guests threw handfuls or rice at them – the rice was provided in cloth baggies at the beginning of the ceremony. Adam and Hannah continued steadily, alone, down the path back to the parking lot. They got in Adam's car, and Adam honked the horn for an extended period as they drove out of the parking lot. All the guests promptly began gathering their belongings and proceeded down the path to head to the reception.

Adam and Hannah were not actually scheduled to arrive at the reception location, Josh's new gallery, until all the guests had an opportunity to arrive. "Can we go see Cody?" Hannah spryly asked as they were slowly driving down the highway. Adam nodded firmly and proceeded to drive back to his condo, where Adam and Hannah had been staying together since their engagement. Cody was so excited to see them when they arrived, almost as if he had sensed that something special was going on and he had not actually expected to see them for a while. Hannah immediately went into the restroom. Adam, with little concern for his tuxedo pants, sat down on the floor and gently pet Cody. He twirled Cody's ears for a couple minutes which effectively paralyzed Cody as he had closed his eyes and became completely motionless.

Hannah walked out of the restroom, fixed a large glass of water in the kitchen, and walked back out to the living room. Adam immediately reached up for Hannah's water. She sighed but conceded and handed it over. She was standing next to Adam when he began talking to Cody, the water in his right hand as he pet Cody with his left hand. "Cody," he said, "so, a little while ago, a minister asked me what I think of your master here, Ms. Hannah. I stood up in front of all her family and all my family and all our closest friends, and I said, 'Ah, …I don't know, …I guess I like her dog.'"

Hannah blurted out a boisterous guffaw. She somehow managed to quickly sit down, in her wedding dress, on the floor behind Adam. She hugged Adam from behind as he kept petting Cody and twirling his ears. Cody was sitting up but still in a trance from Adam's petting.

They sat there quietly for a couple minutes. Hannah then quietly said, "I don't think I've been this relaxed in weeks." They had been very efficient with the wedding preparations, but it had been crazy nonetheless. "Well," Hannah said, "we should be able to head over there now." They stood up, brushed off their formal wear lightly, and headed over to the door. Cody didn't get up as he knew their departure didn't involve him. "See you later Cody," Hannah said sadly as Cody lay down.

Adam and Hannah drove to Josh's gallery that he opened just three weeks ago. Hannah had her last day at the real estate office a week ago, and as soon as she returned from the honeymoon, she would be working part time to help Josh with bookkeeping, payroll, and tax filings and also providing assistance with picture framing and watching the floor. All the wedding attendees had arrived and were standing, or sitting in several chairs, throughout the gallery, enjoying hors d'oeuvres, all catered by the North Fork Tavern, of course. The gathering included a few others that were not at the wedding, so it was crowded for the shop's thousand square feet floor plan. The party was already loud from the numerous conversations, laughing, and music. As Adam and Hannah walked in, the deejay, Tyler, set up to the right of the front door, abruptly stopped the music. Tyler was an old friend of Adam and Drew's from years ago when they all worked together at the resort. He worked various venues and joints throughout the valley, mostly entertaining tourists in the evenings. "Ladies and Gentlemen," Tyler said as everyone immediately dampened their conversations, "may I please introduce Mr. and Mrs. Turner!" Everyone began clapping, and Adam and Hannah were quickly ambushed and separated by guests.

A cash bar was set up in the back right corner, being operated as a side job by a couple of Emily's coworkers from the conference center. A table for wedding gifts was set up in the back left corner. Several displays in the center of Josh's new gallery had been moved for the reception. Framed photos, all taken by Josh, were hung on the walls throughout the gallery. Several of the pictures were marked as sold, having been bought as wedding gifts for Adam and Hannah, for they listed several of the pictures in their gift registry.

Adam and Hannah already bought a home lot in one of the cheaper, new subdivisions in the valley, and Adam completed a design for a three bedroom house to be built, a much smaller home than what he was accustomed to designing, but there would be plenty of wall space nonetheless. Drew already provided Adam and Hannah with his wedding gift, a signed contract to complete landscaping work around the house at a significantly reduced price. Contractors were scheduled to begin breaking ground on the home as soon as Adam and Hannah returned from their honeymoon. For their trip, they would be staying at a resort lodge on a lake in western Montana. Everyone had joked with them for choosing to escape a Colorado forest by trekking to the Montana wilderness for their honeymoon, but Adam and Hannah were elated to have ten days of utter, pure relaxation with nature – no planes, no trains, and no schedule at all.

Everyone enjoyed the reception for the next hour, talking and visiting. At one moment, Adam and Hannah stopped and talked to Lane. He was standing in the back corner, somewhat veiled by the stack of wedding gifts.

"I see you decided to show up," Lane immediately said as Hannah and Adam walked up to him.

"How have you been?" Hannah asked.

"Fine, Great. A couple months ago, I finally got on with a DAs office back in Wisconsin." He shifted over toward his date who was standing slightly behind his left shoulder. "This is Tiffany," he said as he put his arm around her. Adam and Hannah shook her hand. They all enjoyed pleasant small talk for a couple minutes before Jess suddenly called out from the other side of the gallery.

"Hannah! Adam!" Jess yelled. "It's time for you to cut this cake."

"Well, it's good to see you," Hannah said to Lane.

"Yeah, you too. We're probably going to cut out of here in a few minutes but congratulations again and I wish you both the best."

Adam shook his hand and Hannah gave him a light hug, and Adam and Hannah moved through the gallery to cut the cake. There was little excitement over the cake as the deejay continued playing music. Also, wiping cake over each other's faces wasn't Adam's or

Hannah's style. They mostly wanted to hurry and get the cake out to the guests, who were already moving up to the table to get pieces as fast as Jess and one of the bar attendants could get slices cut. Everyone continued talking and telling stories as Adam and Hannah moved around to visit with every guest. Drew's kids had begun dancing with some other children in front of the deejay as champagne glasses were being distributed to all the guests. The deejay suddenly stopped the music and handed a microphone to Josh as he stepped up on a large wooden box platform to the left of the sound equipment.

"Okay, everyone, let's do this," he said. "Everyone obliged and turned toward Josh. I'm on the hook to give a toast. Adam, get up here. Where's your wife?" Adam and Hannah nervously moved up in front of the deejay. Where's Emily," Josh muttered. He located her in the room. "Emily," he said as he was waving for her to join him. She was shaking her head. "Emily, would you please come stand by me and support me while I give this toast."

Emily sighed, walked through the crowd, and stepped up on the platform with Josh. Emily put her arm around Josh and her face was red, not over the anxiety of being in front of the group but primarily because she had no idea what Josh was going to say and he already had a couple drinks. She whispered, "Josh, please show a little decorum." Her comment could be heard through the microphone.

Josh raised his glass. "Adam, Hannah," he said, "you both know that you are two of my favorite people in the whole world." Adam looked around the gathering. "I've known Adam for twenty-two years, and I was never so happy to know such a swell fella as I have been over this past year. We all wouldn't be here in this gallery right now if it wasn't for Adam." Josh turned and looked right at Emily and quietly said, "Emily wouldn't be here with me right now if it wasn't for Adam and Hannah." Emily was more embarrassed than moved by his remarks. Josh looked back at Adam and Hannah. "It makes me so happy to see you together again and know that you will be together forever, exactly as you're supposed to be." Josh looked at Adam and started chuckling. "Okay, there have been times when I wanted to punch Adam in the face myself." Everyone in the gallery started laughing as most were well aware of the punch Adam took from Drew several months before. "But I'll tell you this, Hannah couldn't have ended up with a better guy. When Adam sees a problem, he doesn't sleep, even if it's not his problem." Josh smiled and looked at Hannah. "Actually, Hannah, maybe you can work with him and help him with that." She laughed as she dropped her head. "Adam doesn't look to avoid a problem but he chooses to face it head on, relishing the challenge. He identifies the problem and works toward a solution. He and Hannah did not end up here today by the easiest path." Hannah was now hugging Adam, with her face buried against his chest. "This past year, he identified a key problem – he and Hannah were meant to be together, forever – but they weren't there yet. He went about solving that problem, and Adam and Hannah," Josh lifted his glass and the guests followed, "you're there, right where you needed to be, right where you're supposed to be. Congratulations." All the guests quietly said cheers and took sips of their champagne.

Drew had been standing in the front, off to the right side. Drew took the microphone from Josh and slapped him firmly on the back as he stepped off the wooden box. Drew helped Josh tremendously over the previous few months with several aspects of getting his gallery set up. Drew, very well connected with the business community in the valley, helped Josh get linked up with numerous potential customers, and Josh was very grateful. Everyone remained quiet as Drew stepped up on the box and began to speak.

Drew looked at Adam and then looked right at Hannah as he started chuckling. "Such a sweet kid," he said softly. Hannah was doing fine up until then, but she then started to tear up. "Well, Josh is right. We got a classic, idealistic visionary here, but Hannah, you got your hands full. If he ever gets caught talking your ear off trying to solve the world's problems, you just smack him; it'll work. He'll shut up." Adam was laughing, but several guests were confused and murmuring to each other. "Oh, I'm joking," Drew said. "The truth is, I've actually learned a lot from Adam this past year, and I'll tell you:

he's been one of the most positive influences on my life and how I take on each day. There's something about the way that guy takes it – from me, from everyone. He's about a hard a worker as you'll meet, and he does not get discouraged. He's not going to get distracted from what needs to be done, and that's indeed why we're here." Drew looked at Hannah and in signature fashion said, "Mrs. Anderson–"

"Ms. Anderson," she blurted out.

"Your fella has taught me to open my eyes, listen, and be understanding. I could get caught up discussing the vagaries of life that contributed to your road to matrimony, and maybe I should apologize for not standing by the effort every step of the way, but you both got here. We're all here now, and the world will be a better place as a result." Drew paused. He looked over at his wife Cindy and his two kids and paused, he looked at Adam's parents, and then he looked back at Hannah. The pause was starting to get awkward as Drew took a breath and exhaled. "Well, you don't have to worry about me hitting Adam again because as of today, I would now have to answer to Ms. Anderson." Hannah scowled, pointed at Drew, and nodded, whimsically. Adam, you're a lucky man. Hannah, you're a lucky gal. And Hannah, I hope you'll still share your friend because there's some others out there that need him too. Godspeed." All the guests quietly said cheers and took sips of their champagne.

Jess stepped up and grabbed the microphone. "Okay," she said, "I can't beat that. So, I think it's time for the bride and groom to dance." Adam's eyes got real big. He was shaking his head vigorously. "No, no, no" Jess said, looking at Adam. "Get up here."

He very genuinely said, "Look, I'm sorry, I can't." He pointed to his feet. "My proverbial two left feet." Hannah rolled her eyes, grabbed him, and gently pulled him out in front of the deejay who had already started one of their favorite songs. They danced quietly and the crowd gradually began conversing again.

So that was it. They enjoyed the best day of their lives that went off without a hitch. After their honeymoon, life was as hectic as ever – both working overtime while also building their house. When they moved into their new home right before the holidays, Adam's grand plan still had not come to fruition in Washington, but the debate would never end for Adam. The most comforting aspect of the continued situation was that he knew it would be much easier to withstand the continued impasse, for however long, now that Hannah was at his side.

THE END

## About the Author
Craig Boroughs resides in Summit County, Colorado and encourages everyone to think, formulate different solutions, and demand reform, now, through a final compromise, and between your efforts and your work, go read, love for love's sake, and vote!